John Franklin Bardin was born in Cincinnati in 1916. After an unhappy childhood he had to leave the University of Cincinnati in his first year to find a full-time job. He became a ticket-taker and bouncer at a local roller-skating rink and educated himself by working at night, reading and clerking in a bookstore. From 1968 until 1972 he was a senior Editor at Coronet in New York, and between 1973 and 1974 he was Managing Editor for the American Bar Association magazines. From 1946 to 1948, during a period of intense creative activity, he wrote three re-markable novels, *The Deadly Percheron*, *The Last of Philip Banter* and *Devil Take the Blue-Tail Fly*. Julian Symons described them as 'distinguished by an extraordinary intensity of feeling, and by an absorbtion in morbid psychology remarkable for the period . . . The novels sprang out of nightmare experiences . . . Without, perhaps, being exactly autobiographical, they are clearly a reworking of events in a stormy, painful childhood and adolescence.' John Franklin Bardin died in 1981.

The Last
of Philip Banter

PENGUIN BOOKS

PENGUIN BOOKS

Published by the Penguin Group
27 Wrights Lane, London W8 5TZ, England
Viking Penguin Inc., 40 West 23rd Street, New York, New York 10010, USA
Penguin Books Australia Ltd, Ringwood, Victoria, Australia
Penguin Books Canada Ltd, 2801 John Street, Markham, Ontario, Canada L3R 1B4
Penguin Books (NZ) Ltd, 182–190 Wairau Road, Auckland 10, New Zealand

Penguin Books Ltd, Registered Offices: Harmondsworth, Middlesex, England

First published in the United States of America by Dodd, Mead & Co. 1947
First published in Great Britain by Victor Gollancz 1947
Published in Penguin Books in *The John Franklin Bardin Omnibus* 1976
Published as a separate edition 1989

Printed and bound in Great Britain by
Cox & Wyman Ltd, Reading

The Last of Philip Banter

To
Estella M. Martin

Terror can strike by day as well as by night.
Although the frightful is, perhaps rightly, conjoined
in our minds with the darkly coloured, the harshly
dissonant – with bludgeon blows and the odours of
decay – the most terrible experiences are often bereft
of these properties of melodrama. The words 'I love
you', spoken on a sun-streaked terrace during a
joyous day, can cement a betrayal. The unchecked
gratification of an impulse, conceived in sensation,
can bear the bitter fruit of misery. And a prophecy
can – by auto-suggestion or soothsaying? – deliver a
man to evil.

The First Instalment

'Philip Banter,' he said to himself, 'you are in a bad way.'

He stood on the corner of Madison Avenue and Fiftieth Street blinking his aching eyes against the mild winter sunshine. He was trying to decide whether to cross the street or not. If he crossed the street, he would be confronted by the entrance to his office building and he would have to go through the revolving door and into the elevator and up to his office. But if he did not cross the street . . . if he turned right instead . . . and walked down the side street a few doors . . . he would find a bar and have himself a drink. Just one little drink, no more. That was what he needed. Just one little drink.

He did not cross the street. He turned right and walked to the bar and went inside and sat in the rear booth and ordered a double shot of rye whisky when the waiter came. That was what he needed. That would get it over quickly. That would clear his head.

In a few minutes the ache that had gripped his eyeballs had relaxed until it was only an occasional flickering, the slightest hint of pressure. He found he could think again – he could look straight at things – the bar mirror was what he was looking at right then – without flinching. Now everything would be fine if he could just remember what had happened last night.

He was convinced that something terrible had happened last night. If he could remember one detail, one tiny circumstance which could give him a clue to the calamity that had befallen him, he would feel reassured. But he had no memory of the night before. He knew that he had been drunk, very drunk. And he did not know this because he recalled being drunk – no, he deduced his previous state from the way he had awakened, sprawled across the bed in his rumpled dinner suit, and from his monstrous head and brassy tongue. He also knew that he had hurt himself, or had been hurt, last night. There was the ravelling bandage on his wrist, the steady throb of pain in his arm, the ugly, deep cut he had found beneath the bandage. Putting fresh gauze and antiseptic on the wound, he had tried desperately to remember how he had suffered it. Had he been in a fight and, if he had, with whom and about what? Or was the slash self-inflicted? Had he tried to kill himself? There were no answers.

When he had showered and dressed and come to breakfast, Dorothy, his wife, had not been at the table. The maid had served him sullenly, only bringing him his paper after he had called her twice. There was no doubt about it, he had done it again. But with whom had he gone off this time? If he could only remember how the evening had begun, whether Dorothy had been with him – she must have been or she would have been at the breakfast table – when he had started drinking . . .

He hailed the waiter and ordered another double rye and sat there shaking his head until it came. His wrist still throbbed steadily and he had to resist continually the desire to lift the bandage and inspect the wound. Luckily, he had been able to find a shirt with full, soft cuffs this morning; he could pull his cuff over the bandage to hide it from the curious. Otherwise he would have to answer question after question as best he could. If he could only remember what had happened!

After about five more minutes of introspection, he threw a couple of dollars on the table and walked out of the bar. This time the sun did not hurt his eyes nearly as much as before. He did not hesitate when he reached Madison Avenue but, since the light was green, walked directly across the street. As he went through the revolving door that had seemed such a hazard so recently, the sudden darkness of the building's lobby was marvellously refreshing. And as he entered the elevator, the quick smile of Sadie, the operator, was a welcome challenge. 'Philip Banter,' he said to himself, 'you've still got what it takes.'

Sadie, he saw, was eyeing him. 'How was the love-life last night, Sadie? Satisfactory?' They were alone in the car. By ten o'clock even the late rush was over.

'Mr Banter! What makes you go on like that?' Sadie brushed at her rusty hair provokingly. She was obviously pleased at his sally, indeed she had invited it, yet she felt she should pretend to be shocked and her pretence came off badly – awkwardly and self-consciously. Philip smiled to himself. She acted this way every morning, accepting and responding to his easy familiarity. Their exchange of knowing witticisms had become a ritual.

'Why, I'd think a healthy girl like you would need a little relaxation now and then. Nothing wrong in that.'

Sadie turned away from him to watch the tiny ruby lights wink on and off on the indicator as the elevator sucked itself upward. She played at being embarrassed.

'I'm not going to talk to you any more, Mr Banter, if you must go on like that. It's not nice for a nice girl to hear such talk!' The car subsided at Philip's floor; the automatic doors whispered open. `

'You're not a "nice girl", Sadie.' Philip flipped her backside lightly and left the elevator. This was something new in the ritual.

He heard her voice. 'Misss-ter Banter!' She sounded rather pleased at this added attention. He would have to remember that. Not that Sadie was the type to be considered seriously . . . but you never could tell. There might come a time when she would fit in nicely.

He walked down the hall, his lips pursed, whistling sourly. It was exactly five minutes after ten when he pushed open the door of Brown and Foster, Inc., Advertising.

The house goddess of the agency, Miss Campbell,

turned swiftly in her chair to grant him a tight-lipped smile of good morning. Philip smiled back at the receptionist, feeling – if anything – a little more undone than usual as long as he remained within the orbit of her formal cordiality; he pushed open the swinging gate and ushered himself through it as quickly as possible. He had never considered Miss Campbell either, nor would he . . . she was indubitably frigid. He walked down the inner corridor to his office, no longer whistling, fighting a sudden desire to turn around and leave the office, to go back to that friendly bar on the side street and have another little drink.

As he entered his secretary's office – through which he must trespass to reach his own – Miss Grey, his secretary, looked up at him from a copy of *Tide*, said, 'Good morning, Mr Banter', and watched him cross to his own door. Although he did not see her do it (he shut his door on the sight), Philip knew that as soon as his back was turned she had gone back to *Tide*. This annoyed him. Not that he would say anything – she was so damnably efficient – but did she always have to make such a point of doing nothing when she had nothing to do? The other men's secretaries usually managed to seem busy, why couldn't his Miss Grey? And that awful complexion! Why, in God's name, didn't she do something about that?

As he hung up his hat and coat, Philip was still grumbling to himself and feeling put upon. This being so, it is not surprising that his subconscious aided him in prolonging his martyrdom: he grasped the hanger clumsily and it slipped out of his hands and clattered to the floor; he stooped for it awkwardly and caused a momentary twinge in his side – the protest of a muscle that had grown too used to lax habits – and when he finally managed to hang his topcoat, he discovered a spot on the lapel. Even after he turned around and faced the desk, he did not at first notice that his typewriter was lying open upon it; his mind was too occupied with vague resentments and too inclined to gloat over personal suffering to be quickly observant.

When he did discover the typewriter on his desk, it caused no break in the flow of his inner discourse. Had he left it like that again? If he kept that up, it would need another cleaning, since dust got in it overnight. Here was something else Miss Grey could attend to if she really cared about her job! She could come in after he left each night to see if he had put the machine away. He would want to make a note of that so he would be sure to speak to her about it. She would soon learn to do more to earn her money than burying her nose in the latest issue of *Tide* or the *New Yorker*! Philip did not see the manuscript until he sat down at his desk, then he could not avoid seeing it. There, placed next to the offending typewriter, was a neat pile of pages, double-spaced, well-typed. Why, there was a sheet in his machine that had typing on it, too! Who had been using his typewriter?

He reached for the button that would summon Miss Grey to ask her whom she had let use his machine, when he noticed that it was his own name and address that were typed in the upper, left-hand corner of the first page of the sheaf. He did not press the button. A new idea occurred to him: it might be better to read the pages first before he mentioned their existence to anyone. Someone might be playing a joke on him, trying to make a fool of him . . .

So Philip leaned back, lighted a cigarette and began to read. He was a large man in his middle thirties with a long, good-looking face. His mouth was disproportionately broad, enough so as to be almost disfiguring when he grinned. Yet this horizontal slash added a kind of distinction to his otherwise even features – it unbalanced the narrowing lines of his nose and jaw, suggesting a latent violence, a brooding force. Philip's fond opinion was that women found his face both likeable and disquieting. One of them had been foolish enough to confide this ambivalence. 'Philip,' she had said, 'your face is so innocent and your mouth is so evil.'

But, although Philip frequently remembered this remark and had, on occasion, used it himself at the proper point in a flirtation, he was not thinking of his good looks now. Instead, his attention was focused on the typed page he was reading; and after he had laid it aside and gone on to the second, and then the third, sheets of the pile, he underwent a subtle change. Where before he had been sitting erect in his swivel chair, now he began to slump. Where before he had let the manuscript lie on his desk while he read it from a distance, he now held the pages progressively closer to his eyes. He forgot about the lighted cigarette clenched in his dry lips and let it burn until it scorched him. Then he dropped the smouldering butt onto the floor, impatiently grinding it out with his heel.

There were only fifteen pages of the manuscript, but Philip read them slowly – and then he read them over again.

Philip Banter
21 East 68th St.
New York

Confession

I

I thought I was done with that sort of thing. I thought I had settled down, that I would spend the rest of my days being a model husband.

It isn't that I don't love Dorothy. I even respect her. Although I can imagine life without her (I am not a romantic), if I had to choose I would prefer life with her. I cannot explain my need to be unfaithful to her.

I know the risk I run. Last night, as on all the similar

18

nights before, I gauged the full extent of my jeopardy by the look of sheer hate she threw at me as I left our apartment with my 'latest'. I know how jealous Dorothy can be. I know, too, that some day I shall try her jealousy beyond the self-erected barriers of her admirable restraint. Then it will be too late.

Knowing this, why do I continue the way I do?

*

Sometimes, most times, I must admit, I have brought it on myself; but not last night. When I left the agency at five, I intended a slippered evening: a good dinner with Dorothy, some brandy and a little talk afterwards, then the radio or a book until time for bed. A new flirtation? Impossible! I loved my wife last night when I left work. I loved her all the way home on the subway, and on the short walk to the East River. I was never a more normal American husband than when I fitted my key into the lock of our door, threw my hat and coat on the table in the foyer, went into our room where she was dressing and after kissing her, asked:

'What's for dinner?'

She wrinkled her eyes at me in the mirror, but kept on working the rouge into her cheeks, patting at them with an absurdly large puff, a pink plush blob.

'Something you like.'

'What?'

'Guess!'

'Must I? A roast of some sort?'

'Darling, we had a roast just the other day...'

'A rarebit?'

'No. Try again.'

'No, you tell me. I'll never guess.' I do not like guessing games and though I realized that Dorothy, like all other women, must be coy at times, I was not inclined to encourage her on these occasions. It was tiresome.

'We're having chicken and rice, the Spanish way. You've always liked it so much. But there's something else, too.'

'For dinner?'

She turned halfway around on her vanity stool, throwing her dark hair back, smiling at me. She had just been putting her lipstick on; one lip was smudged vividly like a child playing at being grown-up.

(I tell you I loved her then. I meant no infidelity. I contemplated no sin . . . not that I believe in sin.)

'Yes, in a way, for dinner,' she said.

'Oh, come out with it, Dottie,' I said. 'Stop teasing me!'

She tossed her shoulders and affected to ignore me. But she returned my stare by way of the mirror – her eyes never left mine.

'Jeremy called. He's coming around to dinner and bringing a friend.'

'Jeremy? Jeremy Foulkes?'

'The very same. I thought you'd be pleased. Why, Philip, whatever is the matter? You look positively sick!'

I passed my hand over my damp forehead. I was breathing wildly, my thinking was blurred. What could I say?

'Pleased? Of course I'm pleased. I'm always glad to see Jeremy. You know that. And any friend of his is always welcome.'

'I didn't mean to startle you, darling,' Dorothy said. 'I just thought I'd make it a pleasant surprise.'

*

That was last night, Tuesday, 1 December 1945. A few short hours ago. So much has happened since then.

*

I am confused. I simply cannot understand my own motives. Motives? Drives? Insane urges? Was I wholly sane last night?

*

It may help to clear my mind if I put down a few facts about myself, Dorothy, my friends.

I am in the advertising business, an account executive. Occasionally, I write a little copy.

Before I drifted into advertising, I was a newspaperman: first in Indianapolis, my home town, and then in New York.

*

Philip's hand shook as he laid down the manuscript. The pain in his bandaged wrist had been increasing as he read the typed pages. He pressed his wrist against his mouth. What was the meaning of this 'Confession'? Why did it refer to Tuesday, 1 December – today – as 'last night'. Was he supposed to have written it, or was someone kidding him? He would have to read further to find out.

He picked up the manuscript, slouched down in his chair and propped it against his knee so he would not have to use his injured wrist. He began to read again. His forgotten cigarette smouldered in the ashtray.

*

I met Dorothy during my newspaper days in this city. Jeremy introduced her to me at a party. It was one of those intellectual gatherings Jeremy was always sponsoring in those days; perhaps he still does, I don't know.

I had never thought I'd marry. There was always another woman. Any one woman's individual attractions dulled for me and became enervatingly habitual after a few weeks' intimacy. Matrimony was a fisherman's hook with a fancy lure, and I was a wise old fish who admired the bright, twirling feathers but refused to rise and be impaled . . .

Unless, of course, the woman had money, besides intelligence and beauty. A starved fish will on occasion chance snatching the bait from a hook, if the bait is exceptionally tempting. For that matter, fish have been caught with three or four rusty hooks imbedded in their mouths.

I had never met an intelligent, beautiful girl with money until I met Dorothy. I married her.

It wasn't quite as cold-blooded as all that. I fell in love with her, as might be expected. I still love her. But I am honest with myself: if her father hadn't been a partner in one of the larger, more affluent advertising agencies, if Dorothy hadn't had considerable money in her own name, I can scarcely believe our relationship would have lasted.

I don't mean to imply that our marriage hasn't been a happy one; I think it is as happy as most. We are kind to each other. I believe I have worn worse with Dorothy than she has with me (isn't this the way it should be?). I left the newspaper business at her father's suggestion and became a copywriter in his agency; it wasn't long before he gave me several accounts to handle and I found my salary in five figures. We would be completely happy if I could only be a little more circumspect about my personal affairs. The trouble is I don't try. Dorothy might never know of my flirtations, if I didn't insist on flaunting them in her face.

Or if she learned, I know she would be proud enough to pretend ignorance – if I allowed her the pretence.

But she can't overlook an event that happens before her eyes: the way I made up to Jeremy's 'friend' last night, for example.

Why couldn't I have waited?

*

Our guests arrived while I was still dressing. Dorothy had left the room earlier to see how things were in the kitchen; I heard her go to the door when the bell rang and then I heard muffled conversation. I knew Jeremy and his 'friend' had arrived.

It has been a long time since I last spent an evening with Jeremy. Until about a year ago he was my closest friend; then we had a falling out. Nothing dramatic occurred, no quarrel, not even a disagreement. We just stopped seeing each other. Several months passed before I realized what had happened, and then when I thought about it I knew that our estrangement had been progressing gradually for years. Our community of friends was dispersed by the war, for one thing; I believe that Jeremy and I were the only 4-F's in the group. We might have had the newspaper business in common if I hadn't left it, and Jeremy, too – he went into radio shortly after I married Dorothy. I know nothing about radio, and I must confess I dislike most radio people. They're queer. I've noticed Jeremy growing queer since he has become an announcer. He wears hand-painted ties now, and Irish linen shirts – that sort of thing. I suppose it is another reason why we have drifted apart.

Dorothy might have kept us together. She was our last link. Jeremy had known Dorothy before I knew her, and he had liked her a lot at one time. They were great friends and it was good to see them together. Jeremy was the only one of Dorothy's friends that I did like, for that matter. But then that might have been because he was my friend, too; I don't know.

Thinking back over it I can't understand why I was surprised to learn that he was coming to dinner. As Dorothy said, I should have been pleased. And I was, after a while, yet at first it was a shock and almost disagreeable.

It was as if I had a premonition.

*

She was the first person I saw when I entered the living-room. To that moment I hadn't thought about the 'friend' Jeremy was bringing around. If I had been asked, I should have guessed that Jeremy's companion would be a man. I seldom think of Jeremy with women, principally because he doesn't often have a feminine friend. Jeremy is something of a lone wolf, or he used to be. He had a girl with him last night, though.

I could not take my eyes off her. She was small and slim, and she stood very straight. Her eyes were brown, flecked with a lighter shade that changed from hazel to green and back again within the duration of a glance. She wore a severely simple suit of black broadcloth set off

23

by a tailored shirtwaist. Her hair was darker than her enigmatic eyes and it fell to her shoulders in soft abundance. There was something taut and alive about the way she held her head, something imperious and demanding about the quick, restless gestures of her hands . . .

Jeremy came over and introduced us. He looked well, if a little fat; he had been one of those small, compact men who seem to take the highest gloss, but now his clothes bulged slightly and there was a fold of flesh at his collar.

'This is – –, Philip. She's going to be a writer, too.' (I do not want to write her name. It's not that I have forgotten it – how could I? – indeed, I have been saying it over and over to myself all the while I wrote this, as if it were an incantation. But I refuse to set it down in black and white. A silly quirk, perhaps . . . or a sensible caution?)

I looked away from her to see if he had said this last with malice. But Jeremy was smiling in the best of nature. I tend to remember insults and to cherish resentments, to be sensitive about wrongs long after others have forgotten them. Once Jeremy had lashed out at me unmercifully for taking a job in advertising. He had called me a parasite. But, of course, he no longer remembered that, even if I did.

'What sort of thing are you going to write?' I asked her, sitting down beside her on the sofa. Dorothy had moved over to make room: 'Stories, or something serious?'

Her eyes glinted and changed colour. 'Can't stories be serious?' she asked.

I felt foolish. I had made a snide remark that had turned out to be anything but clever. I had asked a meaningless question, been guilty of an inanity, and her manner let me know she knew it.

'Of course,' I said. 'Of course, they can. I didn't mean that.'

'What did you mean?'

'I meant are you going to write fiction, or – or something more serious?' As soon as I said this, I marvelled at my own stupidity in repeating the very remark I had wanted to efface. Now I wanted to add something else, quickly, that would bury it. But she did not give me the chance.

'I can't understand the typical American business man's attitude that art, writing in particular, is an intricate game, a child's play. I think I detect that in you. And I want you to know that I resent it!' She licked at her lip with her tongue as if a drop of the acid that formed her words had fallen upon the sensitive membrane and must be expunged.

'I didn't mean that,' I protested. 'I wish I could write fiction, good fiction. I admire an honest writer.'

She stared at me incredulously. And then she smiled and looked away. I knew that it had begun all over again.

*

We went in to dinner soon after that, but before we did Jeremy came over to talk to me. He didn't have much to say, just asked the usual questions about business and my health; but he gave me the opportunity to ask him about her.

'Where did you meet her?'

'At a party in the Village a while back,' he said. 'We're pretty good friends. What do you think of her?'

I looked at her again. She was sitting back on the sofa talking to Dorothy (I had walked over to the fireplace with Jeremy). She held her drink in one hand and was gesturing with it, the other hand was poking indefatigably at her long bob. I thought to myself, I've never seen a person who was so alive . . .

'She's attractive,' I answered Jeremy, 'and she's got spirit. I like the way she stands up and fights when she talks.'

Jeremy nodded soberly, but I could see he was pleased. His next words proved it.

'I'm in love with her, Philip. I'm going to marry her.'

'Are you? Congratulations!'

'Oh, I haven't asked her yet,' he said, and his face flushed. 'She may not want me . . .'

'I wouldn't say that,' I said.

He was asking for it, but then Jeremy always asks for it and thanks you afterwards.

*

I said earlier that this time it wasn't my fault. That isn't true. I don't know whose fault it could be except mine. If I had said I couldn't help myself, that would have approached the truth.

All through dinner I could not keep my eyes off her. She noticed my continued attention, and Dorothy noticed it; only Jeremy seemed to be unaware of what I was doing. I don't think I was conscious of the food I was putting into my mouth; I know I paid only enough heed to the conversation to keep up my end. She had pre-empted my mind.

And I could tell that she favoured my attention. Sometimes when you look at a woman she pretends to ignore you – that can be either good or bad; but if she shows you by returning your look that she knows you are watching her – that can be only good. During dinner I think that she returned my gaze as often as I regarded her – that's what I mean when I say I couldn't help myself. I'll admit that I didn't have to look at her . . . that was where I was to blame. But once I had begun our wordless exchange, the only thing either of us could have done to have stopped would have been to leave. And I don't believe that she ever thought of that – I know I didn't.

*

There was a telephone call for Jeremy about nine o'clock. We had been talking about the modern novel: I remember having said something rash about Henry Miller, only to feel her eyes on me again, to hear her soft, harsh voice challenge me.

'At least, he's honest!'

'I didn't say he wasn't. I said only that his books were

execrable, his hatred of America and things American old-fashioned and absurd.'

She was half-smiling. There was a pleasurable antagonism between us. 'I don't believe you've read him!' she exclaimed.

She was right, I hadn't. Although I believe I did read a review of his latest book.

That was where we were when the 'phone rang. Dorothy answered and said it was for Jeremy. We could hear him out in the hall, arguing. 'But I can't. I'm at a party,' I heard him say. And then later, 'Well, all right. If it can't be helped, it can't be helped. But I do think that you could plan these things better. Yes. Yes, I understand. I'll be over right away. Yes, I'm leaving this minute.'

And while this was going on, I was acutely conscious of her and she was comparably aware of me. Each time we spoke we were at each other's throats, but it was a different kind of aggression we intended. This verbal sparring was a substitute; even when we were silent we were at war, the oldest, most fought and best war of them all.

Jeremy returned to find three people with that look on their faces that says, 'We didn't mean to, but we couldn't keep from listening.' He stood in the doorway and made his excuses.

'That was the station. One of the men is ill and I have to fill in unexpectedly. I tried to beg off, but I couldn't.'

'You don't have to go right away?' asked Dorothy.

'I'm afraid so.'

Jeremy walked away from Dorothy and over to her. She stood up – it seemed reluctantly. She looked at me, then shook her head and looked away.

'You don't have to leave, darling,' said Jeremy. 'I'd only have to take you home anyway. And I don't want to spoil your evening.'

She hesitated. She looked from Jeremy to me, ignoring Dorothy. I wondered if she realized how obvious this all was. There was no reason why she could not accomplish the same end more subtly.

Jeremy, the fool, was throwing her at me. There is an example of why he never has a woman of his own. He knows nothing about them. He should not be trusted with them.

'Why don't you stay, darling?' he was saying. 'Phil will take you home, won't you, Phil?'

She was watching me again, this time eagerly. 'If you're sure it's no trouble,' she said.

'Of course it's no trouble.'

Jeremy seemed relieved. 'Then I'll be going. I've really got to dash! Thank you, Dorothy, for a magnificent dinner.' He waved his hand at us and was gone – an absurd little man in a shirt too big for him.

As soon as he left, she sat down beside me. I was uncomfortably aware of Dorothy, standing by the fireplace, too pointedly paying us no attention.

'Dorothy,' I asked, 'what do you think of Henry Miller?'

'I haven't read him either,' she said. 'I'll reserve my opinion.' I could feel —'s leg against mine.

*

There are times in my life that I remember well and of which I can recall every detail, yet I have to force myself to think of them at all. The rest of last night is such a time. Until about eleven o'clock we sat and listened to the radio and talked. I think I can remember every word that was said, but I cannot make myself put that conversation down. What we said had no relation to what was happening. Last night was an emotional crisis, a conflict between three people that existed by itself without the aid of words or overt action.

I believe we talked about the plight of the American writer, of his peculiar homelessness and the strange feeling of futile striving you get from our fiction – as if the author were inarticulate. Actually, it was ourselves who were inarticulate. We felt a need to talk, as if our talk clothed and made decent our naked emotions, but what we said was frustrate. There seemed no end to it.

At times I felt myself to be a bystander; these were the times when Dorothy and – were concerned only with each other in their contention over me. And there were other times when Dorothy must have felt herself excluded – when – and I were alone despite her presence. (I still cannot bring myself to confide her name to paper.) Yet no anger was expressed. No words of love were spoken. We talked about Cain and Dos Passos and Wolfe; it was all very intellectual and civilized like a scene from a bad play.

About eleven o'clock, she stood up abruptly. 'I'm going home.'

'It's early yet,' I said. At that moment I wanted to delay the inevitable. I believe I would have backed out if I could.

Dorothy yawned. 'You might as well take her home, Philip.' Dorothy wasn't being impolite; she was acknowledging defeat, and letting me know that it would be an armed truce. 'I'd like to get to bed, too,' she added.

I went out to get our coats. She was standing in front of the mirror over the fireplace fussing with her hair, and I saw that Dorothy was watching her. Dorothy was looking at her the way she would inspect an obstacle in her path, coldly, dispassionately – but the emotion she was hiding was hatred instead of annoyance.

I brought her coat back into the room and helped her into it. In the mutual struggle with the fur she brushed against me more than was necessary. Dorothy saw this as well. I felt I had to say something to take the curse off the silence.

'I'll be back within the hour,' I said. Dorothy smiled at me, and then looked at her. 'You know you won't,' she said.

I turned around to look back at Dorothy as we left. She had craned her neck to watch us leave. She was still smiling, but that was because she had forgotten to stop.

I looked down at the woman beside me. I resolved that I would take her to her house and leave her. I told myself that I would really come back to Dorothy within the hour. I was married. I loved my wife. I was getting too old for this sort of thing. And I believed myself for the moment it took to shut the door on Dorothy.

She stood still beside me, her eyes answering my look, her lower lip trembling. After acting like that all night, now she was shy . . .

But I tasted blood when she kissed me in the taxi.

*

Later, while I was dressing, she asked, 'Why did your wife say that?'

'Say what?'

'What she did just before we left. When you said you would be back, and she said you wouldn't.'

'I don't know.'

'Oh yes you do, Philip.'

'But I don't.'

'It's because this happened before, isn't it? Many times before?'

'I don't know what you're talking about.'

'Oh yes you do!'

'What are you getting at?'

'I mean – this isn't the first time you've been unfaithful to Dorothy, is it?'

There was no use lying. 'No, it isn't.'

'You do it all the time, don't you?'

'Not quite "all the time".'

She threw me a strange look and ran into the bathroom. 'Why does she put up with it, Philip?' she called to me over the sound of running water.

'I suppose she loves me.'

'If I loved you . . . and you did that to me . . . you know what I'd do?'

'No. What?'

'I'd kill you, Philip.'

I didn't say anything. I finished brushing my hair. I was ready to leave.

30

'Philip.'

'Yes.'

'I wouldn't try her too far, Philip. She might kill you, too . . . sometime.'

'I know. I'm leaving now.'

She came to the bathroom door. She had thrown a rough, terry-cloth robe over herself.

'You have my number, haven't you?'

'Yes, I have. Good night.'

She was smiling at me, imitating the way Dorothy had smiled. She mimicked Dorothy's voice. 'Go straight home, Philip. Don't stop at any bars.'

'Good night,' I said, and slammed the door.

*

The manuscript ended there without reaching a conclusion. As if there would be more – later.

Philip threw it down on the desk and reached for the calendar pad. He sat staring at it, fingering its leaves. The 'Confession' purported to be written by himself about events that had occurred the night before. But the date given in the manuscript was Tuesday, December 1 – today. Did that make the 'Confession' actually a prediction?

He had thought while he was reading it that he might possibly have written it himself, and the thought still plagued him. He had also thought that the 'Confession' might be a distorted account of what had happened last night, what he could not remember. Of course, if he had written it himself, he might have mistaken the date – that would account for the discrepancy. But if he had written it himself, when had he had the opportunity? Had he returned to the office to record the details of his latest conquest before he went home to bed? Hardly. He had been drunk the night before, but not that drunk. Nor had he ever been inclined to keep a diary. No, this must have been written by someone else and was intended as a prophecy.

But by whom? Dorothy? Dorothy would not stoop to so

cunning a device; besides, hadn't he always been most cautious to be at all times discreet? He was sure Dorothy suspected nothing, but even if she did she would have too much good sense to jeopardize her own happiness by threatening him. For that was what the 'Confession' did – there was no escaping this conclusion – it constituted a threat.

Jeremy might have written it. Jeremy had always been a little jealous of him, especially since he had married Dorothy. But why should Jeremy come forward with such a preposterous device as this now? He had not seen Jeremy in a year or more. And was Jeremy that subtle? No, Jeremy could bluster – he had once in the past – he could try to bully, but he would never think of planting a 'Confession' on a man's desk. A 'Confession'! Why, the very idea!

What the hell was it all about?

Philip stood up. His face was very red and he had run his hand through his hair again and again. Now he seized the sheaf of manuscript and, turning the pages quickly, re-read a line here, a paragraph there. It was a strange sensation, that of reading an account of actions that were supposed to be his – a sensation that left him with an emptiness in the viscera and a heady feeling of pleasure, much as he supposed he might experience if, upon the completion of a dangerous exploit, he had heard himself praised for his daring. Even while he was first reading it, he had been particularly pleased by certain passages and significantly disturbed by others, although why he should feel either pleased or frightened he could not say. The whole thing was ingenious, and surprisingly accurate, in places. Of course, most of it was nonsensical. He knew no one who fitted the description of the mysterious woman and it was fantastic to predict that he would meet such a person. For the 'Confession' did predict . . . the day it concerned itself with was today . . . the events it described had not happened yet. And wouldn't, if he had anything to say in the matter!

But who had placed it on his desk? Suddenly, he thought of Miss Grey, and, as he did, his face grew livid. He tossed the 'Confession' violently aside and jabbed the button that would call her. While he waited for her to appear at the door, he cursed her under his breath.

When she came into the room, her pencil and notebook in her hand, he asked, 'Did you put anything on my desk this morning, Miss Grey?'

'Just the mail, Mr Banter.'

'Nothing else? No papers, or anything like that?'

'No, Mr Banter, just the mail.'

Philip hesitated. He felt he could not refer openly to the 'Confession'. He did not want anyone else to know about it. But he did want to discover who had put it on his desk.

'Did anyone else come into my office this morning before I arrived?' he asked.

'No, Mr Banter, not while I was here.'

'Or last night – after I had left?'

'Nobody's been near your office, Mr Banter. Is there something wrong?'

Philip thought quickly. 'It's just that someone else has been using my typewriter, that's all!'

The girl look puzzled. 'Nobody has used your typewriter, Mr Banter. I know.'

'I found it open this morning, Miss Grey!' He felt himself growing angrier. She was playing innocent. He knew she was. She had to be!

'Why, Mr Banter, is that what's the matter? That doesn't mean someone else has been using it. That just means that you left it open last night yourself. I remember noticing it.'

Although the girl's blotchy face was wholly earnest, Philip felt she was laughing at him. She wanted to make a fool of him, did she? He would show her a thing or two!

'You're sure of that, Miss Grey?'

'Yes, Mr Banter, I remember you left it open.'

'Why didn't you cover it up then? Isn't that one of the

duties of a good secretary? To see that my desk is in order before you leave?'

'But, Mr Banter –'

'Don't "but" me, I mean it! And another thing, from now on you can spend your spare time cleaning out the correspondence files or helping Miss Campbell. You're not to sit around all day long with your nose in a magazine as if I didn't give you enough to do!'

The girl looked as if she might cry. Philip felt foolish now that his anger was spent. What had been the good of that? Not that he had not been justified, but had he learned anything?

'I'll ring when I need you, Miss Grey.' He watched her leave the room. He was right about it; she had been growing awfully slack of late. Still, he could have gone about it more successfully. He was convinced that she knew more than she said. But what could he do about it?

Someone had to write that story, someone had to put it on his desk. The only possible times this could have happened were after he left the previous afternoon, and that morning before he came in. Miss Grey had said she had been in the office both times. She had to be lying . . . unless he had written it himself. And then forgotten about it . . . impossible!

Philip thought he heard the door to his office click. He did not look up. He waited for the door to open . . . for the person who was there to step into the room. But the door never opened . . . instead, his vision grew dull, the light grew grey and scummy, there was a faint . . . but persistent . . . ringing in his ear. And he felt as though he were breathing cobwebs . . .

He tried to get up, and he could not. He tried to cry out, and he could not. And then he heard the voice . . . a familiar voice . . . one he had heard many times before . . . although he never recognized it as his own until it had stopped . . . his voice when he had been a child . . . a petulant, whining, coaxing voice . . .

'Philip,' the voice said, 'why can't you remember last

34

night? I want you to remember, Philip. We had so much fun.'

Philip buried his head in his hands to shut out that foggy light. He knew that if he opened them before the tinkling in his brain went away, he would still see the light that soiled every object in the room. For a month or more he had been having these spells – that was why he got drunk so often. He never saw the light when he had been drinking, never heard that voice . . .

There it was again. 'Philip, why can't you remember? It was just last night, Philip.'

He clenched his teeth and forced himself to stand erect. Despite the vague fuzziness of his vision, he found the calendar pad and began to check off the day's appointments. Lunch with Peabody at one. Copy conference at two-thirty. Mr Foster's office about the new campaign at four. He looked at his watch – it was a few minutes to twelve. Time enough to have a quick drink and then catch a taxi for the ride downtown.

He stumbled across the room, grabbed his hat and coat and plunged blindly out of his office. 'Philip, why can't you remember?' the voice was saying. As he waited for the elevator in the corridor, he shut his eyes and listened for the voice again. It did not come. By the time he had reached the street his vision had begun to clear and the tinkling sound was fading. The sun was still bright and he had to blink his eyes to see anything. Then he saw a taxi pull up across the street, an empty taxi.

As he stepped forward, the dull, black truck turned out of the next side street – moving with clumsy rapidity. It bore down on him. Philip did not see it. His eyes were intent on the taxi. The taxi driver saw it and shouted at Philip. At the same moment, a woman screamed. The great, dully painted truck swerved – in an attempt to miss Philip, or to make sure of hitting him? Philip looked up and saw the looming headlights, the tarnished radiator grill, the kewpie doll on the front of the hood.

He jumped, sprawled, stretched himself forward and down. A great blast of wind tore at him as he hit the hard pavement. The woman screamed again – and again.

Then the cab-driver was standing over him, helping him up. Automobile horns were honking and a policeman's whistle shrilled. 'Cripes, that was a close one, buddy!' the cabby was saying. 'He looked like he was out to get you – like he swerved right at you! And he kept on goin', didn't even stop for the cop! Are you all right?'

Philip smiled weakly and thanked the driver. He climbed into the cab and told him to get away as fast as he could. 'I'm already late to my appointment,' he explained.

In reality, he wanted some time to think about what had just happened. Was the cabby's hunch correct? Had someone aimed that truck deliberately at him? Was this near-accident and the 'Confession' all part of a scheme – a scheme either to kill him or to drive him out of his mind?

Philip just did not know.

Dr George Matthews was looking at his appointment book. '11 a.m., Mr Steven Foster and Mrs Philip Banter,' he read. Mrs Philip Banter? – that would be Phil's wife, Dorothy, wouldn't it? And Steven Foster – wasn't he Dorothy's father? Dr Matthews was surprised to find their names in his book, but then his appointments were usually made six or more weeks in advance and during the interval he often forgot them. He lighted a cigarette and tried to remember when and why he had made this one. Phil and he had had lunch together a few weeks before – they had kept up their college friendship and they liked to talk over old times. Had Philip asked him to see his wife and her father then? George Matthews doubted it. He made a policy of not accepting his friends as patients and if he had broken this rule, he would remember why he had broken it. No, he had not made this appointment. He picked up his telephone and buzzed Miss Henry, his nurse. She might remember . . .

Miss Henry did remember. 'I made it for you only yesterday, doctor,' she said. 'Mrs Campbell called to say she could not keep her eleven o'clock today. Then Mr Foster called right afterwards and said he wanted to see you as soon as possible. So I squeezed him in today.'

'Thank you, Miss Henry. Will you ask them to come in now?'

Matthews hung up, and ground his cigarette out in the ashtray. Miss Henry had no way of knowing that Mrs Philip Banter was an old friend, but he wished she had checked with him before making the appointment. Dr Matthews did not like analysing his friends or his friends'

friends. Psychoanalysis and friendship belonged in different worlds. But there was little he could do about this now.

The door opened and Miss Henry ushered a beautiful, dark-haired woman and a tall old man into the office. Matthews stood up and shook hands with Steven Foster, while smiling warmly at Dorothy Banter. She acknowledged his greeting. He saw at once that Dorothy was tense and unnaturally excited. She kept glancing back to her father (they had come into the room separately, Dorothy with Miss Henry, her father a discreet distance behind). Now Dorothy sat down and as she did, jerked open her purse, spilling its contents. Matthews came around his desk and stooped to help her pick up the money, powder and cigarettes that had scattered over the carpet. He saw that she was embarrassed, her face flushed as she stammered her thanks, and he wondered at this because Dorothy had always before had remarkable poise.

But if Dorothy's behaviour was puzzling, Steven Foster's attitude was even more interesting. Dorothy's father had not spoken a word. He had nodded his head and smiled grimly when Matthews had shaken hands with him, but he had said nothing. Rather than sit in a comfortable chair, he had walked to the other end of the large, book-lined office and sat on the couch – he was sitting on the edge of it, his cane imprisoned between his knees, his gloves entangled in his fist. It was as if he wanted himself considered a spectator, not a participant.

And yet Dorothy looked at her father and waited until he nodded his head again before she began to explain their presence. 'We have come to see you about Philip,' she said, smiling apologetically. 'You have known Philip as long as I have, and you are a psychiatrist. We thought you might be able to help us.'

Steven Foster thwacked his fist against his thigh. Dorothy, nettled by the unexpected sound, glanced at him. But still he said nothing.

'You see, my husband has been behaving strangely lately,' she added a moment afterwards.

38

'I saw Philip last month,' Matthews said. 'We had lunch together. He struck me about the same as usual. Although, as I remember, he didn't have much to say. But then I don't think about my friends the same way I do about my patients.'

Dorothy smiled at that, and for an instant regained some of her normal composure. She leaned forward and spoke eagerly. 'You don't expect to find psychoses in your friends, you mean?'

'I don't seek them in my friends.'

'Then, perhaps, you can understand how unnerved I am. I didn't expect to find my husband psychotic. But little by little that is the conclusion that is being forced on me . . .'

Dr Matthews made a tent of his hands and peered through it. He was a well-proportioned man in his middle thirties with a face that had once been handsome but had suffered a scar that made it saturnine. Yet there was a kindness in his eyes, a gentleness about his mouth, that told you that here was a man to whom you could talk and he would listen.

'What does your husband do that seems psychotic to you?'

Dorothy fretted with her necklace. 'There are so many things I've noticed, it's hard to decide which to tell you about at first. I suppose I should tell you that he drinks. He drinks a terrible lot. The way an alcoholic drinks.'

'Have you any idea *why* he drinks?' Matthews asked.

Dorothy shook her head. Her dark eyes were half-closed and her full lips were tightly compressed. She seemed to have to fight down a desire to withdraw before she could speak. 'He is unhappy. I can tell that, although he never says so.'

'Do you know why he is unhappy?'

'I thought he might be worried about business. But Dad tells me that he seldom comes into the office any more – and that he's losing all his accounts.'

39

Dr Matthews turned to Steven Foster. 'Has he talked to you about this?'

The old man pulled at his stick. '*I* have talked to him. I told him he was a loafer. I warned him that if he lost another account, he was out of a job.'

'And what was Philip's reaction to your warning?'

Foster tossed his head in disdain. 'He begged me to give him another chance. He said that he had not been himself.'

'Did he say he was ill?'

The old man snorted. 'Ill? Do you call hitting the bottle being ill? If so, Banter's dying!'

Matthews smiled to himself and turned back to Dorothy. He could see that Steven Foster had no wish to cooperate, and he surmised that his antagonism for Philip had deeper roots than he would admit.

'So far, you have told me nothing about your husband's behaviour that would support your fear of insanity, Dorothy. Hasn't he other symptoms that have alarmed you?' Matthews asked. Or else, why are you here? he added to himself.

'The scoundrel has been seen with other women,' growled old Foster.

'That, even when coupled with chronic alcoholism, is not necessarily psychotic,' Matthews said drily. 'Although such men are often neurotic enough.'

Dorothy smoothed her dress, looked at her father and then at Matthews. 'It's been going on a long time. A long, long time. Since before we married, perhaps. And I have never known until recently . . .'

This was growing more and more embarrassing, Matthews thought. If only Philip were here to defend himself! 'Are you sure of what you're saying?' he asked.

Dorothy nodded her head.

'I would think you needed a lawyer instead of a psychiatrist.'

'You don't understand.' Dorothy stood up and walked around her chair, stood holding on to it. 'There is no "other woman". There have been scores – hundreds for all I know. I found his address book. It was full of . . . of their names.'

'The scoundrel!' fumed Steven Foster.

George Matthews was shocked. Philip had been a gay enough blade in college; in fact, he had a reputation then for this sort of thing. But he had seemed to settle down, to be in love with Dorothy. It was difficult to be professional about his wife's confidences: as a friend, he felt he should spring to Philip's defence; as a doctor, he felt his interest should be strictly clinical, probing. He solved this dilemma by straddling.

'Promiscuity is relative,' he said. 'It can be a sign of arrested adolescence, of perpetual self-love, narcissism. Or it can be the end result of a driving fear of impotency. However, by itself, it can hardly be regarded as a sign of insanity – unless it attains the proportions of satyriasis.'

'Of what?' asked Dorothy.

'Satyriasis. Abnormal, excessive sexuality. Fortunately very rare.'

Dorothy thought for a moment. 'There are other signs, too.'

'Yes?'

'Philip disappears.'

'Disappears. What do you mean?'

'He did it only last night. We had dinner together. Afterwards, we sat together for a while, then Philip discovered that he hadn't any cigarettes. He said he was going down to the corner to get some. I waited a half hour for him to come back – and then an hour. He did not return. I went down to the drugstore. He had not been there. I went to the bar across the street. The bartender knows us. Philip had been in, he said. He had had several drinks and then had left with a woman he met there. The bartender was reluctant to tell me this, but I wheedled it out of him. He said he thought Philip had picked her up . . .'

'I see,' said Dr Matthews. He did not know what else to

say. He knew that he did not want to have anything to do with this. Philip had been his friend for a long time. If his actions were peculiar, who was he to say they were amoral – let alone that they were evidence of insanity? And Matthews did not like the way old Steven Foster sat on the couch and glared at him without saying a word.

'This isn't the first time this has happened,' Dorothy was saying. 'Philip disappears like that often – increasingly often. Once he left me at the theatre. Just said he was going out for a smoke. I didn't see him until the next morning. He was drunk and he smelt of cheap perfume. I asked him where he had been and he said he didn't remember. I pressed him, and he began to tell me a wild story. He said he kept seeing a "dingy light" and hearing a "persistent ringing as if a tiny bell was tinkling somewhere far off". He also said that he heard a voice – he asked me if I heard it! – that repeatedly chided him for not remembering what he had done the night before. And that was all I could get out of him.

'Another time he was to meet me on a street corner. I saw him across the street. I saw him look at me and then go into a bar. I waited a few minutes and then crossed the street. But when I went into the bar he wasn't there. He must have gone out a back entrance. He didn't come home for days that time. And, as usual, he said he could not remember what he had done or where he had gone.'

Dorothy had been speaking furiously. Now she stopped, to catch her breath, and glanced at her father. The old man's posture and mien had not changed. His hand still clutched his gloves. His cane still shot upright from between his knees. His unyielding gaze seemed to Matthews outrageously malevolent. But Dorothy was relieved – she sighed and some of the stiffness left her face – when Steven Foster nodded his head curtly.

'What do you think, doctor?' Dorothy asked.

Matthews spoke slowly, emphatically. 'I've known Philip for a long time. He was always sensitive. When I first met him his adjustment was dependent and precarious –

he leaned heavily on his friend, Jeremy Foulkes, used him as a model and mentor. But then Jeremy did the same with him. It is not unusual in college to see two friends who mutually idolize and patronize each other in this way.

'But after Phil met you, it seemed to me that he matured quickly. If he was something of a Lothario in college, I thought he was now a devoted husband. I am surprised, and a little shocked, to hear your testimony to the contrary. And I am put in an uncomfortable position. Your husband is still my friend, Dorothy – even as you are my friend. A doctor, especially a doctor of the mind, must put aside all emotional allegiance when he accepts a patient. If Philip had come to me, and told me that he was ill, I might be able to work with him. But when you and your father come to me, and tell me these things without Philip's knowledge, there is little I can do. It is not that I doubt your word, but just that I do not see how I can act honourably, as a friend, or effectively, as a physician.'

'You could talk to the man!' exploded Steven Foster, projecting his resonant voice across the room. 'You could call him down, tell him he is ruining his life!' The old man's rugged face was infused with colour.

'A psychiatrist never calls anyone down, Mr Foster,' Matthews said abruptly. 'Nor would I, as an individual, think of dealing that way with Philip. Neither is it sound medicine, nor sound friendship.' He looked at Dorothy, who had also arisen. 'I would like to talk with Philip though, Dorothy. Perhaps, the next time we have lunch together, he will ask my advice. You must understand that it is psychologically necessary for the patient to come to the doctor. All you can do is inform me that Philip is ill. Of all that you have told me, only the "voice" that he hears seems symptomatic to me. That doesn't mean that you aren't right in your suspicions that Philip is facing a break. But you should realize that while drinking – even heavy drinking – and promiscuity are often neurotic, they are not by themselves signs of a psychosis.'

George Matthews had walked to where Dorothy was

standing: now he took her hand. Her dark eyes were quiet and brooding. Her mouth trembled. 'I'm afraid he doesn't love me,' she said simply. 'He has changed so. I don't know what I've done.'

Matthews did not know what to say. He was concerned, too, but he was not sure whether it was Philip who was ill. He tried to be matter-of-fact. 'Talk to him. Encourage him to talk to you. Try to get him to tell you why he leaves you. Don't be jealous. Don't attempt to watch him every moment. Give him his freedom. Suggest that he come and speak to me.'

They were at the door. Matthews glanced at his watch and saw that it was time for his next appointment. Then Steven Foster, who had at last gotten to his feet and walked over to them, broke in irately.

'You doctors are all alike!' he cried. 'You never have any time for common-sense, direct methods. I thought you might be different from what I read in the newspapers, and what my daughter told me, of how you solved the Raye case.* But no, all you can do is to mumble scientific terms and beat about the bush. Why don't you come right out and tell the girl that the only thing she can do with a man like Philip Banter is to divorce him or have him horsewhipped?'

Dr George Matthews, for the first time in his life, held the door of his office open for a patient. He was exceedingly angry, although he did not show it, and he wanted Steven Foster to leave immediately. But he answered his outburst with courtesy. 'I never prescribe horsewhipping as therapy. Corporal punishment is at once mediaeval, cruel and ineffective. As to divorce, that is not for me to decide – certainly not on such skimpy evidence. Since you have been rude enough to allude to my experiences with the police, and my abilities as an amateur detective, all I can

* Steven Foster referred to the mysterious death of Frances Raye, in which Dr Matthews was innocently involved. The psychiatrist solved this mystery with the aid of the police and gained some fame. cf. *The Deadly Percheron.*

say is that both have been exaggerated – and that I hope I shall never have the opportunity to add to them.'

Dr Matthews smiled again at Dorothy, turned and went to his desk. His mind was already on his next patient. Dorothy took her father's arm – the obstinate old man was still enraged – and led him from the room.

When they had reached the street, Steven Foster hailed a taxi and told the driver to take them to the Algonquin. He sat in a corner of the cab, his lean fingers caressing the polished knob of his stick, his eyes intent upon the taximeter. Dorothy smoked a cigarette nervously and tried not to keep glancing at her father. She knew now that she should never have come to him that morning and told him about Philip. She had found him at breakfast, alone at the long table in the formal dining-room of the town house in which she had spent her girlhood – and the sight of her father at the head of the table had, as always, vanquished her. He had looked at her and asked, 'What have you done?' The question had stripped her maturity from her, made her a guilty daughter again, forced the conversation into a well-known pattern that allowed the full expression of parental authority.

Within a few minutes she had told her father all the most secret of her fears and suspicions about Philip – the accusing words had come tumbling out in response to his probing, skilful questions. And, as she confessed, she felt the full shame of her self-betrayal. She realized that she was damning both Philip and herself by giving in to her father, yet this knowledge did not deter her. She had only wanted to come to her father's house for a few days, to stay away long enough for her absence to worry Philip. Her father would not have known, indeed, she had not wanted him to know, what was wrong. If she had not forgotten that she had never been able to withhold the truth about any of her misdeeds from her father, she also had not recognized that she felt guilty about her relationship with Philip. And yet she must have felt guilty, why else had she

45

confessed? It was this unpremeditated action of hers that bewildered her.

Once she had told Steven Foster about her husband's loose habits and queer ways, the old man had become coldly angry. He had wanted her to see his lawyer at once. This she had refused to do since she felt a need to defend Philip against her father's authority. Not that she had not thought of divorce before; she had on many occasions when Philip had deserted her or by some chance she had uncovered fresh evidence of his chronic infidelity. But to have her father suggest that she see a lawyer was, in some way she did not understand, treachery. Instead, she had said that she wanted to consult George Matthews – whom she knew to be Philip's friend – and her father had gone to arrange the appointment, grumbling about 'that modern fad, psychoanalysis'.

Dorothy had never expected to get an appointment that day, in fact, she had hoped that the time set would be weeks in advance and that by then she would have solved her difficulties with Philip. When her father had come back from the telephone and announced grimly that 'Dr Matthews will see us at eleven o'clock,' she had been horrified. Her mouth had gone dry and her pulse had pounded. She had wanted at that moment to call Philip, to ask his help. But this she could not do, nor was there any way she could escape the appointment.

The taxi jolted to a stop at a traffic light and the sudden jar interrupted her thoughts. She looked out the window and saw that they were nearing the hotel. Her father still sat rigidly in his corner, and the sight of him made her want to shudder. In the past such fits of taciturnity meant that he was arriving at a decision which he would ultimately force upon her. Now he was probably planning how to deal with Philip. Dorothy leaned forward and deposited her cigarette in the bent and battered ashtray that clung to the side of the door. This time, no matter what Steven Foster decides, I will not do it, she said to herself. And the part of her that always quarrelled with her highest ideals and most fervent resolutions, her materialistic conscience, reminded her – 'If you don't, it will be the first time since you married Philip that you have gone against your father's wishes.'

The light changed to green, the taxi lurched forward and turned down the side street to the hotel. Steven Foster did not change his position until the cab had come to a full stop in front of the Algonquin, then he flicked a bill at the driver, clambered out and stood stiffly while his daughter stepped down. Taking her arm he said, 'We shall have luncheon here and while we eat we can decide what to do about Philip.'

Dorothy shook her arm free of his firm grasp and walked ahead of him into the lobby. She walked rapidly, as if she wanted to escape him. He stepped forward slowly and resolutely, as if he knew that for her escape was impossible.

While Dorothy and her father lunched at the Algonquin, Philip and Mr Peabody had luncheon at Angelo's in the financial district. The Peabody account had not been a fortunate one for Brown and Foster. Sales had fallen off during the first year's campaign, despite an enlarged budget and additional space in the latter half of the year. A few weeks before Philip had submitted the suggested programme for the next twelve months, a campaign which Philip had worked out himself, supervising it down to the last detail with the copywriter and the art director. But Philip had not given it much thought since it had been submitted. The fact was that recently he had found it impossible to think about advertising matters at all. He sat at his desk, when he was at the office, and tried to remember the intervals that he had forgotten. Sometimes, his vision would fog, the dingy, dirty light would soil everything he looked at, and the voice would begin to pester him about yesterday or the day before.

'Philip, why can't you remember. Think hard, Philip . . .'

So Philip was not prepared to defend the merits of the

campaign, and this was exactly what he was called upon to do. He had left the taxi at One Wall Street, still shaken by his narrow escape from death a few minutes before, and had taken an express elevator to one of the topmost floors of the tall building. As he stepped out of the car at his floor, a large man pushed past him hurriedly, knocking him off his balance. He fell backwards into the elevator just as the automatic doors were closing. He knew that these doors did not bounce back from an obstruction like subway doors, but kept closing inexorably. He struggled desperately, off-balance, to lunge forward – spurred on by the helpless cry of the elevator operator who was reaching to reverse the controls. Suddenly, he was struck in the back, slammed forward onto his knees. And at almost the same moment, the heavy doors whispered together and he heard the car drop down the well. He knelt on the floor, breathing heavily, cold sweat on his forehead. Had there been two attempts on his life inside of a half-hour? Or had the burly man, who had entered the elevator successfully and without Philip's seeing him full on, only accidentally knocked him off-balance? Both his near collision with the truck and his almost being crushed to death *might* have been accidents – but they also *might* have been attempts on his life. He was going to have to be very careful.

Philip stood up, brushed at his knees and walked down the corridor to Peabody and Company. He gave his name to the receptionist and she showed him into the board room where Evergood Peabody, the president of the company, was surrounded by his vassals. The campaign was spread out on the long table and the men were hunched over it, exhaling cigar smoke at it, peering at it malevolently. As he entered the room. Philip heard one of them saying, 'I agree with you, Mr Peabody. Even the theme, the basic gimmick, hasn't the "Peabody push".'

Philip saw at a glance that the campaign was being torn apart. All the men, every one of whom depended on Evergood Peabody for his opinion but – once the line of argument to follow was established – were quite capable of destroying good copy and art in any number of ingenious ways, jumped on Philip at once. 'The headlines have no zing,' said one, another said; 'The copy's too long, it takes too much time getting in the sales punch.' 'I miss the "Peabody push",' said a third voice. 'This thing hasn't enough class, no real distinction,' complained another.

Fighting off these generalities as effectively as he could, Philip tried to concentrate his sales talk on the essential – tried at all times, even when he was addressing a subordinate, to aim his argument at Evergood Peabody. For, as everyone knew, the president made all decisions at Peabody and Company.

At one o'clock, Evergood called off the discussion. 'I just wanted you to get my department heads' reactions,' he told Philip, chummily putting his arm around him. 'Let's you and me go to Angelo's for lunch where we can talk this over quietly. Then we can decide what to do.'

Philip followed the client out of the board room and down the hall. He knew that the dogfight he had just been in might mean nothing at all, or it might be highly significant. The real decision would come from Evergood Peabody himself in the next half-hour or so. Even now he was making up his mind.

And Philip did not really care. He was preoccupied with his own problems: the two 'accidents', the voice he heard, the 'Confession'. He was especially concerned with the voice, because – as they walked down Wall to Pearl Street and Angelo's – the voice kept sounding in his ear. 'You have to be more careful, Philip,' it was saying. 'You're so forgetful – you even forget to look when you cross a street. Please remember what I say, Philip.' He was glad when they reached the restaurant and found a table quickly. Now, for a few minutes, Peabody would be busy eating and drinking and telling his interminable stories, now he could relax and perhaps the voice would go away. But he did not relax and the voice did not go away.

While Peabody talked at length about a hunting trip

49

he had taken in Canada, Philip listened to the voice. There had been moments when he had not been able to hear it since he left the office. But the sound of bells had persisted, as had the queer, dirty light. He picked up a knife from the table and held it in front of his eyes. If he could only see the silver gleam, he would feel better. But, no, the same greasy film seemed to cling to it, too, just as it covered his hand, the tablecloth, yes, even Peabody's face!

Only then, as he looked hard at his face for quite another reason, did Philip realize that Peabody had asked him an important question, a very important question.

'I beg your pardon,' Philip said, 'I didn't understand.'

Peabody coughed pompously and patted his chin with his napkin. 'I would have thought you'd hear that! I asked you if you can think of any good reason why my company should retain your agency's services.'

The ringing ceased. The fogginess faded and in its place were the hard outlines of Peabody's heavy-jowled face, brightly, sharply defined. Philip's mind baulked at the meaning of the words it heard. Why, the man was firing the agency, they were losing the account! And only a moment before he had been talking about the seven point buck he had shot!

By now Peabody was glowering at him. 'Maybe you don't hear so well today, Mr Banter,' he said. 'If so, I'll repeat my charges. Our sales are off twenty per cent – thirteen per cent in the last five months with December yet to come in. They're falling in the face of the biggest Christmas season this country's ever known. All the time our advertising costs are going up. Every time you have recommended more papers, a bigger budget, fancier artwork. The copy remains the same. Oh, you change a few words here and there and tack on a new headline – but that's all. Now, you submit a new campaign. And what do I see?' He stopped and flopped his fat hand down on the presentation. The diamond on his middle finger glared at Philip. 'I see the same old crap!' he snarled. 'The very same pretty girls, the same old reason why copy, the same boilerplate layout. There's not a new idea in that whole campaign. Peabody and Company couldn't use an inch of it – let alone hike the budget by five hundred grand the way you have the gall to suggest!'

He peeled the band from a panatella and stuck it in his mouth. He did not offer Philip a cigar, although there were two in his pocket. 'In view of that,' he went on, 'I ask you if you can tell me any reason why we should continue your contract?'

Philip said nothing. All he could think was: if Peabody walks out on us that will be the third client in two months. What will the old man say?

The silence grew. Peabody puffed away at his cigar until the booth they were sitting in was clothed with smoke. Philip tried several times to speak, to say something like 'If you could be a little less destructive in your comment, Mr Peabody' or 'Now, suppose we look at just one ad. and you tell me what is wrong,' but each time he failed to get the words out of his mouth. Finally, Peabody reached for his hat.

'If you haven't got anything to say for yourself, young man, we're just wasting our time.' He pushed the cloth-bound presentation across the table. 'Here, maybe you can use this some place else. It isn't a bad programme. It's just not the thing we need right now with sales falling off.' The heavy jowls relaxed into a grin. He was being proud of himself for being sympathetic.

'We can have another programme on your desk next week, Mr Peabody,' Philip managed to say. 'If you will just show me what's wrong, where we took the wrong turning –'

But Peabody was shaking his head. 'You heard what the department heads had to say, son. They're the ones that know – they're the ones that have their hands on the public's pulse. I'm not saying it's your fault, son. I know you try your best to sell our stuff, but you just don't seem to have what it takes.' His eyes glinted. 'Get your hat and I'll walk you to the Battery. The sea air will do you good.

Looks to me like you haven't been getting enough exercise, son.'

Philip reached for his hat and the check. Three accounts gone in two months. What would old Foster say? And, as he walked glumly out the door behind Peabody, he heard the voice again. 'Philip,' it coaxed, 'we had so much fun last night. Why can't you remember?'

Steven Foster returned to his office in the middle of the afternoon. He walked through all the departments of the agency, looked into all the offices, stopped and talked to a man here, a girl there. Foster had been in advertising for over thirty-five years. He had started his own agency with Brown, long since dead, twenty years before. There had been times when he had written most of the copy – he had even helped with layout – when the agency was hard-hit by the depression and they were losing most of their clients. He was of the old school of advertising men, a man who could write a book or a rateholder, sell banks or soap.

He took a paternal pride in his force and showed an interest in their welfare that was frequently unwelcome. It was not uncommon for him to stop a secretary whose eyes seemed tired and whose face was pale and command her 'to get more sleep at nights'. And he had been known to sniff a copywriter's breath. He walked into the art department without knocking and loved to make detailed comments on finished artwork that drove the art directors out of their minds. Each ad. had to be personally approved by him – he was reputed to know every schedule in the agency. On occasion he had kept the production men working day and night to get an intaglio layout proofing up right – he had once even invaded the precinct of a syndicate's rotogravure shop to demand a sharper definition in the printing of a client's trademark. But he made up for this driving mania for perfection, or so he reasoned himself, by his generosity. His wages were among the highest in the business, his employees shared equally in the agency's profits, his Christmas bonuses were enormous. But as one paste-up boy put it, 'I'd rather do without an extra finn at Christmas so's I didn't have to worry every day in the week that the next minute I'd find old S.F. breathing down my neck telling me to move the logo a sixteenth of an inch and watch that I set that cut down at exactly a 40 degree angle.'

The aloof severity that marked Steven Foster's manner was actually a kind of restraint. He was naturally a man who itched to get his hands into everything, who was supremely confident that he could do any man's job better than that man. Often he could, but he had learned that he could not always prove his abilities. And he was the same way about his loves and hates. He liked few people. He loved many and hated many. A man could become his deep friend, without the man's knowing it, within the duration of a handshake – and a man could become a bosom enemy in as short a space. But Foster kept his feelings hidden, revealing them, if at all, only in crisis. As a result, everyone feared him, even his daughter – for whom he held the deepest love.

When he had finished his stroll through the agency, Foster returned to his own office and seated himself behind the broad desk. He kicked open the bottom drawer on which he rested his foot, picked up his telephone and asked the switchboard girl to tell Miss Grey to come in to see him. While he waited for Philip's secretary to arrive, he bit the end off a fresh cigar, lighted it and exhaled clouds of smoke at the ceiling.

Like many wealthy men, he was unused to having people say no to him and when it happened he was hurt; although he usually hid his feelings behind a gruff taciturnity. His temper was particularly short at this moment because Dorothy had refused to agree to divorce Philip. Foster had argued with her for an hour at lunch, yet she had remained steadfast. 'You know that I have usually followed your advice, father, but you must realize that this is one problem that I have to solve for myself. You can grumble and berate me as much as you like, but I shall make up my own mind.'

Her adamancy especially rankled Steven, since he had never liked Philip and was pleased that Dorothy's marriage was not working out. His reasons for not liking Philip were, for him, the best ones. He knew no Banters, had never heard of the family, and none of his friends had either. But Dorothy had insisted on marrying him, and he had been unable to prevent her since she had been of age. He had toyed with the idea of disinheriting her, but had dismissed that as being petty. Actually, he had been more than generous. He had given the puppy more than enough rope: a good job, a handsome apartment, a responsibility in the agency. He chuckled. It was working out just as he thought it would . . . although no one could say he had not been willing to give Philip a chance . . .

'Yes, Mr Foster?' Miss Grey had come into the room without him hearing her. She was standing in front of his desk, a slight smile on her face. Good girl!

Steven Foster glanced at her, and then nodded his head. He did not speak.

'Mr Banter came into the office about four o'clock yesterday afternoon. He had not been in all day. He seemed as if he had been drinking. I am not sure as I did not get close enough to him to catch his breath.' The girl spoke mechanically as if she were reciting. 'I waited around until five-thirty, at which time he came out and told me to go home. Remembering your instructions not to do anything suspicious, I left. However, I gave the charwoman a dollar and asked her to tell me if Mr Banter was still there when she cleaned his office. She told me this morning that he was still in his office at six o'clock, and that he was very drunk. She said he had his typewriter out on his desk, but he was just staring at it. He had not written a thing.'

The girl paused and looked at Foster. He nodded his head again, and she went on. 'This morning Mr Banter arrived about ten o'clock. He had been drinking. He went into his office and, a moment later, called me in. He asked me why I had let somebody use his typewriter. I told him that nobody had used his typewriter but himself. Then why was it open on his desk? he asked. I told him that he had left it open the night before. He got very angry and told me that I was to make sure that his typewriter was shut up before I left. Apparently he had forgotten that I left ahead of him last night.'

Miss Grey stopped, and stood waiting for her employer to speak.

'Where is Mr Banter now?'

'He went to lunch with Mr Peabody shortly before noon. His appointment was for one o'clock. He has not returned.'

The old man smiled. 'Thank you, Miss Grey. That will be all for now.' He held up his hand as she started to leave. 'Except that you might tell Mr Banter to see me as soon as he comes in.'

Miss Grey opened the door. 'Yes, Mr Foster,' she said.

She shut the door and Steven Foster sat staring at it, chewing vigorously at the end of his cigar. 'I'll teach the puppy!' he said.

Philip had a drink, and then another before he returned to the office. He would not have come back that day, if he had not had an appointment with old Foster at four. As it was, he needed the false courage of the whisky.

He joked half-heartedly with Sadie on his way up in the elevator, and was careful not to look at the starched elegance of the receptionist as he entered the offices. He did not go back to his own cubicle, so Miss Grey did not have a chance to deliver her message. Philip knew that there was no use putting off the inevitable. He strode right into Steven Foster's private office.

The old man was still sitting, chewing on the end of a now dead cigar, his feet propped up on an open drawer. He did not look around when Philip came into the room, but he did glance up when Philip laid the presentation down on the polished surface of the desk.

'How many O.K.s did you get?' Foster asked.

Philip shook his head.

'Not a one?'

Philip did not answer.

'What does he want us to do?'

Philip cleared his throat. Everything was bright and clear now. He heard no ringing, no voice. But still it was all he could do to hold on to himself. He stared at the hard lines of Steven Foster's face, the etched wrinkles and the wide, compressed angle of the mouth, the obscenity of the limp cigar. He felt himself sinking into that face, being devoured by it . . .

'There will be no new campaign,' he said. 'We have lost the account.'

The old man took his cigar out of his mouth and laid it gently in the gold-plated ashtray. He stood up slowly. He walked slowly around the large desk until he was standing directly opposite Philip.

'I am going to give you a month's notice, Philip,' he said pleasantly. 'Through the end of December. Call it a Christmas present if you want.' He held out his hand.

Philip took it and shook it grimly. There was nothing else to do.

Miss Grey saw Philip go into Steven Foster's office. She went to the water-cooler, which was near the president's office, and stood by it. She had finished two Dixie Cups of water and was about to start on a third, when she saw Philip come out of the door. His face was flushed, his lips compressed, his eyes defiant. Miss Grey turned slightly so that as he went past the water cooler, he would not see her. As soon as he had gone down the hall to his own office, she followed him. But she did not go back to her desk. Instead she knocked on the door of the office next to Philip's. And when a masculine voice cried, 'Come in!' she went inside.

This office was as large as Philip's and hers put together, but four desks occupied it. Two of these were empty, at a third a young woman was diligently typing – she did not look up when Miss Grey entered – and at a fourth a young man was sitting staring out of the window with his hands behind his head. Miss Grey went to this last desk. The young man looked up at her.

'What is it, Alice?' he asked.

'I'd like to see you tonight, Tom. For just a few minutes.'

The man smiled, he had a nice smile, and looked at his watch. 'The usual place? After work?'

Alice Grey nodded her head.

'Good,' said the young man.

The girl at the other desk went on typing.

'The usual place' was a restaurant on the lower level of the R.C.A. building. Alice Grey was there at ten minutes after five, and she waited another ten minutes before Tom Jamison arrived. They found a booth and ordered beers.

'What do you have to tell me that couldn't wait until I came for you at eight? Or did you forget we have a date tonight?'

Miss Grey reached over and squeezed his hand. 'I didn't forget, of course. But I just learned something that was too good to keep.'

'What?'

'I think that Philip Banter is going to be fired!'

Tom looked at her, barely suppressing a smile. 'Are you sure?'

'No, I'm not sure. But he's been getting worse and worse. And, you know, I've had to report everything he did to Mr Foster each day. Well, when I told him he was drunk again last night, you should have seen his face! He thanked me, but he was very angry. Then I saw Philip go into his office and come out within two or three minutes. Something had happened, Tom – I'm sure! I could tell by the way Philip acted. I'm thinking that he fired Philip this afternoon!'

57

Tom sipped his beer. 'What has this to do with me?' he asked coldly.

Miss Grey bit her lip. 'But, Tom, this is just what we've been working towards.'

'Just because Philip loses his job – that doesn't mean I get it again.'

'Who will S.F. put in his place but you? Someone will have to take care of those accounts. You always did it well, before Philip came. Oh, Tom, this is what we've been working towards for months!'

Tom Jamison allowed himself a smile. Actually, he agreed with Alice that if Philip had lost his job, old Foster would give it back to him. And why not? Had Foster ever had any reason for taking him off those accounts in the first place, except that of making room for Philip? Now, Tom would get a little of his own back.

But all he said was, 'Drink up, Alice, and let's get out of here. Someone might hear us talking.'

3

'Oh, Philip, how beautiful! How sweet of you!'

Dorothy could not keep from beaming. Philip was pleased by her pleasure. It was ever-surprising to him to see how ingenuously happy a woman could be over a simple gift of flowers. Childish, yes, but wonderful – a constant in an inconsistent world.

'Whatever made you think of them, darling?'

She was fussing with the stems, filling a vase with water, arranging them on the mantelpiece. While he watched, he noticed for the first time that she was wearing a dinner dress. Were they going out? He would have to remember to ask her.

'I saw them in the window,' he said, 'and I thought of you.'

Dorothy had finished arranging the blood-red flowers, but she seemed loath to leave them; she stood looking at them, her head tilted upwards. Philip could discern the whiteness of the part in her glossy hair. He walked over to her, placed his hands gently on her bare shoulders, turned her about and kissed her. She was warm and sweetly scented.

'It was nice of you to think of them tonight, Philip – when we are having company that we can show them off to.'

There was a circular mirror above the fireplace; Philip looked into it, over her shoulder, and saw his own long face grow grim. 'Company? Tonight? Whom?'

'Jeremy and a friend. He called up this afternoon and asked if we'd be in. I tried to get you at the office, but the switchboard girl said you and father were in conference. Why, Philip, what's wrong? Are you ill?'

Dorothy put her arm around him and helped him to the sofa. Her dark eyes were suddenly anxious, her hands quick to feel his brow, to unbutton his shirt – her voice was sincerely worried.

'Your face changed so abruptly, Philip. You're still pale – tell me what's wrong.'

'I'm all right. I was . . . startled.' It had been a shock. He had quite forgotten about the 'Confession'. He must hold on to his wits. He dare not let her know.

'Well, if you're sure you're all right . . .?'

He patted her hand. He was very fond of her: the gentleness of her ways, the ease with which she moved, her sincerity. 'I'm all right, Dorothy. I don't know what came over me, but it's passed.'

'I was telling you about Jeremy, when all at once I thought you were having some sort of an attack.'

'You said Jeremy called and told you he was bringing a friend. Are they coming to dinner? Did he mention his friend's name?'

'Some girl. He said we hadn't met. He said he wanted me to see her. Philip, do you know what?'

'No.'

'Philip, I do believe Jeremy's in love! It certainly sounded like it over the 'phone. Oh, I hope he is! It would do him so much good. You know I've always said . . .'

Philip stood up. He staggered. Dorothy jumped up, caught at him – but by then he had found his balance.

'Philip, are you sure you're all right? You almost fell.'

'I'm perfectly all right. I'll go in and change my clothes now. Nothing is the matter with me. It was just that something you said startled me.'

'But, Philip, I was only telling you about Jeremy. Why should that have startled you?'

'I must have been thinking about something else at the time. I'll go in and change now.'

'I'll be in the kitchen with cook if you need me, Philip.'

He looked back at her as he left the room, and he saw

that she was watching him. She looked like a little girl in a sophisticated dress. A worried little girl.

Philip felt sorry for his wife. He almost felt like crying.

He sat on the bed, his fingers fumbling with the buttons of his shirt, thinking. Was the impossible about to happen? Was all that the 'Confession' predicted about to come true? No, he couldn't believe that. This was a coincidence. To think otherwise was superstition. And it was to deny his own will. The rest of the prophecy would not happen because he would keep it from happening. If he knew the danger he had to face, as he did, he could avoid it. He would not allow himself to look at this girl Jeremy was bringing, not even one glance.

But it had been a shock. Wasn't it strange how he had managed to forget that damnable story? Not so strange, after all. You don't get fired every afternoon, and when such a calamity does befall you tend to think of nothing else. If the 'Confession' was so good, why didn't it predict that? No, of course, the manuscript had said nothing about what would happen that afternoon. It concerned itself only with what was to happen that evening.

Why couldn't he have continued to forget about it? If it was going to happen anyway . . . He had been completely happy in Dorothy's happiness, her unalloyed joy over his gift. He had even managed to stop thinking about the things Foster had said, the curt way he had discharged him. And then she had said that – practically the way she had said it in the manuscript. Or had she used the same words? Was this only a trick of his imagination? He could not tell without re-reading those pages still safely locked in his desk drawer at the office.

Why not plead illness? Why not go to bed? Dorothy would believe him since she already feared that he was ill. If he said he was sick, then he would not have to meet Jeremy or his friend.

Or his friend. Was he admitting the possibility that Jeremy's friend would be the woman in the manuscript?

Did that mean that, so soon, he was ready to give up? Was superstitious panic this close to the surface? A few mysterious occurrences, none of them definite proof of the manuscript's predictions, and he was ready to abandon all logic, all reason, to a savage irresolution!

It did not have to happen. It could not be ordained. There was no such thing as fate (and even if there were, the author of the 'Confession' was not privy to it). He could not be made to do something he did not want to do.

But what if he wanted to do it? Suppose he was attracted to this girl, would he then have the will to ignore her? Suppose she was attracted to him (as the manuscript said she would be), would he then be able to ward her off?

He had to. There was no escaping that conclusion. If it all came to pass (it was impossible – it could not – these events could not possibly occur!), would he be able to withstand the temptation?

When Philip finished dressing, he lay down on his bed and tried to smoke a cigarette. He found that he was breathing too rapidly and too irregularly to accommodate the habit of smoking: he gasped and choked until his eyes watered. He threw the cigarette away and stared at the ceiling, his hands clasped behind his head. He waited. He could hear his wife moving about in the living-room, and he could catch occasional fragments of her conversation with the cook, who must be setting the table. He felt detached and lonely. As a boy he had often had the same feeling when visitors came to call on his mother and he hid himself in his room because of his reluctance to meet strangers. He had been modest and reticent in those days, and he suffered from feelings of inadequacy. Now, emotionally, he was the groping adolescent again. His mother's face (she was long dead) hovered in his mental eye, a vague, disembodied face that seemed to be trying to tell him something, to communicate with him . . . He shut his eyes to concentrate on the evasive image; it enlarged in size and foreboding, but it became no more distinct. Warmth, an uncomfortable warmth, pressed down on him and, at the same time, he knew that he was sinking into timelessness, an unnatural kind of sleep. Then, all upon an instant, he was awake again, wholly alert, sitting forward, strained and tense with shock. He had heard the ghost of a tinkle, the last faint vibration of the doorbell – and now, voices – not a voice, not *the* voice he had come to expect to hear, a man's voice and a woman's voice . . . in the hall.

Not until Dorothy called to him, concerned about him, 'Philip, are you all right? – Jeremy and Brent are here, Philip! are you about ready?' did he go out to meet his guests.

As he entered his own living-room he was still existing partly in the emotional context of his youth; it was as if he had walked into his mother's parlour: the warm, un-aired, shut-in odour oppressed him (the sliding doors had been kept closed, the windows shut and locked against the dust so that everything would look nice when company came). He found himself comparing Dorothy to his mother – the likeness about the eyes was particularly remarkable. He promised himself again that he would not look at Jeremy's friend, even while being introduced to her. He glanced at Jeremy once; as soon as he saw how fat his friend's formerly open, boyish face had become, and had seen the fold of flesh that bulged slightly above the purposely loose collar of his shirt, he turned back to Dorothy (remembering how as a child he had kept his gaze steadfastly on his mother while forcing himself to mumble the polite words, to say 'I'm glad to know you').

No one noticed his shyness. Jeremy was being boister-ous, as usual. He had walked over and clapped Philip on the back, and had pumped his hand. 'Where you been keeping yourself, Phil? Long time no see! Auld acquaint-ance shouldn't be given the brush-off, you know!'

'Philip has been kept very busy at the agency, Jerry,' Dorothy was saying. 'Neither of us meant to neglect you. It's just that we hardly ever have a day to ourselves.'

Philip saw that Dorothy was frowning at him. Then she had noticed that something was wrong. He would have to do better than this. He would have to look at the woman, at least.

Jeremy again. 'Phil, I want you to meet Brent Holliday, a little something special I've picked up since last we met. Smile your prettiest for the nice gentleman, Brent dear!'

Had Jeremy always been like this? Philip did not remember him as being quite so blatant, so downright vulgar. Had a year really made that much difference?

And then, thinking about Jeremy, trying to compare the man before him with the memory of a friendship that was over, Philip forgot and looked at Brent. His mind neglected its principal concern for the duration of an instant and, in so doing, dropped its defences of shyness and withdrawal. He turned and looked directly into her eyes, and he did it as much to get away from Jeremy as for any other reason. He did not look away.

Brent was not beautiful. He saw at once that she was even careless of her personal appearance: her mouth needed fresh lipstick, her long bob fell naturally, loosely, to her shoulders – it had not been trained to fall that way by a hairdresser – the gold pin above her breasts was fastened crookedly to the high-necked tunic of her dress. But her eyes were alive, brown flecked unevenly with a glinting, changing colour, commanding. She was half-leaning against the back of the sofa, regarding him mockingly. He realized that she had noticed his awkward reticence, too, and had been amused by it. Where, at first, he had thought no one was aware of his shyness, and he had been able to hope that it was but an inward state of himself, now he knew that both Brent and Dorothy had sensed his fear at once, and that only Jeremy was unconscious of it.

'I'm glad to know you, Philip,' Brent was saying, looking past him at his wife. 'Tell me, Dorothy, is he always this shy? Why, he's just like a little boy. A frightened, little boy!'

64

But as she said these cruelly jocular words, Philip saw her face change; or was it that he was seeing her as she was instead of the façade she wished him to see? The badly rouged lips were actually quite controlled; the slurred words were slurred consciously. Her eyes held his like a man's; it was almost as if she had put out her hand, grabbed the stuff of his stiff shirt, held him at arm's length and cried, 'Here you are – I have you!'

'Philip – shy?' Jeremy exploded into laughter. 'Oh, he's shy all right. Tell her how shy he is, Dottie. Go on, tell her!'

'It isn't that he's shy, Brent. It's just that he had a dizzy spell before you came and he still feels a little shaky. Are you all right now, Philip?'

At this cue, Brent's expression changed again, became demure, penitent.

'Oh, I'm sorry, Mr Banter, I didn't know you felt badly. I wouldn't have said what I did.'

Philip thought he detected a sense of disappointment in what she said, as if he weren't all that she had expected. Or was he reading too much into a few casual words? He looked away from her and went over to sit down next to Dorothy. Jeremy was still laughing. 'Phil, tell her about how you met Dottie. Go on and tell her, Phil. Oh, he's shy all right!'

Brent's face stiffened. She seemed annoyed by Jeremy, sympathetic to Philip. 'Do you have to go on so, Jeremy?' she asked.

'It is rather amusing, Brent,' said Dorothy. 'What Jerry's referring to. You see I met Jerry before I met Philip. In fact I met Philip through Jerry. Jerry was always telling me about Philip. It was always "Philip did this" or "Philip said that" – so I got curious about this man I was always hearing about, but never seemed to meet –'

'Do we have to rehash all that, Dorothy?' Philip asked. He felt enough of a fool already.

'He's just shy, Dottie!' Jeremy insisted. 'Don't let him stop you now.'

Dorothy looked at her husband. She smiled at him. 'I suppose it's really only amusing to us. It would only bore you, Brent.'

'No, really, Mrs Banter.'

'Call me Dorothy as you did before.'

'I really feel like I've known you quite a while, Dorothy. Go on. Tell us about how you met Philip.'

'I finally persuaded Jerry to take me to a party that Philip was giving. It was in one tremendous room that hadn't been cleaned in weeks. There were scads of queer people milling around or being very quiet in corners. And Philip! The first time I laid eyes on Philip he was standing in the centre of this crowd, with his shirt torn and his trousers sagging, ashes and cinders sprinkled in his hair and all over his clothes, reciting T. S. Eliot's *The Waste Land* in sepulchral tones!'

'Good old Phil! The life of tne party!' laughed Jeremy.

'I tell you, Brent, I never saw a drunker man in all my life. I was mortified when Jerry insisted on taking me over to him right away and introducing us.'

Brent had nothing to say. She was watching Philip and smiling. He turned away from her deliberately.

'But that was only one side of you, wasn't it?' Dorothy was smiling at him, too. Only her smile marked the indulgence of a wife, not the mocking acknowledgement of Brent's manner.

'I wasn't always drunk,' said Philip. He wished he could have kept Dorothy from dragging in that extraneous bit of his past. She meant nothing by it – her reasons were probably sentimental – but it annoyed him.

'No, darling,' she said. 'And you made love beautifully.' She turned to Jeremy and asked him coquettishly, 'He took me away from you, didn't he, Jerry?'

Jeremy seemed about to bulge out of his dinner jacket as he made a comic bow to them. A lick of his sandy hair fell onto his brow, and Philip could see beads of sweat on his forehead.

'To the brave, the fair,' he said.

Philip felt Brent's eyes upon him, but this time he did not turn away from Jeremy. He did not dare look her way. He wanted to too badly.

They talked more naturally during dinner and Philip found himself taking part in the conversation. Jeremy seemed to forget his delight in retelling sensational details of Philip's past. Dorothy was the inquiring, solicitous hostess. Even Brent ventured to talk about herself and her work. She was a writer who had been published in several of the 'little' magazines and was now working on a novel.

Philip drew her out about the novel, but cautiously. He could not forget certain lines in the prophetic manuscript. He felt that if he heard her say anything that was even an approximation of the predicted dialogue, then all of it would also come to pass, inevitably.

'I feel vaguely uncomfortable when I hear someone say "I'm working on a novel",' he said, taking care to address the remark to them all, not to Brent alone.

'Why say that, Philip?' Dorothy asked. He could see that she feared he was going out of his way to be rude.

'I think I know what he means,' Brent interrupted. 'I feel the same way at times. You're wondering what the person has found to say.'

This was not what Philip had meant. Philip had not intended anything so definite. His question had been an attempt to draw Brent out about her writing, and it was succeeding.

'There are so many kinds of novels,' he said.

'It is difficult, I admit,' said Brent, 'and if you asked me what it is I want to say in my novel, I don't believe I could answer you. Not in so many words. I could give you the plot, of course. I could describe the characters for you . . .'

Brent lifted a spoonful of pudding as she said this, but it never reached her lips. She made a small gesture with the spoon and the chocolate stuff fell off onto the front of her dress. She stopped speaking and stared at the mess she had made, frowning. At the same time a lock of her dark bob slipped forward, obscuring one of her eyes and making her seem more than ever like a wilful child. Suddenly Philip wanted to kiss her, to hold her in his arms . . .

'I'll get some hot water,' said Dorothy, getting to her feet. 'If you apply it immediately it will come off.'

'Never mind,' said Brent. 'I'll just scrape it off. It doesn't matter.' And she did as she said, not too carefully, leaving a brown smear on the light cloth of her bodice. 'I'm going to have to send this to the cleaner's anyway.'

'It would only take a minute.' Dorothy continued to protest.

'No really, Dorothy. It does not matter.' She had become aware of Philip's steady gaze and her own expression now changed, became serious, intent. It was as if she had only then made an interesting discovery. When she spoke, her words were made indistinct by the smile on her lips. 'What was I saying, Philip? Not that I suppose it matters . . .'

'You were telling us what your book was about.'

Brent laughed a little too loudly. 'Or rather I was telling you what it wasn't about. I was being awfully vague.'

'You said you could tell us about the characters,' Philip said hopefully. As long as she was talking to him, he could maintain the fiction that she was talking to the group. And he could look at her without rousing Dorothy's suspicions.

'They are very stuffy characters. I'd only bore you.' She was teasing him. She wanted him to coax her openly, before his wife.

'Let me decide that,' he said.

Brent glanced at Dorothy – to see if she gathered what was going on? And if she did – to see how she was taking it?

Jeremy yawned. 'Brent's always going on about that damned book, but she's never let me see it. I'm beginning to doubt its existence.' He began to eat his pudding again. After making this one morose comment, he was definitely uninterested in the conversation.

'It's about a man and two women,' Brent said. 'The man is in his thirties and attractive. One of the women he has known for a long time; the other he meets in the subway quite by chance. He loves both of them and cannot choose between them.' She paused.

'There's more to it than that?' Philip asked.

Brent twisted the pin on her dress. 'Much more. You see, he only meets the second girl in the subway. At first, he meets her accidentally, and then, later, he plans to. She talks to him, lets him kiss her, but she will never leave the train with him. He trails her, follows her, tries to see where she gets off. But she never gets off.'

'She would have to leave the train sometimes, wouldn't she?' asked Dorothy.

'No,' said Brent, 'she never does. She stays on the train. One night the man stays up the whole night with her on the train waiting for her to get off. But she never does.'

'She's a symbol?' asked Philip.

Brent looked down at her empty plate. 'Yes, you might call her that. You see, he talks to her on the train about everything, simply everything. The world, politics, art, the education of the young – just everything. She's well-informed, intelligent, nicely dressed, beautiful . . . his ideal woman.'

'But she never gets off the train . . .'

'That's right. She never gets off the train.'

'What happens in the end?' Philip asked.

Brent smiled secretively, and traced a pattern on the damask with her fork. Then she looked directly into Philip's eyes. 'He dies. He commits suicide by jumping under the train. He has realized his love is hopeless.'

'And what about the other woman, the one he has known a long time?' Dorothy asked. 'Does she just stand by while all this is happening and . . . and let it happen?'

Brent turned to Dorothy. 'She never knows what is

wrong. She thinks she is at fault. At the end, she blames herself for his suicide. And, in a way, she is right . . .'

Jeremy jumped to his feet and threw his napkin down on the table. 'Rot! Unpleasant, pretentious rot!' He glared at Brent. 'And what's more. I think you were making it up as you went along!'

Brent made no response, nor did she seem discouraged by Jeremy's comment. He excused himself, and they watched him leave the room. And then, since dinner was over, they followed him.

Coffee was served in the living-room. Philip and Jeremy could find little to say to each other, but this was not the case with Brent and Dorothy. They sat together on the sofa and talked about those subjects women always talk about and men never listen to, while Jeremy and Philip sat on either side of the fireplace, in the two large chairs, facing each other glumly. Jeremy, who had been boisterous before dinner, had grown surprisingly taciturn. Philip concentrated on beginning a conversation with him. He was glad that Dorothy and Brent were taken up with each other – if he could get Jeremy to talk, perhaps he would be able to forget his obsession: Brent.

'I have some brandy that should go well with this,' he said to Jeremy, setting his coffee cup on a low table and getting to his feet. 'Would you like some?'

Jeremy gazed vaguely at his own cup and slowly shook his head. 'Never touch the stuff any more. My doctor advises against it.'

'Ulcers?' Philip tried to make his inquiry sound sympathetic.

'No, palpitations. And high blood pressure. I work too hard.'

'Still doing the same thing?'

'I'm on sustaining. And then I get calls for extra shows at odd hours. I did ten extras last week. They pay well, but I'm on the go all the time.'

'Do you still live down in the Village?' Philip asked.

'No. I found a place uptown last fall. It's closer to the studio, in the Fifties near Madison Square Garden. It's a loft that I fixed up. Roomy, and you can play the radio loud or have company to all hours. The only thing is you have to pay off the inspector.'

'The inspector?'

Jeremy lighted a cigarette and drained the rest of his coffee. 'The building inspector. You're not supposed to live in lofts. I keep my bed covered with a studio couch cover and pretend to be an artist. When he comes around I say the bed is a couch for my models to rest on. I keep an easel under the skylight to further the impression that I'm an artist and I only work there.'

'Where does the pay-off come in?'

'The last guy who came around was nosy. He prowled into the kitchen and saw the stove and refrigerator and the dishes in the sink. He asked some questions so I made him a present.'

'What's the advantage of living in such a place?'

'It's roomy. The rent's cheap. Nobody bothers you and I can walk to work.'

'Sounds interesting.'

Jeremy nodded his head. 'It is. You and Dorothy should come up some time.' He was not enthusiastic.

'We'd like to,' Philip said. 'I've been busy myself or we would have looked you up long ago.' He hesitated, not knowing what else to say.

Jeremy threw his cigarette into the fireplace. 'I know you've been busy. I can understand that. I've been busy myself. If Dorothy hadn't –'

'Philip! Jeremy!' cried Dorothy. 'What on earth are you talking about over there by yourselves? Brent and I feel we've been deserted!' Dorothy's manner was very bright and gay, but her eyes glittered at Philip. Why is she so intent on having me make up with Jeremy? he wondered. Why did she interrupt us like this? Did she think we were having a row?

Jeremy crossed over to where Brent and Dorothy sat;

Dorothy moved to make room for him on the sofa. 'Why don't you get us some of that precious brandy of yours, Phil?' she asked.

'I offered some to Jerry, but he tells me he has stopped drinking,' Philip replied. He walked over to the credenza and began to fumble with the bottles. He had almost forgotten about the 'Confession' again, and he was certainly not thinking of Brent at that moment. But before he found the bottle of cognac he had been saving since before the war, the telephone began to ring.

He ran into the foyer and answered it himself. At least that much of the prophecy would not come true, he told himself as he picked up the receiver; Dorothy would not answer the 'phone. And if it were for Jeremy, he would make sure the call was genuine and not tricked-up. 'Hello?' he said.

'I'm trying to reach Mr Jeremy Foulkes,' said a woman's voice. 'Is he available?'

'Who is this calling?'

'This is Mr Foulkes' studio calling. Can you ask him to come to the 'phone, please. It is urgent.'

Philip started to ask what was so important, but then he realized that Jeremy was standing beside him. 'Is that for me, Phil?' he asked.

Philip handed him the telephone. 'It's your studio,' he said. He walked back into the other room.

Dorothy and Brent looked up at him expectantly. 'Philip,' Dorothy asked, 'what was the name of the awful book you were telling me about the other day? The one you said I should read? Was it by Henry Miller? I can't remember.'

Philip sat down on the edge of the sofa. He tried to make his face blank. He did not want to show the sudden panic that had again seized him. 'What book?' he asked. 'I don't know what one you mean.'

'You know the one I mean, Philip – I'm sure you do. It had something to do with an American living in Paris – it was Bohemian, I think.'

Brent smiled archly at Philip. He had not noticed that he had sat down beside her, that she was close to him – that if he leaned forward he could touch her shoulder. 'Dorothy was telling me that she found the modern novel difficult, Mr Banter, and often revolting.' Brent's tone indicated that she wanted Philip to help her deride his wife's opinion. What bothered Philip most was that what Brent had said did not sound like Dorothy's opinion of contemporary writing. Dorothy liked most modern novels.

Philip's mind was whirling. He was afraid to speak or to try to answer Brent's question. The 'Confession' had predicted that Jeremy would be called to the telephone after dinner, and the prediction had come true. It had also predicted that the conversation would turn to Henry Miller, and that Philip would venture an opinion which Brent would attack – but what the devil was the opinion he was supposed to come out with? He could not remember. Did that mean that anything he said *might* be what the 'Confession' had predicted he would say? How could he keep this part of the prediction from coming true, if he could not remember what he must not say? He took his handkerchief out of his pocket and patted at his damp forehead.

Brent was puzzled by his silence. Dorothy was smiling at him vacantly. Philip tried again to speak, but all he managed was a mumble. He saw Dorothy frown. Then, before anything else could happen, Jeremy came back into the room.

'Sorry folks, I've got to go to work. One of the boys has reported sick and they've got no one to do his trick for him.'

Brent was dismayed. 'Oh, Jerry, again? Why don't they leave you alone one evening in the week, at least? We haven't had an entire evening together for a month!' She stood up to go.

'You don't have to leave, do you, Brent?' asked Dorothy. 'Why don't you stay and talk for a while?'

Jeremy patted Brent on the shoulder. 'That's right, honey. I don't want to break up the party. Why don't you stay with the folks?'

Brent was watching Philip. She was smiling the way she had at dinner, baring her teeth at him. He heard himself saying, 'Yes, Brent, why go now? I'll be glad to see you home, if that's what's bothering you.' It was the polite thing to say.

Still Brent was undecided. She looked at Jeremy again. 'I don't see why you should leave if you want to stay,' he said. 'I could only take you home, you know.' He glanced at his watch. 'No, I don't even have time for that. I'd have to leave you in the taxi – you might as well stay and get to know these good people.' He started for the door; obviously he did not have much time.

Dorothy went after him. Philip heard her saying, 'You will come again, won't you, Jerry?' Brent sat down on the sofa beside Philip. Whether by chance, or because she wanted it that way, she sat uncomfortably close to him – he could sense her body next to his. 'I don't think your wife likes me,' she said.

Philip was startled. The 'Confession' had not predicted this remark. 'What makes you say that?' he asked. 'I don't think it's true, you know.'

'May I have a cigarette, please?' Philip handed her his case and held a light for her. She inhaled, then blew out the lighter's bluish flame with a harsh exhalation. Her eyelids lowered as she looked at him through a brief cloud of smoke. 'Oh, I can tell. She's jealous of you. I don't think it's just me she's jealous of. I think she doesn't like any woman near you.' Perversely, she leaned against him. He could hear the cloth of her tunic rustle as she breathed.

'I think you're imagining things,' he said. He stood up to get away from her, although escape was not what he most wanted. 'Dorothy isn't like that at all. She hasn't a jealous bone in her body.'

He went over to the credenza, found the brandy and poured three glasses. As he was carrying a glass to Brent, he happened to glance at the mirror above the fireplace. He saw Jeremy and Dorothy standing by the door in the mirror. He saw Jeremy take Dorothy in his arms and begin to kiss her. Then Philip was past the mirror. He gave the brandy to Brent, and went back for his own – passing the mirror twice and twice glancing at it. The first time Jeremy was still kissing his wife. The second time he had released her and was opening the door to go.

Brent raised her glass for a toast. 'To us,' she said softly. Philip did not understand what she had said.

'I beg your pardon.'

'To us,' said Brent, her glass still raised, a tempting smile on her lips. 'To you and me.'

'I'll drink to that,' said Philip.

4

It had been inconceivable to Philip that Dorothy might ever be unfaithful to him; it had not occurred to him that other events, aside from those specified in the 'Confession', might take place on the same night that the 'Confession's' predictions came true. Seeing Dorothy kiss Jeremy came as a double shock to him. Not only was this an event that had not been foretold, but it was also one he had not thought possible. Of course, if he wished, he could excuse Dorothy's conduct on the grounds that she had known Jeremy for many years and could kiss a good friend if she so wanted. But he did not find himself wanting to excuse Dorothy. Instead he found himself wanting to kiss Brent.

He did not kiss her then. Dorothy came back into the room before they had finished their brandy, a moment after Brent had repeated and clarified her toast, in fact. Philip discovered that it was difficult for him to look at his wife. He gave her a glass of brandy, and then sat down in one of the chairs by the fireplace.

'What sort of a job has Jerry got that he has to run off to it at all hours?' Dorothy asked Brent.

Brent was sipping the last of her brandy. 'He's the head announcer at one of those small stations that play records all night,' she explained. 'They've had a run of illness lately, and he has been having to substitute for somebody almost every night. Then, sometimes, he has a half-hour show at one of the big stations.'

'He must work awfully hard.'

'That's not like Jerry,' said Philip.

Dorothy glared at her husband. 'Philip, what's come over you? Whatever made you say a thing like that?'

'It's true, isn't it? Did he work in college? You ought to know about that, you wrote as many of his papers for him as I did. Did he work when he was a reporter? How many times times did I file his stories for him when Jerry had a little too much party? It just seems damn queer to me that all of a sudden he should develop into such a hard worker!' Philip gulped the rest of his brandy and banged the empty glass down on the table.

'Philip, I don't understand you. I watched you all evening, and I saw you were as unpleasant as you could be with Jerry. It seemed to me that you were deliberately trying to pick a fight with him.' Dorothy was angry. Brent was amused. She kept sniffing her empty glass of brandy and glancing from one to the other of them.

Philip did not know what to say. He could not remember having tried to pick a fight with Jeremy, although – since what he had said to Jeremy had not been uppermost in his mind – he realized that his actions might have been taken that way and even, possibly, his words. But why did Dorothy come out with all this in front of Brent?

'I wasn't impolite to Jeremy,' he said. 'If anyone was impolite it was he. I tried my best to get him to talk after dinner. I was as pleasant to him as I could be.'

Dorothy was quietly indignant. 'Philip, that's not true and you know it. I watched you all evening and I know.'

Brent stood up to find an ashtray. Philip and Dorothy were oblivious of her in their concern for each other. After she had extinguished her cigarette, Brent walked over to Philip and rested her hand lightly on his shoulder. 'What do you think of Henry Miller?' she asked. 'Don't you find his work exciting?'

Philip was hurt and angry at Dorothy's unfounded accusation; he answered Brent's attempt to change the subject without thinking about what he said. 'Miller's just a little old-fashioned, isn't he? Rather an overdue romantic, I think.' Not until he had spoken, did he begin to wonder if what he had said had comprised what the

'Confession' had predicted he would say. He kept his eyes on Dorothy. She had withdrawn, as she usually did after losing her temper, and was affecting to ignore him.

'At least, he's honest,' Brent pressed him. 'He says what he thinks.'

Philip gave his attention to her. He had to keep his wits about him, he reminded himself. Or else he might say something that would lead to disaster. 'He makes a cult of it, doesn't he?' he asked. That had not been in the 'Confession' he was sure.

'A cult of what?'

'Of saying what he thinks. Of calling a spade a spade. I'll admit that he's thought out his position, and I'll admit that his position may be a sound one for him, personally. But I rather resent having him shout his invective at me at the top of his lungs. I'm an American. I live in America. I like it. If he doesn't, that's all right with me. I don't go shouting at him!'

Brent was leaning against the fireplace, her head tossed back, her dark hair falling crookedly against the mantel. 'Why do you American business men insist that the artist sing your praises? America is business. That's all we have. Is it surprising that Miller doesn't like it – that he refuses to pay lip service to your phony values?' Philip could see that she was not angry; instead she was enjoying the argument. He felt as if she were slicing away at him, peeling him to ribbons with the cutting edge of her tongue. Queerly enough, he enjoyed being attacked.

'It's been a long time since I read Miller,' he said. 'I still can't remember the title of the book Dorothy asked me about. You may be right. I'd have to read more of him to tell.'

Brent smiled, allowing him to elude her. But he knew she was aware of the full measure of her victory. She advanced to the sofa triumphantly. 'May I have another cigarette, please?'

Philip offered the case to both Dorothy and Brent, and then he got some more brandy for the three of them. 'Why don't you see what's on the radio, Phil?' Dorothy suggested. 'You might be able to get some music.'

Philip turned on the set and they listened to the last movement of Brahms' Fourth. This monumental music seemed absurdly incongruous to Philip amid the confusion of his thoughts, which called for cacophony and a mixing of tongues. As the mighty chords of the *passacaglia* died away, Brent stood up. 'I think I had better go,' she said. 'I want to get some work done tomorrow.'

Dorothy did not rise. 'You will persuade Jerry to bring you again, won't you?' she asked. 'And I hope your novel turns out well.'

Philip escaped to the foyer to get Brent's coat. After he had found it he stood watching the duel of platitudes between his wife and Brent: the spectacle of two women who dislike each other yet are intent on maintaining the pretence of sociability. The sight disgusted him.

Brent finally completed her good-byes and came into the foyer. He helped her on with her coat. They went out the door. He tried to kiss her in the hallway, but she evaded him. He succeeded in the taxi.

Dorothy waited ten minutes after Philip and Brent left before she put on her old tweed coat and a mannish hat that made her look drab and different and went out herself. While she waited, she drank two brandies and paced the room. When she reached the street, she set off westward, walking swiftly. She walked with her head down, her hands thrust into her pockets, blindly. She ignored traffic lights and several times bumped into other pedestrians. By the time she had gone four or five blocks, her pace had quickened to a rapid trot. When she reached the stone steps of her father's house, she fled up them as if she were pursued.

The butler let her in and told her that her father was still in the library. Dorothy did not wait to let him take her coat and hat, but pushed past him and walked down the high-ceilinged hall, her heels clattering on the tile floor.

She threw open the heavy oak doors of the library and strode into the large, comfortable room. A fire blazed in the fireplace, and Steven Foster sat beside it in a high-backed chair. His hand clasped a book, by his side was his glass of port. His posture was as rigid, as uncompromising, as ever. He did not lift his eyes from the page he was reading until Dorothy stood before him, her breasts rising and falling from the exertion of her pell-mell haste, her breathing sibilant.

'What have you done to Philip, father?' she demanded.

The old man returned his attention to the book. The gilt letters on its spine glinted in the firelight. She could read the first words of its title, *Statistical Report on* –

'I've discharged him. Gave him a month's notice this afternoon.'

Dorothy paled. 'Oh, father, why?'

'He lost the Peabody account today. His work has been going steadily downhill. There was nothing else I could do.'

'I asked you not to . . . I knew at lunch that you were going to do this . . . I begged you not to . . .'

Foster glanced up again. His mouth curved slightly. 'Why are you so concerned? You know I'll take care of you. Philip can very well get himself another job.'

'But to do a thing like this . . . now.' Dorothy's voice trailed off. She put her hand to her mouth, pressed it hard against her colourless lips. Her body wilted. She crumpled and fell at his feet.

Foster looked down at his daughter. He laid aside his book and mumbled, 'Damn!' Then, he knelt stiffly beside her, put his arms carefully under her, picked her up and, carrying her high against his breast, walked over to the leather couch. He laid her down gently, bending his body until his face was close to hers; his lips lingered over hers. He stayed this way for a long moment, before he crushed her mouth with his own. 'He never deserved you!' he muttered savagely.

*

Later, after the butler had brought smelling salts and

brandy, Dorothy was able to sit up. Her father sat beside her for a long time, holding her hand, imploring her to stay with him and not to go back to Philip.

'I can't do that,' she said.

'Where is he now? Is he waiting for you?'

'I don't know.'

'Has he gone off again?'

'I don't know.'

'What do you mean "you don't know"? Either you know where your husband is or you don't.'

'We had people in tonight. Jerry and a friend. Jerry was called away unexpectedly and Philip promised to take his friend home. Her name is Brent. They left just before I did.'

'He's coming back?'

'He said he would.'

'But you don't believe him?'

Dorothy stared at her father, then, putting her hands to her eyes, she stood up. 'I don't know, I tell you. I don't know!'

Steven Foster clenched his fists. 'If you tell me where he went, I'll go fetch him myself!' he cried.

Dorothy backed away from him. Now her face was determined, her mouth set, her body as straight and as unyielding as her father's. 'No, I know what to do. And I have to do it myself. There is no other way out.' She walked resolutely to the door.

'What are you going to do?' Foster asked, running after her.

'Oh, father, I'm going home, of course. I'm going to wait for him like a good wife. What else can I do?'

And she slammed the heavy door in her father's face. Foster gazed at it and smiled. Things were working out uncommonly well.

Brent's apartment was on Jones Street in the Village, a street that exists for one short block between Bleecker and West Fourth and is lined its entire length by six-storey tenements only occasionally interspersed with newer, efficiency apartment buildings. Philip was panting before he had finished climbing the five flights that led to three small rooms on the top floor of the newer buildings; he was glad for the pause outside the door of her apartment while Brent fumbled with the lock; he sank down on the studio couch by the window as soon as they were inside. Brent went into the kitchen and came back a few minutes later with two highballs.

She looked much younger in the tidy, cramped flat. Her body was thin and angular in places. She moved awkwardly, in sudden spurts and sidesteps, as if she were confined by the box-like room. He drank half his highball while watching her pick up and arrange some books and papers that had been lying on the seat of the maple armchair. When she sat down beside him, he put his arm around her and pulled her to him. She allowed him the intimacy, but she did not respond. She squirmed away from him when he tried to kiss her again.

'Why are you doing that?' she asked.

'Because I want to.'

'Must you always do what you want to do?'

'It's generally more satisfactory that way.' Her attitude puzzled him. Why had she acted the way she had, if she had not wanted him to make love to her? Even in the taxi she had been inexplicably cold and, while she had not repulsed his advances, she had given him no encouragement.

'Suppose I don't want you to?' she asked.

'Don't you?'

'I don't know. I know I don't love you. I'm not sure I even like you. And I'm surprised you're not content with Dorothy. She is nice.'

'She wasn't nice tonight.'

'I wouldn't have been either the way you were making up to me.' She jumped to her feet and sat in the other chair.

'I thought you wanted me to make up to you,' he said. 'You certainly acted that way.'

'You're attractive. I like to play with the idea of you making love to me . . .' She watched him, a smile on her lips, her eyes half-closed.

Philip went over to her, seized her hands and pulled her roughly to her feet. He held her tightly against himself. He could feel her trembling. He grasped the collar of her tunic and tried to rip it from her throat. 'It won't do you any good to tear my clothes, you know,' she said matter-of-factly – although her body was wire-taut and throbbing. 'I'll sleep with you if I want to – you can't make me.'

He continued to hold her. He relaxed his grip on her dress, but his hands refused to release her body. She stood stiffly against him; her eyes stared openly at his flushed face; her mouth was a line of anger. 'And now I know that I do not want to,' she whispered.

Philip felt exhausted. Although he knew that he could overpower her physically, he also knew that he could never possess her. The advantage had exchanged hands – had it ever been his? – and he could only withdraw. As if to jeer at him, the memory of the manuscript and its misleading prediction returned to his mind. He smiled and let his arms drop to his sides. Brent walked nobly away from him. She went over to the closet and picked up his hat and coat. 'In a way I have scored a victory,' he mumbled to himself.

Brent was holding his coat for him. He could see that he had not even succeeded in tearing her dress, although he had wrenched the collar loose from the rest of the material and it was hanging awry. 'I wouldn't call it a victory,' she said. 'Or did I hear you right?'

He turned his back on her and shrugged himself into the coat she held. 'I was thinking about your novel,' he lied. 'About the poor devil who keeps chasing the girl until he falls off the train. In one respect, at least, I'm better off than him. I haven't fallen off the train.'

'Haven't you?' asked Brent. She was holding the door open for him.

5

After Philip left, Brent went into the bathroom and brushed her teeth, making wry faces in the mirror as she manipulated the brush. When her mouth felt clean again, she undressed and put on a pullover sweater and a pair of corduroy slacks. Her hips were small and the slacks outlined them pertly. She went into the kitchen, mixed and drank another highball. Then she turned out the lights and left the apartment.

She took a taxi to Jeremy's place in the Fifties. This was a loft located in the tenement district near Madison Square Garden. She unlocked the battered door and climbed a steep flight of broad stairs. Inside the loft she went to the rear of the barn-like room and switched on a lamp that made a small circle of warm light in the greater darkness. A half-partition hid a kitchen, a tub and shower, as well as an improvised closet. Brent filled the tub with warm water, took a pair of pyjamas out of the closet and laid them on a chair, then soaked herself in the tub until the water grew lukewarm. She jumped out and rubbed herself down with a rough towel that dry-scrubbed her flesh until it was brick-red. She put on her pyjamas and combed her hair, then went into the other part of the room where she turned down the cover on the studio couch and made it up for the night. Her movements were quick and showed her actions to be habitual; she was obviously accustomed to the place as she knew where everything was and lost no time in deciding what to do next. After she had made the bed, plumping up the pillows that served by day as the back of the couch and sheathing them in slips, she took a book off the shelf and twisted the lamp so that its pool of light fell on the head of the bed and climbed under the covers.

Brent read for ten or fifteen minutes before she fell asleep. Jeremy awakened her when he came in about four o'clock. He turned off the light that had burned all night, bent over and kissed her brow. 'Jerry,' she said sleepily, 'you took so long.'

Later, she wanted to know about Philip and Dorothy. 'I've seldom felt so uncomfortable, Jerry – what's going on between those two? And why did you let him take me home? Didn't you know he would make a pass at me?'

Jeremy's face paled at her last remark. 'Did he do that, the bastard! What did you do?'

Brent laughed softly. 'I didn't let him, silly! I think I gave him a shock. He looked very strange when he left.' She told him about Philip's unsuccessful attempt to make love to her. 'But that doesn't help me find out what interests me,' she said later. 'Tell me more about his wife, Jerry. She hates me and I want to know why.'

Jeremy hesitated before he answered her. His hair was tousled and his eyes were tired. He was still a young man, but he was the kind of young man who already shows some of the signs of middle age. 'First, let me ask you a question,' he said. 'What do you think of Philip?'

'I think he's fascinating in some ways. He's so sullen and dissolute-looking. But I don't like him.'

'Because of last night?'

'Partly.' She sucked in her lip, thinking. 'But I felt I disliked him before he tried to make love to me. I think perhaps, because of his attitude towards you.'

'I didn't think that showed.'

Brent nodded her head. 'Yes, it did. After you left, Dorothy bawled him out for it. She said he had been trying to pick a fight with you all evening.'

Jeremy smiled. 'I wouldn't have believed she would take my part,' he said.

Brent bit her lip and began to pound him playfully with her fists. 'Stop being so mysterious!' she cried. 'Tell me what's behind all this. What kind of people are they? And how long have you known them? Does Dorothy look that way at every woman who comes into her house? Each time she looked at me, I felt like she was thinking up ways of murdering me!'

Jeremy laughed. 'She probably was.' Then he grew more serious. 'Dorothy's one of the nicest people I know. We've been friends ever since we were in college together. She was my best girl then. Does that make you jealous?'

Brent leaned up against him. 'A little,' she admitted. 'But not seriously, as long as it's in the past tense.'

'It's in the past tense all right. She didn't stay my girl, you see. I introduced her to Philip, my closest friend, once when we were in New York for the holidays. The next year they were married.'

'I know most of that from what Dorothy told me last night,' said Brent. 'But why is she so jealous of him?'

Jeremy was silent for a few minutes. Brent waited patiently, sensing that what he was about to tell her was painful to him and that he would prefer not to speak about it. It had begun to grow light outside; the skylight in the front part of the loft had become an ill-defined grey patch latticed with darker shadows, as had the great, wide front windows, the sills of which rested on the floor. Slowly the cavernous darkness of the loft began to recede, to grow dim and vague; objects began to take their daytime forms beyond the previous frontiers of sight: an easel, a door, the slanting roof of a tenement across the street seen foggily through the rain-streaked windows. 'I believe Philip loves her.' Jeremy spoke at last, quietly and contemplatively, spacing his phrases with intervals of silence. 'And I believe he loved her when he married her. I have never blamed him . . . for taking her from me . . . she was there to take . . . and I have never blamed her for preferring him to me . . . Philip had so much more to offer her . . .

'We had the same ambitions, Philip and I – I suppose that is why we were friends. Both of us wanted to write . . .

86

Philip even started a novel. It was a good novel; at times I thought it came close to being profound . . . but who am I to judge profundity?'

'I would never believe that!' Brent exclaimed. 'Philip's a fool! Why, I asked him his opinion of Henry Miller last night, and the comments he made were the standard clever remarks with which they always try to write off Miller. I don't think he has ever read a book by him. I know that when Dorothy asked him the title of one of Miller's books, he did not know it and pretended not to have heard of it!'

'Philip is not a fool. That is part of his act, which you mistake for the whole man. He likes to make one think that he knows the least, to make a pretence of ignorance, in the hopes that he will be able to lay a trap for you and catch you in it. But that's beside the point. The point is that Philip could have written a good book had he wanted to.'

Brent rested her head on Jeremy's shoulder. 'But, of course, he didn't,' she said.

Jeremy stared at the growing patch of daylight on the floor. 'And I have never understood why not. It sometimes seems to me that all Philip cares about is to prove to himself that he can possess something that he desires and which seems unattainable. But once he knows he can have it, then he is no longer interested in it and is more than likely to throw it away. Most of us have some touch of this folly in our natures, but the objects of our desires are inanimate: books, pictures, automobiles or, at the most, a way of life – a complex of people and things. Most of us learn to accept a modicum of dissatisfaction and we manage to adjust ourselves to imperfectly attained goals. Not Philip. I wonder if I am right when I say he loved Dorothy? What I mean, I think, is that he desired the things Dorothy stood for and, if he was in love, he was in love with the process of achievement. Once the exploit was over, the goal attained, Dorothy lost all value to him. He is throwing her away . . .'

Brent sat up, surprised. 'What are you talking about, Jerry? How is he throwing Dorothy away? I don't understand.'

'You saw the way they were last night. You saw how jealous Dorothy was of him. Fear lies beneath her jealousy, fear of losing him. Once Philip made sure of her, you see, once he had married her and held a secure position in her father's agency, he began to be consistently unfaithful to her. And Dorothy knows this. That is why every woman she sees him with she looks upon as a threat to her own security.'

Brent considered what he said. Her fingers busied themselves with pulling a ravelled thread from the blanket, but she was deeply concerned. Did what Jeremy was telling her mean that he still loved Dorothy? If it did – and how else was she to interpret it? – what would happen to her?

Jeremy responded to her silence, came close to her, held her to him so that her dark hair smothered his face and her warm breath moistened his cheek. 'Don't worry, Brent, dear,' he said. 'That is all past. It's you I love, not Dorothy.'

'But you were just saying . . .' she began.

'You asked me to tell you. I loved Dorothy once, and so did Philip. He married her, not I. I feel badly that he gets into bed with every piece of fluff that comes his way – I feel even worse that Dorothy knows this and still wants him enough to be savagely jealous. But I can assure you that I no longer desire Dorothy, now that I know you.'

'You mean you did . . . before?'

Jeremy nodded his head. 'Sometimes when I went to their house for dinner, it was all I could do to keep from kissing her every time Philip's back was turned. And Philip was supposed to be my best friend! That's why I stopped seeing him.'

'You know what I think, Jerry,' said Brent. She was smiling and baring her teeth the way a kitten does. 'I think Philip is your personal devil. I don't believe in his talent the way you do. I think he has been lucky. He didn't finish that novel because he couldn't – not because "he was no longer interested in it". I talked to him last night and I think he is a fool!'

Jeremy stared at her and slowly shook his head. 'You've seen him only once. You don't know what he's really like.'

'I saw all of him I intend to see, I can tell you that. As for Dorothy – well, I think she's a nice person.' Brent spoke cautiously. She did not want to say anything that would alienate Jeremy. She was afraid of Philip's wife, and the hold she had over her lover. But she did not want to let Jeremy see her fear. 'She's a nice person, and I like her. Perhaps you're right, and the only reason she doesn't like me is because she thinks of me as a threat to her. But I do believe that what goes on between Philip and her is their business, and you had better not concern yourself with it. If Philip wants to be unfaithful to his wife, let him! Why should you bother about that?'

Jeremy rumpled her hair and kissed her. Then she pretended to resist him and he pretended to overcome her resistance. Then they both laughed for a long time.

'All right,' he cried finally. 'You win! Philip, I hereby give you the right to sleep with anyone you desire!' Jeremy was kneeling on the couch, the blanket draped over his shoulder toga-wise, his face severely pontifical. He made an imperious gesture, then pulled Brent to him and kissed her. 'As long as it isn't you!' he added.

6

As Philip came out of Brent's apartment building and turned down Jones Street, there was a sudden sound of glass splintering above him and a small hard object struck him a glancing blow on the temple. He crouched instinctively, over-balanced and fell to his knees. The street was now totally dark. Glass continued to fall near him. Then he heard a shrill whistle, which was followed by spasms of childish laughter. As his eyes grew accustomed to the dark, he saw that a street lamp overhead had been smashed – out of the corner of his field of vision two small boys disappeared from view, running wildly towards Bleecker Street. He stood up, touched his stinging forehead tentatively with his handkerchief. He was not bleeding. He laughed self-consciously. Only kids shying rocks at the street lamp . . . he had thought they were stoning him!

He walked down the deserted, darkened street, his mind intent on the strange scene he had just had with Brent. The 'Confession' had been wrong. Although many of its predictions had come true, its major prophecy had not: he had not been unfaithful to Dorothy with Brent. But he could take no credit for this. He had made all the necessary advances, as the manuscript had foretold: if he had not done his wife an injustice, it was because Brent would have none of him, and this the manuscript had not foretold.

What was the purpose of the 'Confession'? Had someone deliberately egged him onto Brent, knowing that she would not find him acceptable, as a crude joke? Would this fit Jeremy's sense of humour? He wondered.

At Sixth Avenue, a flashing neon sign that advertised a

bar met his eye and beckoned him inside. The bar was crowded, but a booth was empty at the rear of the room. He sat down and when the waiter came, he ordered a double scotch.

His mind had grown numb and the whisky tasted like tap water. He gulped it down and ordered another . . . and then another. He knew very well that he was going to get drunk again, that he would forget again. But somehow it did not matter. He had a problem to which he had to find a solution, a problem that would require reasoning. Now, of all times, he should stay sober. That was all very true, and yet it was all very false. He had another whisky. Now he would stop drinking and try to think it through. First of all, there was Jeremy. But who was Jeremy? Just what did he know about Jeremy . . . ?

He had another whisky. This one burned a little and did not taste like it had come out of a faucet. As he sat and stared at the seat on the other side of the booth it seemed to him that he began to see Jeremy vaguely. This is an hallucination, he told himself. Jeremy is not really sitting there. I am alone. But the vision became clearer and clearer. Jeremy was still wearing the same suit he had been wearing earlier in the evening. The same fold of fat bulged around his collar. And, while Philip was trying to assure himself that he was not real, it seemed to him that Jeremy spoke.

'Remember me, Philip?' he asked. 'Do you remember how I was when we first met? I was the fat boy who was your room-mate all through college – the kid you were jealous of all through the first term because I had so many friends and I played on the Freshman team.

'And do you remember the night that you came home to find the fat boy – that was me, of course – crying over his books? It was just before exams and I was failing. I told you that I would be eternally grateful if you helped me. And you helped me, with bad grace even then, but you helped me, Philip. And I am still grateful.'

'I remember,' said Philip, hoarsely.

'I was your best friend for years to come, wasn't I, Philip?' The vision smiled mockingly. 'You imitated me, dressed as I did, made my friends your friends. I encouraged you to go out for sports. You pledged my fraternity. You wouldn't have received that bid, Philip, if I hadn't sponsored you. Oh, I know what you're going to say. You helped me, too. Of course, you did. You had to keep up the pretence of the friendship. You tutored me. You had me major in English Lit. and taunted me into becoming a journalist. Oh, I'm very grateful to you, Philip – don't think that I'm not. But it was you who became president of the senior class. And would that have happened if you hadn't been my friend? Or would I have had the honours you received, if I hadn't boosted you?'

Philip stared at his empty glass and slowly shook his head. He knew that Jeremy was not there and that the apparition was due to his nervous tension. He had been thinking about Jeremy, arguing with himself about Jeremy – and suddenly his imagination let him see Jeremy, argue with Jeremy. It was all in his own mind.

But what about the argument? All the things 'Jeremy' said were true, and yet they weren't motivation enough for him to have written the 'Confession'. Philip raised his finger and summoned the waiter and ordered another double scotch. And then 'Jeremy' seemed to speak again.

'What about the women, Phil boy? What about the women? I not only refused to compete with you when it came to campus politics, but I let you take my women, too. I guess I just liked being a sucker – but does anyone really like being made a fool of, Phil? I knew you excelled me at all my own specialities. I even tried my hand at one of yours. Do you remember the chapter of a novel of mine – that's about as far as it got, one chapter – I read to you, Philip? Do you remember what you said, Philip? Now was that kind? After I had listened so patiently to the sections you read me of your novel, too. Oh, I could have written the "Confession", if that's what you're wondering.'

Philip smiled to himself and averted his eyes to avoid looking at the apparition. He felt a little good now that the scotch was taking hold. He had been a different man in those days; his face had been as long then as it was now, but the line had been firmer, his jaw had been less heavy, his hair had been . . . thicker. And then he thought he heard Jeremy's voice again.

'You were quite a boy with the girls, weren't you, Phil? You had had several affairs by the time you were a senior. You seemed to like taking your friends' best sweethearts away from them. Why were you so successful with the women, Philip? Was it your eyes, that way you had of looking that left no one up in the air as to what you wanted? And what you wanted was usually someone else's woman, wasn't it? Sometimes it seemed to me that you made a point of ignoring the beauty of a woman until some other fellow, whose taste you respected – myself, for example – had selected her for his own!'

Philip let the glass slip out of his hand as he laughed loudly. Now he knew what he had been evading. Now he knew why it must be Jeremy who was writing the 'Confession'. Dorothy had been Jeremy's girl. He had not fallen in love with her when he first met. He might never have fallen in love with her if Jeremy had not mentioned that her father was the head of one of New York's largest advertising agencies.

Philip rolled his glass back and forth under his hand as he looked up for the waiter. Oh, he was a realist about his own motives. He knew how large an element of profit there had been in his choice of Dorothy for a wife. But she had been attractive to him, too. He had loved her . . .

He pointed his finger at the apparition. 'You never did like the idea of Dorothy loving me more than she did you, did you?' he demanded. 'I saw you change, Jeremy. At first you were pleased that Dorothy and I liked each other. Then you were miffed when Dorothy and I had dates on nights when you wanted to be alone with Dorothy. Finally you were angry when you realized that you no longer

93

rated with Dorothy. There was the night I proposed to her. I took her for a long drive in the country and asked her to marry me – we stayed out quite late. When I came home, I found you, Jeremy, waiting up for me. "By God, Phil!" you said. "I've had enough of this! If you want to marry her, marry her. But if you won't, then leave her alone. If you make a slut of her, I'll kill you!" Do you remember what you did next, Jerry? You started swinging wildly and I had to hit you – to knock you out. I didn't get the chance to tell you that Dorothy was going to marry me until morning. Then you insisted on being a gentleman and buying me a drink. Do you remember all that, too, Jeremy?'

But, as Philip watched, Jeremy disappeared. He faded away all at once, blending into the dark wood of the booth. Philip had known all along that he was not actually there. But now that he could no longer see him, he felt relieved.

It was late and the room was growing hazy – with smoke? Philip sat staring at his empty glass. Only a few stragglers were left at the bar in the front of the room; a fat blonde leaned on the juke box next to the booth where Philip sat and crooned the words of the tune the machine was playing. Her voice was raw and beery. After a time, she came over and sat down next to Philip without asking for an invitation. She put her arm around him automatically and hugged him to her. Philip's thoughts had been in the past and he was only partly conscious of her presence until she ventured intimacy, then he was too startled to take any action for a moment. 'Would'ja like to meet a nice girl, dearie?' the blonde whispered in his ear. He pushed her away from him, stood up and went to the bar and paid the bartender. He did not look back although he could hear her cursing him drunkenly. Outside it was drizzling and a low-hanging fog partially obscured the street lights. He began to walk uptown, looking for a taxi.

'. . . if you make a slut of her, I'll kill you!' Those words of Jeremy's, spoken many years ago, still rang in his ears.

94

Jeremy had meant them at that time, but did he still mean them? After all those years did Jeremy still love Dorothy enough to conspire against her husband? If he did, then it was probably he who was writing the 'Confession'.

Philip shivered, only partly because of the cold, clinging fog. His eyes searched the misted streets for a taxi. He wished the mist would blow away. It made everything loom dim and vague, made him fear that he was about to hear the voice again. Very few automobiles were about, mostly early trucks. He kept walking uptown.

What he could not understand was what Jeremy, if he were writing the 'Confession', hoped to gain by it. Did he think that a reading of it would reform Philip and make him faithful to Dorothy? That was laughable. Did he hope to drive Philip into some action that would make him a fool in Dorothy's eyes? If that was his objective, Philip had to admit that he had already come close to succeeding. But there was another possibility that Philip considered even more disturbing: suppose Jeremy *was not* writing the manuscript, suppose he was writing it himself – and then forgetting he had written it! This was what he might have been doing the night before, what he had been trying to remember all day.

And it was not impossible. He had thought so at first, but now he was not sure. Who else, besides himself, could have written it? No one else knew his mind that well, but even if someone did, how could this person have forced him to make love to Brent? No, he had made love to Brent because he desired to, not because the 'Confession' had predicted that he would – to think differently was madness.

He had a theory – it might not seem sensible in the light of day when he was cold sober, but he could see no holes in it now. He was afraid that he had written the 'Confession' out of some latent, autobiographical urge, and then suffered a kind of amnesia about it. Later, he discovered it again, but then it seemed new to him and the work of someone else. He had some reason for thinking

95

this since once before he had had a similar experience. This had happened back in his college days when he was still rooming with Jeremy and while he was working on the novel he never finished. One day, he had gone to his desk to resume writing only to discover a newly-completed chapter that he must have written himself – but which he could not remember writing. His first impulse had been that Jeremy had written it as an ill-humoured joke. He had sat and stared at the totally unfamiliar pages until Jeremy had come into the room; but when he had told Jeremy about them, Jeremy had been able to solve the mystery. 'You wrote them last night,' he had said. 'I remember waking in the middle of the night. I heard the sound of your typewriter. I got up and slammed the door of my room in hopes that you would take the hint and stop disturbing my sleep. But you went on typing until dawn.'

Last night, drunk as he must have been, he might have decided to go to his office and write. Then he might have gone back home after he finished, gone to bed and, when he awakened the next morning, have forgotten about it. The flaw in this reasoning – if there was a flaw – lay in the time sequence. How could he predict that he would meet and make love to a woman he did not know? And yet, who was better equipped to make such a prediction?

But then there was the disturbing fact that not all the events foretold in the 'Confession' had come true. He had not slept with Brent. This he still found hard to believe. He had never before been rejected so ignominiously – why, the woman had lured him on, teased him, led him to expect an easy conquest by her every action, only to refuse him coldly. If he had written the 'Confession' he would have been certain that he would be successful with Brent. Did this mean that he had written the 'Confession'?

A taxi came into view. Philip hailed it and ran into the street to meet it in his eagerness to climb inside. He gave the driver the address of his office building. He intended to find out if his mind was playing tricks on him again. By going to his office now, and staying there all night – he planned to sit at his desk and await the culprit if the second manuscript were not already there – he would either catch the author or frustrate him. He expected that there would be another instalment as the first manuscript had been titled 'Confession I'. Of course, if he were the author . . .

The building lobby was deserted. One elevator was open and the light was on inside, but the operator was not to be seen. Philip rang the night bell several times, listening to its metallic clangour resound in the vaulted lobby. After about five minutes, the night operator appeared – an old man who limped as he walked. Philip strode impatiently into the elevator.

'Aren't you supposed to be on duty at all times?' he demanded. It was insufferable to have to wait so long for an elevator in a building that advertised twenty-four-hour service!

The car started its flight upwards with an unseemly jerk. 'I ain't got no relief from twelve to six. It ain't human to ask a man to stay in one spot all that time,' the operator complained.

'It's your job, isn't it?' Philip demanded.

'Mister,' said the old elevator operator, turning around as the doors opened at Philip's floor, 'there's always the stairs.'

Philip walked down the hall towards the frosted doors of Brown and Foster. He was angry at the old man's impertinence as he fitted the key in the lock. Philip had never seen the office after hours and its dark emptiness dismayed him. He could not find the switch to the bank of lights that illuminated the corridor leading to his office. Never before had he had an occasion to turn on those lights since it was always done for him. He gave up trying to locate the switch and groped his way down the hall, striking matches until he found his own name on one of the doors. He stood looking at it long enough for the flickering flame to burn down to his fingers, remembering the brief, calamitous interview with Steven Foster. Then he pushed the door open and went in, turning the light on in Miss Grey's office and looking around carefully before he went into his own.

It seemed as though the light dimmed as he went through the door to the inner office. A bell started ringing somewhere, a faint tinkling. He felt as if he were falling forward as he groped across the room to his desk. A scream began in his mind, but stifled in his throat. And then he was swimming in furious circles in a pool of blackness that lapped over him and swallowed him until all was deafeningly quiet.

Out of that quiet came a voice – the simpering voice – speaking clearly and distinctly. 'Oh, Philip,' it wailed, 'you aren't going to forget again, are you? Please, Philip, try hard not to forget . . .'

The Second Instalment

I

Brent, Jeremy and Dorothy stood in a circle about him, pointing their fingers at him, chanting words he could not distinguish, although he sensed their meaning was shameful. An overpoweringly bright light, originating he knew not where, shone in his eyes and dimmed his vision so that when he shut his eyelids he could not escape the haunting, blue after-images of his friends ringed about him, pointing accusing fingers. Then Brent stepped forward, seized his shoulders and began to shake him, shouting more words at him that he could not understand. His head swelled with a pain that throbbed like the motor of a relentless engine, coming and going with piston-like regularity. Once again he dared to open his eyes and this time they were dazzled by bright sunlight. He felt hands – Brent's hands? – release his shoulders. He twisted his neck to see who it was who had been shaking him, and again his head was possessed by spinning pain. Brent, Jeremy and Dorothy had disappeared. He realized that he was alone in his own office. But, if he were alone, who had been shaking him? Again he tried to turn around, this time more slowly, and this time he succeeded despite the persistent pain in his head. Miss Grey was standing beside him, her blotchy face sympathetic and solicitous. 'Are you all right, Mr Banter? You gave me such a turn when I came in and found you slumped over your desk!'

Philip stood up. His whole body felt cramped and his muscles ached. How had he gotten here? He searched his memory in an attempt to recall the events of the night before. A number of scenes and jumbled incidents jostled for precedence: he had been in a bar, he had looked for a taxi, Jeremy's words – had they been spoken last night? – 'If you make a slut of her, I'll kill you!', Brent's face at dinner, slowly smiling so that her teeth were bared, the elevator man telling him, 'There's always the stairs.'

Philip tried to pretend to Miss Grey that his conduct was in no way unusual. But, even as he straightened up and smiled, he knew from the wondering expression on her face that she was aware that something had happened and that he did not know what it was. Still he had to make the best of it he could. He said, 'I came back to the office after you left last night. I had some work to do and I kept at it until late. I must have fallen asleep.'

Miss Grey began to walk towards the door. 'I didn't know what to think when I saw you there-like that. I guess you scared me. Did I hurt you shaking you? It seemed the thing to do at the time.'

Philip managed another smile, another attempt to put the girl at ease. She was not a bad sort, if she would only do something about that complexion. 'Thank you for waking me,' he said. 'I'll just wash up and then go out for some breakfast.'

Miss Grey answered his smile with an embarrassed grimace of her own and then left the room, closing the door behind herself. Philip sat down again and ran his hands through his hair. What had happened to him? He still could not think very clearly. He could remember coming to the office building, waiting an unbearable length of time for the elevator, unlocking the door to the office and searching for the light switch – but after that his mind was a blank. Why had he come to the office at such an odd hour? He thought for a moment about this and then remembered that it had had something to do with the 'Confession'. That was it! He had come back to the office to see if another instalment of the manuscript would be awaiting him, possibly to have the good luck of catching the author in the act of writing it. But what had he found? He could not remember.

He looked down at his desk. Only then did he realize that his typewriter was open as it had been the day before – when he awakened he must have been lying on it, but only now did he see it – and there was a sheet of paper in the machine also as before. Beside the typewriter was a second neat pile of manuscript that bore his name on the upper left-hand corner of the first page!

This must mean that he was writing the damned thing himself! How could he reason otherwise? He remembered coming into the office after midnight, turning on the light . . . no, he did not remember turning it on, he just remembered reaching for it . . . and nothing else. His amnesia must have set in as he began to write. But why should he want to torture himself in this devious fashion? That was yet another question to which he had no answer. He sighed and picked up the first page of the new manuscript. He might as well read it to see what he had dreamed up for himself this time . . .

Philip Banter
21 East 68th St
New York, N.Y.

CONFESSION

2

My head aches today; I feel ten years older overnight. I cannot blame it all on the liquor. I was drunk enough last night, but not too drunk to know what I was doing. Have I lost all control over my impulses? I know I cannot experience many nights like last night and survive.

But didn't I make much the same sort of vow yesterday? I seem to have a store of good resolutions . . .

I must be losing my mind. Certainly there is something

badly wrong with me if I don't learn a lesson from last night.

Philip laid the first page aside. He stood up and walked to the window and looked down on Madison Avenue. The street below him swarmed with people, all types of human beings, leading all kinds of lives. Why had this happened to him? Why not to one of them? He inserted his finger between his collar and his neck and ran it nervously along the starched edge. The 'Confession' was positively uncanny! Reading it this morning was almost like hearing his own unspoken thoughts declaimed in an echoing, resounding room. Certain sentences, phrases, were still reverberating in his ears: 'my head aches today' – his head did ache; 'have I lost all control over my impulses?' – well, had he? – his actions left the matter open to serious question; 'I must be losing my mind . . .' Philip pulled the cord that controlled the Venetian blind, jerked at it, shuttered the view of hurrying pedestrians from his sight. Was he losing his mind? His fists clenched his temples – he could feel the blood pounding in his ears. He stood like that for several minutes, cataleptically rigid, a panic-stricken statue. Then his fists relaxed, his arms drooped and his hands, now open, dangled at his sides. He turned slowly around and stared at the pile of manuscript beside the typewriter. For a moment longer he resisted it, a tense moment during which he felt as if he were about to collapse; but instead of collapsing he sat down again at the desk and seized the second page . . .

When I reached the office yesterday morning, I was ashamed of myself. I had not seen Dorothy since the night before, when I had left our apartment to take – home, and I didn't know as yet how she was going to react to my behaviour. It did not seem possible that she could overlook my misconduct this time. As long as I kept my affairs to myself, as long as I did not force her to acknowledge my infidelity, I was confident of Dorothy's reasonableness. I did not bother her and she would not bother me. But now I had broken our tacit agreement: I had made love to – before her eyes. I did not know how she would take it.

I did not work all morning. A few minutes after eleven o'clock my telephone rang. It was Dorothy on the other end of the wire. Her voice seemed pleasant and cheerful. She was going to do some shopping and would need extra money, would I stop at the bank and make a withdrawal and then meet her at the Three Griffins for lunch? I asked her how much money she needed. She mentioned a staggering sum which would all but take our balance. I started to protest, then hesitated and finally said nothing. She said she would have to hurry if she were to be on time and hung up. I sat looking at the receiver until the switchboard operator asked me if I wanted another line, then I hung up, too. I could not believe my ears. Dorothy had seemed natural, as if nothing had happened. Yet why did she need so much money?

I reached for my hat and went out the door, telling Miss Grey I would not be back until after lunch and to get the name of anyone who called. I would go to the bank and from there to the Three Griffins – I would see Dorothy and judge for myself.

The Three Griffins is a small restaurant on East Fifty-Third Street run by a hunchback. The *décor* is pseudo-Gothic: the booths along each wall fit into *papier-mâché* groined arches, the lighting fixtures are hidden in candle wind screens of pierced metal, the atmosphere is murky, romantically dismal. Dorothy had discovered it during our first year of married life and the place had some obscure, sentimental significance for her that I quite forget. Yesterday, she was as late as I had feared she might be, and I sat there under one of the mouldy-looking arches chain-smoking cigarettes and staring at the repulsive proprietor perched on his high stool behind a very modern cash-register. I was on my second martini when Dorothy arrived.

'Darling! I'm so sorry to have kept you waiting! But

Mimi dropped by to show off a hat she had just bought, and to tell me about a hairdresser she has discovered who has simply done miracles for her – you know how ratty her hair always looks? – well, you should have seen it today! it was miraculous! – and I could not get rid of her for the longest time . . .' Dorothy was being bright and gay and artificial as hell. I knew there was a reason for this pose; Dorothy is not usually like that. She went on, 'Order me a martini, darling, won't you? That one looks so good!'

I ordered her a drink, and then later the hunchback brought us a cutlet and vegetables, a salad, coffee and brandy. It was a good lunch, but I did not enjoy it. Dorothy kept on talking frippery in that phony, very-very manner with a 'darling' tacked onto the end of every other sentence, while all the time I was uncomfortably aware of what thin ice her chatter skated on so glibly. Sooner or later we would get down to cases; I could have done nothing to hurry her, just as I could do nothing to defend myself when the time came.

This was when I lighted a cigarette and Dorothy was finishing her brandy. She had just asked for the money I had drawn out of the bank and I had given it to her; she had thrust the thick wad of bills into her purse without counting them. But she spent an inordinate amount of time fussing with the catch on her purse, and said without looking up. 'And how is – ?'

'Well enough, I suppose.'

'She got home safely, I trust?'

'I took her to her door.'

'Just to the door, Philip?' Dorothy had taken a cigarette from her bag and was bending forward for me to light it. I struck a match – the spurting, spluttering crack it made sounded deafening. I did not answer her.

'You admit it then?' Dorothy had turned her eyes away from mine. It was queer. A stranger might have judged us conspirators from the way she was acting.

'I don't know what you are talking about!' I said loudly and distinctly. Too loud, in fact – I saw the hunchback swerve around to look at me. I smiled back at him to assure him that he had not been addressed.

'Oh yes you do, Philip,' Dorothy was saying softly, insinuatingly. 'Don't you think I know what goes on?'

'Nothing is going on,' I insisted.

She was silent. She held her anger for a moment or two longer as if she savoured it and was loath to part with it. This interval could not have endured more than a span of seconds, a minute at the most; but to me it seemed ten, twenty times that long. I could hear my pulse in my throat, feel the hot throb of blood in my temples . . . but I could also hear two shopgirls eating their lunch in the next booth talkatively comparing the salient points of their 'gentlemen friends'.

'You slept with her last night, Philip. You needn't deny it, I know you did. And it isn't the first time, Philip. This sort of thing has been going on for years. You've been quite . . . brazen . . . Philip.' Her manner was deliberate, like a judge on the bench; only this judge had a swarm of dark hair in place of a powdered wig, dark eyes that in the past had been merry more often than judicial, dark lips . . .

I said nothing.

'I'm leaving town tomorrow, Philip. Don't try to stop me. You'll hear from my lawyer. This time you'll have to talk to Dad yourself.' She had swept up her gloves and her bag and was gone, leaving me staring at a piece of green paper that I had folded and refolded so many times in the previous few minutes that the scribbled figures on it were nearly worn away – the check.

I went over to the hunchback and paid it; I walked outside and stood looking up at the tall, blue sky; I was not surprised or angry. Now that it had happened, it seemed inevitable.

*

I didn't go back to the office; instead I walked over to Third Avenue, entered the first saloon that I saw and started in to drink. I drank very methodically. I drank rye and water, and I would take two drinks in one place and then go to the next one. By four o'clock in the afternoon I had worked my way down to the Twenties and I had run out of money. The bartender in the place I was in then would not cash my cheque, so I went outside and into a pawnshop next door and hocked my watch; the heavy-jowled, bent-over pawnbroker gave me ten dollars after much hesitation although I had paid fifty for it. I kept on drinking. I reached Astor Place by nightfall – the clock on Wanamaker's told me it was after six. I searched my pockets but could find only a dollar and some change. There was a cigarstore on the corner of Ninth Street and Third Avenue where I went to telephone Jeremy. He told me yes, he could lend me ten until the end of the week if I would meet him at a bar on Sixth Avenue in the Radio City neighbourhood within half an hour. I promised to do that. He sounded surprised. I took a taxi uptown – the fare and the tip took my last cent. If Jeremy didn't meet me, I told myself, I would have to stop drinking, and the thought of stopping drinking made me tremble.

But Jeremy was waiting for me at the bar. He glanced at me and handed me a crumpled bill. 'What in God's name have you been doing to yourself?' he asked.

I stared at his fat face. One crease of flesh which rolled over his collar revolted me particularly. I could not understand how this man could ever have been a friend of mine.

'You look like you've slept in those clothes,' he went on when I didn't answer his first question. 'My God, Phil, what's come over you?'

I had intended to have a drink with him – I needed one badly – but I could not stand there and let him question me in his sneering way. I pushed past him towards the street.

'Hey, Phil! Wait a minute!' I walked faster. It became a matter of paramount importance to put as much space as possible between myself and him; when I was through the door and on the sidewalk, I began to run; there were many pedestrians – it was the tag-end of the rush hour – and I had to weave through the crowd like a broken-field runner. I heard him shout, 'Hey, Phil!' one more time, that is I heard a faint shout – it might have been somebody else; but I didn't stop running until I neared Central Park. Then I went into a package store and bought a bottle and took it with me into the park where it would be quiet and I would be left alone to drink in peace.

*

I am not too clear about all that happened in the park. I remember that I found a secluded bench behind a rocky upcropping that was not close to a street light; sitting on the bench I drank about half the bottle before I began to feel alive again (the ride uptown in the taxi and the energy I had spent in escaping from Jeremy had sobered me; I felt dead). I looked around me and saw that the trees, the distant lights of the theatre district, had all receded into a soft and comfortable haziness. There was a small, but intense, fire in the pit of my stomach that warmed me and encouraged me to feel that everything fitted into place and that I belonged to the world again. I remember stretching out on the bench, my head on my rolled up coat, lying there gazing entranced at the starry, clear, cold sky. It was December, yet I had drunk enough to make it seem like June.

I must have fallen asleep for the next that I remember is the impression of being on a subway train: the roar of steel wheels on steel rails bottled up and rushing past me in the tunnel, the pale light of the cars. — was sitting across from me, but I was aware of Dorothy's presence also; although I could not see her anywhere, I sensed that she was there watching me. Then, as I sat trying to decide whether to speak to — or get up and look for Dorothy, the car began to cave in. First, the vestibule careened wildly inwards, then the walls began to collapse and the floor rose to meet them; there was a shrill, screaming rending and I found myself thrown against — on the lurching floor, a warm wetness spreading over me, flooding me, fogging my sight. I tried to get up, to stand on my feet, to force my way out – but I was pinned down, helpless. I opened my mouth to cry out my anguish, but no sound came . . .

Still trying to scream, I swam upward through the blackness, a blackness that was now relieved by the pinpoints of bright stars. I kept struggling to rise, but something held me down. I fought to free myself, as yet only half-consciously, and then suddenly awake and aware that this was no dream. I heard someone curse and I felt a staggering blow that knocked me from the bench onto the sloping ground; I rolled with the momentum of the blow down a small grade behind the bench, clutching at the slippery earth, trying to stop my fall. I continued to roll all the way down the hill and fell, at last, face down in a pool of icy, revivifying water. Someone was scrambling away up above me; I could hear running footfalls dying away in the distance.

I sat up, cold sober. My clothes were torn and muddy and drenched with rye whisky where the bottle I had been drinking from had spilled over them. My hands were bleeding for they had been scratched in my long, tumbling fall down the grade. I stood up and made my way painfully to the top of the hill. Only when I reached the bench where I had been lying, did I realize that my wallet was gone and with it my money. I had been robbed by a thug.

I set off towards the entrance of the park in search of a policeman. I did not find one; one found me. He walked up behind me, seized me by the collar and pushed me in the direction of the nearest drive out of the park. 'Get along with you,' he growled, 'before I have to run you in!' There was no use arguing with him. He took me for a bum. At that, I must have been a pretty sight: my clothes were muddied, one trouser leg was torn, I reeked of whisky and my face was scratched and dirty. I left the park and started walking downtown again.

*

I did not know where to go. If I went back to the apartment, Dorothy might be there and I didn't want to face her after what she had said at lunch. On the other hand, if she weren't there, I didn't want to be there either – I had too many associations connected with that apartment, too many mementoes of our life together. I couldn't go back to the office in my present condition. Jeremy might have let me sleep at his place, but I didn't want him to see me looking the way I did. Sooner or later he would have told Dorothy about it, and I never wanted her to have the satisfaction of knowing how her decision had affected me. There was no place I could go.

*

Philip let the pages fall onto the desk. He pressed his hand against his forehead and eyes to shut out all light. As he had read, he had been overcome with a feeling of unreality – as if he did not exist in this room, but only in the pages he was reading. Even now, with his eyes shut and the friendly, self-consoling pressure of his hand to remind him of his own, incontestable existence, he was not certain. The 'Confession' goaded him, tormented him. After another moment, his hand dropped, he picked up the manuscript and began to read again.

But I kept walking downtown along Sixth Avenue. Distances which I had covered many times by bus or taxi, I now had to cover on foot. I was near exhaustion from exposure and the after-effects of the quantities of liquor I had swilled, yet I forced myself to keep moving as if there were a great spring inside me that once it started to unwind was to continue inexorably until the last erg of tension was released. When I reached Forty-second Street, I considered going into Bryant Park; but I was afraid that if I did the police would only chase me out again. I kept on walking, stopping for street lights and when the press of traffic required. I was hungry and I had begun to feel sick when I was in the garment district around Herald Square; I went down into the subway to go to the comfort station before I realized that I would have had to pay a fare to get in there, and I had no money to pay a fare; instead, I stood looking at the exit gate with its 'No Admittance' signs, watching it swing open widely and invitingly whenever anyone pushed out. I didn't have the courage to try to sneak through when the man behind the change-window wasn't looking. I went back upstairs to the street and started walking downtown again.

When I reached the Village, I went straight to Jones Street. It might have been that my subconscious had been directing my steps that way all the while, although if this were true I had not consciously planned it or semi-consciously abetted it. Nevertheless, it made no difference to me then whether I saw – or not; either way I had lost Dorothy, hadn't I? And, queerly enough, I felt that – was the one person I could trust. I waited in front of her building until there was no one near to see me go in, and then I rang her doorbell. As soon as the buzzer sounded I pushed the door open and started to climb the stairs to her apartment; on the second landing an Italian woman with her arms full of groceries stopped to stare at me – but I didn't give a damn what anybody thought by then.

I remember – letting me in, her mouth agape when she saw how bedraggled I was. 'What happened to you?' she asked. I mumbled something that satisfied her for the moment. She helped me into the other room and let the water run in the tub while I took off my clothes. She was wearing a housecoat that featured a slit from her ankles to above her knees and showed the outside of her thigh when she walked, but I was too tired to do anything about that. She made me some coffee and some hot soup while I was in the tub; later, I sat in the kitchen drinking it and matching her questions with what I thought were convincing lies. Afterwards she took me into the next room and made me get into bed.

The next thing I remember it was morning and I was

awake and staring at —'s dark head beside me on the pillow. One of my other suits was lying on a chair across the room, neatly laid out for me. I jumped out of bed and began to shake – to waken her. She looked up at me drowsily. 'Whassa matter?'

'Where did you get that suit?'

'I went to your place last night. Dorothy gave it to me. You couldn't go out looking the way you did when you came in.'

'But how did you know to go to my place? I mean didn't I tell you not to go there?' If she had been given that suit by Dorothy, that meant that Dorothy knew how cut up I had been over her decision to divorce me. I had not wanted her to know that.

— was smiling at me, that cocky smile of hers that is half a sneer. 'You talked in your sleep last night, darling,' she said. 'You told me all about Dorothy's leaving you. There's just you and me now, Philip. Isn't that nice?'

I hit her when she said that. I knocked her down on the bed and beat the bejesus out of her. It made me feel like a man again.

Philip's hand shook as he laid down the last page of the manuscript. If Dorothy were to leave him . . . he did not know what he would do. He might take it like that. It would mean that he was not only out of a job, but that he had lost his home as well. It would mean the end of his comfortable life and the start of a whole new chapter.

But what concerned him most was the apparent fact that he must have written what he had just read. What kind of mental disorder did he have that would prompt him to try himself in this fashion? It was a kind of slow suicide. And there was a sly masochism about it – a delight in tormenting himself with personal revelations – that was dismaying. If anyone else should see it! And if any of the events predicted in it should actually occur! Yet wasn't this exactly what he must want to happen – if not, why else would he have written it?

His one consoling thought was the fact that of what had happened the night before in *reality*, as far as he could remember, there had been a serious discrepancy: he had not slept with Brent. As far as he could remember – ah, that was the catch. He could recall having gone to Brent's apartment, drinking a whisky and soda with her, holding her to him and having her refuse him. He could remember getting drunk and returning to the office . . . but he could remember nothing else. What had happened during the rest of the night? Had he written the 'Confession', or returned to Brent's apartment – or both? It could be that his memory was playing him false again, that he did not remember what he thought he remembered. It could be . . . as the idea occurred to him, he snatched at his desk calendar to check the date. If he had gotten mixed up on his dates and everything that had been 'foretold' in the manuscript had already happened it might not have been last night that he had met Brent at a party at his house – but the night before. His heart stopped beating as he looked at the calendar, and then it started beating again. The day was only the second of December – not the third – the events prophesied in the 'Confession' had yet to happen. If he wished, he might still prevent them. Somehow he must prevent them!

Then Philip thought of Dr George Matthews. He had known George when he was finishing up his pre-med course and they had kept in touch ever since, even writing back and forth to each other while Matthews was doing post-graduate work in psychopathology in Zurich. Once or twice Philip had nearly dropped his end of the correspondence; but Matthews had always persisted, writing letter after letter until Philip was shamed into answering: Matthews had said that Philip interested him since he was 'perhaps, the archetype of the narcissistic personality'. Philip had intended to look that up and find out what it meant, but he never had. Now that George Matthews had offices in New York and a booming practice, they met about once a month for lunch. George was a full-fledged psychiatrist, certainly the one best person to consult about this. He might be able to tell Philip what to do.

Philip reached for the telephone and had the girl get him Dr Matthews' number. He was lucky and George, although he said his appointment book was filled for six weeks in advance, was free for lunch. Philip said he would meet him at their club at twelve and hung up. He checked his watch and saw that it was already after eleven and he had not washed or shaved since the evening before. Well, he could have a wash, at least, before he met George. He put on his hat and went out the door, telling Miss Grey that he was going to lunch and then to the barber, but he would be back afterwards.

As Philip passed the switchboard girl, she signalled to him. 'Pardon me, Mr Banter, but I have a call for you.'

Philip remembered the 'Confession's' first prediction. 'Ask who it is,' he said.

The girl spoke into her mouthpiece, listened for a moment and then looked up at Philip. 'It's your wife, Mr Banter. She wants to meet you for lunch.'

A chill warped at Philip's neck. 'Tell her I've just left,' he said quickly. 'Tell her I didn't say when I'd be back.'

Philip slipped through the door hurriedly and walked rapidly down the hall towards the elevator. He was still seeing the look of startled, slightly pleased – here was something to gossip about! – surprise on the frigid face of the receptionist; he could still hear her haughty voice exclaiming, 'But, Mr Banter!'

He jabbed the down button. That had been a close call.

As soon as Philip left the office, Miss Grey reached for the telephone and asked the operator to connect her with Tom Jamison. When he answered, she said, 'I have some more news.' She listened for a moment. 'I'm going out at twelve; I know that's early for you, but can you make it then? All right. Twelve-fifteen at the usual place.'

She hung up the receiver, stood and went to the door. She looked up and down the hall before she closed the door quietly and walked into Philip's office. Sitting down at his desk, she began to go through the drawers methodically – shaking her head in displeasure from time to time. The large bottom drawer was locked. She pulled at it several times, banged it hard with the heel of her palm. She took a hairpin from her hair and inserted it in the lock, but then she thought better of it. She shook her head again and withdrew the hairpin. Standing, she walked to the window – 'Damn!' she said.

After looking out of the window for a few minutes, she went back into her own cubicle, opened the door to the hall and seated herself at her desk. A copy of the *New Yorker* caught her eye and she picked it up. This would help pass the time until twelve o'clock.

Tom Jamison was a young man whose face wore a perpetually worried expression. If the corners of his mouth had not turned down, and his forehead had not been scored with wrinkles, he might have been considered handsome. As it was, his habitual frown belied his even features and good bone structure. Now, his frown deepened. He regarded Alice Grey, who was sitting across from him at the table, and tried to speak above the din of the crowded restaurant. 'Why didn't you pick the lock?' he asked.

The girl did not understand him. She asked him to repeat his question.

'I don't want to speak too loud,' he said. 'You never can tell who might hear.'

'Silly!' Miss Grey smiled at him. 'No one's listening to us. They're all too busy making themselves heard.'

'Why didn't you pick the lock?' he asked again. This time the girl heard his words.

'I was afraid that I'd scratch the finish of the desk and he would notice it. Then I had no way of knowing that he had put it there.'

'It was the only locked drawer, wasn't it?'

'Yes.'

'Well, wouldn't that be the logical place for him to put it?'

'I suppose so. But he could have taken it with him.'

'Did he have anything under his arm when he left?'

The girl thought about this for a moment. 'I don't think so. If he did, I didn't see it. But I wouldn't be sure.'

Jamison was angry. 'Why not? Weren't you making it your business to keep your eye on him? Now we may never get it back! And, if we don't, sooner or later he's going to put two and two together . . .'

'Oh, Tom, I'm sorry. I do the best I can.'

'I wish we had never gotten into this,' he said.

'But when I told you about it, you had no objections.'

'If you got each one of them back. Anyway, you had already gone ahead with the first one before you told me.'

'But, Tom, a hundred dollars – now it's two hundred dollars. You know how long it takes us to earn that!'

Jamison cut a piece of meat with his knife and started to put it into his mouth. Then he thought of something and his fork stopped halfway between the plate and his lips. 'You never did tell me what you did the other night,' he complained.

'What other night?'

'Day before yesterday. The night I couldn't get away.'

The girl looked down at her plate. She spoke without looking at him. 'I waited around for your call – you could have 'phoned, you know, even if you couldn't make it. After more than an hour I gave you up and went out. I took a bus up to Central Park and walked around. Later – I don't know when – I left the Park and went to a bar. I – I had a few drinks and – and then I went home.'

He looked at her questioningly. 'Is that all you did?'

'Don't you believe me?'

'I suppose I do.'

She looked up at him. Her eyes were wet and her cheeks glistened. 'Tom, you must believe me. I work so hard. I look forward to the time when we can be married. Now that it is almost within our grasp – and I'm sure it will be, Tom, if you get Banter's job – please trust me.'

Tom laughed. 'You're so certain Foster will give me that job – that Philip will leave. How can you be so sure?' he spoke bitterly.

'I've told you as much as I can. You know that by rights it's your job – it always was your job.'

'Not when the white-haired boy's around. And he's still around as far as I can see.'

Miss Grey shook her head. 'But not for long, Tom. I can assure you of that, I think. Philip Banter is on his way out.'

They finished their meal in silence.

Dr George Matthews finished tamping tobacco into his meerschaum, struck a match and puffed strenuously until his head was wreathed with a laurel of heavy smoke. The delicately tinted bowl of his pipe glinted merrily in a ray of sunshine that slanted from one of the club's vaulted windows. Matthews held it out at arm's length and admired it: this was a fine pipe, an excellent example of a kind of workmanship found only in Switzerland before the war and now, doubtless, irreplaceable. Still paying homage to his pipe, Matthews addressed Philip. 'Your secretary does seem a bit of a nuisance, Phil,' he said. 'and I can't say I blame you for being irked with her. Yet there is a tenseness about you, a drawn and hectored air, that leads me to wonder if there isn't some other flaw in your – at least up to now – enviably prosperous existence.' The corners of Matthews' wide, heavy-lipped mouth (he always reminded Philip of a Saint Bernard about the mouth) curled with sly humour. 'Then again I noticed a quality of *angst* in the hasty telephone call with which you summoned me to lunch this morning, and – if I may say so – almost traumatic apprehension. "Banter," I told myself, "has got the wind up over something."' He drew his pipe slowly back towards his mouth, inserting the stem carefully between his thick, sensual lips as if it were a piece of laboratory apparatus. 'Tell me, am I not right?'

Matthews had been pleased when Philip called him. He had not expected to have the patient come to him so quickly. Yet all through lunch Philip had talked around the subject that Matthews knew, from his interview with Dorothy and her father the day before, must be uppermost in his mind. So, although he firmly believed that the patient must bring his troubles to the psychiatrist, Matthews decided to make a leading comment that might make it easier for his friend to speak of his disorder.

Philip's reaction was complex. He laughed, and lifted his coffee cup to keep Matthews from seeing his confusion. 'No,' he said, 'you're not right. Or, rather, yes, you are – but not in the way you think.'

'"Yes and no" is a good enough answer to a general question. In fact, I can think of few questions of the kind I just posed that deserve any other answer. There are times when "yes" can be an evasion and "yes and no" quite forthright.'

As usual, Philip realized, George had managed to relieve his embarrassment. He set down his coffee cup and lighted a cigarette. For once he decided he would be frank. Sometimes it was wisest to lay all one's cards on the table. But, although candour was his earnest desire, when Philip spoke he found his words taking a devious path.

'I am disturbed,' he began, 'greatly disturbed. But not about myself or anything that has happened to me.' He paused after saying that and wondered at how he could resolve one moment to be frank and yet be so incapable of simple honesty the next. 'I've come to you about someone I know who . . . who is suffering from a delusion.' Philip's face went damp and his breath caught in his throat as he lied. However, now that he had framed it, the subterfuge seemed necessary. I shall tell the rest of it straight enough, he promised himself. And Matthews, at the same time, recognized the most familiar device of the inexperienced confessor and redoubled his interest in his friend's conversation.

'What kind of delusion does this person experience?' he asked.

Philip hesitated. 'I may be wrong in calling it a delusion,' he began again. 'It is a very real experience to my friend.'

'Would it be a delusion if it weren't?' Matthews asked soberly.

'Of course. But what I mean is – suppose a man came into his office one morning and found a manuscript there, piled beside his typewriter, one sheet still on the machine. His first impulse is to ask his secretary who has been using his typewriter, then, on second thoughts, he decides to read some of it first to see what it is about.'

'Natural enough. Might be blackmail,' George commented.

Philip nodded his head vigorously. 'Exactly. So he reads it. He finds it is a self-termed "Confession", supposedly written by himself, of events that the manuscript says have happened to him – only they haven't.'

Matthews laid down his pipe and studied Philip closely. 'What kind of events?'

'My friend says the manuscript predicted that he was to meet a girl at a dinner given by his wife. He was to make love to her, to have an affair with her. And his wife was to be aware of what was happening.'

Matthews spoke deliberately, soothingly. 'You say "predict". And yet you say the manuscript purports to be a "Confession" written by your friend. Isn't this a contradiction in terms?'

'You would think so, wouldn't you? That's one of the reasons why I called what has happened to my friend a delusion.' Philip pushed his chair away from the table and restlessly crossed his knees. 'But he says no. He says that although the manuscript was entitled "Confession" and although it was supposed to be about events that happened the night before, the events told about in the manuscript did not actually happen until after he had read about them, that evening in fact. So the "Confession" was really a prophecy.'

Matthews picked up his pipe, stuffed more tobacco into it, tamped and re-tamped it. He genuinely enjoyed the strongly aromatic smoke and he fancied himself as a pipe-collector; but his habit had a practical, as well as an aesthetic, advantage. A man who plays with a pipe is able to keep silent for long intervals and is free to observe his companion's actions – a necessary trait for a psychiatrist. Thus Matthews' pipes were wont to go out more often than those of most smokers so that when he fiddled with matches and cleaners his patients would be unaware that their doctor's eyes were upon them. Now, as he used this device to regard Philip obliquely, he grew more certain of his friend's anxiety. Where he had been sceptical about Dorothy's fears, and inclined to reassure her, he was now sure that Philip was badly neurotic. This onslaught of neurosis was not entirely unexpected; on the contrary, George had never understood why his friend had not had a break sooner. He had first known him as a shy, with-drawn lad who was sensitive about his unusual good looks; he had watched at the sidelines, figuratively speaking, while Philip drew on an inexhaustible supply of com-pensatory energy to spurt with unnatural rapidity into a position of leadership and to acquire a Byronic repu-tation; later, at a veritable distance, he had kept in touch with the mature life of this compulsive Casanova whose narcissism combined a perpetual, wily aggression against the distaff side with an uncanny acumen in the masculine, competitive world. Philip reminded him of his first acquaintance with him today: he had a diffidence that was disarming, and his attempt at dissimulation in telling the story of his hallucination was completely ingenuous. Matthews was frankly fascinated.

'You think he has been writing it himself, don't you, Phil?' Matthews puffed the words out with the first fog of rank smoke from his re-lighted meerschaum. He wanted the blunt question to have full shock value.

Again Philip hesitated. Now that he was talking about what was happening to him, it all seemed silly. But he had begun, he had said enough to pique George's curiosity so that he would have to continue. 'No, it's not like that, or rather maybe it is. He could be writing it himself. He won't ever admit that he ever suspected himself of it, but I am sure he has thought of it. Yet I am inclined to think that someone else is writing it, you see.'

Matthews shook his head. 'I wonder if you really think so. I know you say you think this is being done to your friend, but then you come to me to ask my advice. Am I right in supposing that the contents of the "Confession" are slanderous? Well, then, if you really believe that your friend is not be-devilling himself – but is being be-devilled – why don't you go to the police?'

Philip's hand was trembling. He thrust it into his pocket so that the doctor would not see. 'I wanted to rule out the possibility that he might be writing it himself before I advised him to do that. If it's a matter for the police – well, then he will have to talk to them himself. But I promised him that I would speak to you about it first.'

'Oh, he knows that you are consulting me? Doesn't that mean that he does suspect himself to be the author of this mysterious manuscript?' Matthews made a sound that resembled a deep chuckle, but his expression remained grave and the chuckle might have been an indication of digestion.

Philip knew that he had been caught up and that this was his friend's way of telling him to come clean. Instead, his explanation became more involved – partly out of the perversity that makes us defend a lost argument for just a little longer after we know it is lost. 'I've tried to make him see the bad logic of his position. But he insists every time that although I suspect him, he does not suspect himself. When I mentioned you, he even urged me to talk to you about it – but he professed to want me to see you only because I needed to be reassured that "it was impossible that I should be writing it". Those are his very words.'

This time George Matthews laughed openly and resonantly. 'He's an obstinate cuss, isn't he?'

Philip smiled and nodded his head. 'Tell me the truth, George. Could my friend be writing this story about himself – could he be telling himself what he planned to do and at the same time pretend that what he planned had already taken place – without his ever knowing it?'

Matthews rested his pipe against his cup and saucer; although he no longer held it in his hand, one of his fingers lingered beside the bowl and caressed it, taking pleasure in its warmth. 'You will have to tell me more about your friend before I can answer that. What does he do for a living?'

'He's a writer.'

'What does he write? Advertising?'

'Yes.'

'Is he married?'

'Yes, he is.'

'Is he happy with his wife – and is she happy with him?'

Philip paused. How could he answer that? Until yesterday there would have been no doubt in his mind that Dorothy and he were happy. But now? 'Yes . . . I think so,' he said slowly.

'Why aren't you sure?'

Again Philip thought before he spoke. He did not want to come too close to his own personality in describing this mythical friend, or Matthews would realize that he was talking about himself – if Matthews hadn't realized that already. Yet he did want to strike a fair parallel to keep from misrepresenting his problem. At last he decided to risk it. George had given signs of seeing through his pretence anyway. 'He, my friend, that is, has played around a little lately. He hasn't been doing all his sleeping at home. He is afraid his wife might know.'

'How do you know this?'

'I've heard gossip.'

'Do you hear voices, Philip?' Matthews asked casually.

'I beg your pardon.'

'Do you hear voices? Do you hear someone speaking to you when you are alone?'

'Why should I hear voices?'

Matthews smoked his pipe in silence. He did not speak,

but his eyes were kind. Why must I continue to pretend when I know there is no reason for pretending? Philip asked himself.

'Sometimes.'

'Do you want to tell me about them?'

Philip coughed. A great hand seemed to seize his stomach and twist it. He coughed again. 'I hear a voice. A child's voice. But first I hear a bell ringing in the distance. The sound keeps coming closer and closer. The lights dim and everything I see looks as if it were covered with scum. It's then I hear the voice.'

Dr Matthews carefully kept his own tone casual. 'What does it say, Phil?'

'It says, "Oh, Philip, why can't you remember? We had so much fun! Why did you have to forget?"'

'And what have you forgotten?'

Philip fumbled for a cigarette. His hands shook as he struck a match, the flame wavered and danced as he held it up. He dropped the match in the ashtray and stared defiantly at Matthews.

'You drink a lot, don't you, Phil?'

'Why do you ask?' Philip's voice had an edge to it. Inwardly, he was frightened.

Matthews nodded at his hand, which was still trembling as it held the cigarette. 'Your hands,' he said. 'They shake so.'

'Yes, I drink a lot.'

'Too much, do you think, Phil?'

'No. No more than many people I know.'

Matthews smiled. 'Why do you drink, Phil?'

Philip felt bright shafts of anger spear their way into his brain. He wanted to pound his fist on the table and shout George Matthews down. But he spoke quietly because he was afraid to shout or show his rage. 'I do it to get away from the voice. I never hear it when I'm drunk.'

Matthews nodded his head. He was silent, gazing at the design he had traced on the tablecloth with his fork.

'I know whose voice it is,' Philip said.

Matthews still did not speak.

'It's my voice. My voice before it changed. My voice as a child, saying "Philip, why don't you remember?"' Banter said.

'And you drink to escape the voice, drink until you forget what you do – and then the next day you hear the voice again. Is that it?'

Philip nodded his head. 'And now I'm writing this "Confession", threatening myself. It looks as if I want to drive *me* mad!'

Matthews picked up his pipe and stroked it against his cheek. He looked away from Philip at the deeply recessed windows of the club's dining-room. 'Tell me more about this "Confession" – what did it predict? And what happened?'

Philip told him the circumstances surrounding his discovery of the manuscript and related briefly the predictions it had made about his meeting Brent and his attempt to make love to her.

'And did these events take place exactly as predicted? Or were there disparities?'

'There were disparities,' Philip said. 'But I met the girl as the manuscript predicted, and I made love to her.'

'You had not known her before?'

'I am sure I never met her.'

'You could have met her and then forgotten about it, couldn't you?'

Philip had not considered this. Yes, he might have met Brent during one of his 'forgotten' periods.

'But if I had done that, why wouldn't she have said something when we were introduced?'

'There might have been a reason, mightn't there? Your wife was present . . .'

Then Philip had to tell him what had happened after he took Brent home the previous night. He ended by saying, 'She finally ordered me out of the apartment.'

'And this the "Confession" did not predict?'

'That's right. The "Confession" had stated definitely that I would sleep with her.'

Matthews sucked noisily at his pipe and again studied the high sunny windows. But he said nothing, nor did he seem to expect that Philip would have anything more to say. His reaction was disquieting – it made Philip feel uncomfortable.

'After I left her place I had a few drinks and then I went back to the office,' Philip went on. He felt a need to continue talking in the face of his friend's, the psychiatrist's, taciturnity. 'I do not remember what happened at the office clearly. I must have been pretty drunk. And I must have fallen asleep eventually. I know I do not remember having written anything. But I found a second instalment of the "Confession" on my desk this morning when I awakened.'

'And what did it predict this time?'

'That Dorothy would meet me for lunch today and ask for a divorce. That I would get drunk in Central Park and be rolled by thugs. That I would wind up at Brent's apartment as before.'

'And what do you intend to do about it?'

'I am going to do my level best to keep any part of it from coming true. I avoided having lunch with my wife. I won't go back to the office today or home tonight.' He hesitated and stared grimly at Dr Matthews. 'I won't let it happen again!' he cried.

Matthews laid down his pipe. 'I've heard of cases similar to yours, but not in all particulars. Of course, every love-sick swain since time began has kept a diary of his peccadilloes. I have encountered adolescents who laid down time-tables for themselves to follow in these matters. "Watch the girl who works in the candy store and find out where she lives. Manage to meet her alone. Ask her to the church supper." That sort of thing.' Matthews sensed the extreme anxiety of his patient (for he now regarded Philip as his patient), and he was trying to allay it in part by relating the strange facts of the 'Confession' to other more natural diaries.

But Philip stiffened. 'I see no similarity,' he said with dignity. He mistook Matthews' easy casualness for joking familiarity.

Matthews grew more serious. 'It really isn't as different as you would think. The basic mechanism is the same. Narcissus looking into the pool. Your predicament is only more complex. For example, you have always been quite a lad with the ladies, haven't you?'

Philip's hand, hidden in his trousers' pocket, began to tremble again. 'Yes. Why?'

'And you're in your middle thirties, I take it?'

'Yes.'

'And once or twice lately, you have experienced unexpected failures?'

'Yes, I – I have,' Philip stammered. And then wondered why he had not lied.

'That might have a bearing on your case,' Matthews said. 'If you have a growing fear of impotency – as well as earlier feelings of guilt . . .'

'But if I did – and if I have, I don't know it – why would I write a "Confession" about an affair I was afraid I could not have? Wouldn't that be ridiculous?'

'Not as ridiculous as it seems. I'll admit that the part about actually writing down your wishes and then forgetting that you have written them is unusual – although I dare say I could find a similar case if I looked it up. But the mechanism is classic! The young boy who has never experienced sex and the old man who doubts that he will ever experience it again share common feelings of guilt and inadequacy. They both spend an inordinate amount of time daydreaming about exploits they don't have the courage or opportunity to make real. Sometimes this happens to a man in his maturity, and then his fears are often false. They are only symptomatic of a deeper wound, a hidden conflict. Some men never get over adolescent feelings of inadequacy and guilt, and with such men, every time they have a new relation it is a fresh trial of their ever-doubted prowess – you might call them sexual athletes since they are always trying to break their own records. These men often become psychically impotent prematurely. They day-dream compulsively – you do it on paper! – about imagined triumphs and then force themselves to make them real. Often they come a cropper . . .'

'Then do you think I'm writing the "Confession" myself?' Philip clenched a table knife spasmodically as he asked this question. His heart was jumping in his throat.

Matthews was lighting his pipe again. 'You do, don't you?'

'Yes, I suppose I do.'

'Philip, I don't think that "Confession" is so terribly important – if you are writing it. If you are not writing it, and that is possible – who could it be?'

'I don't know. I have no evidence against anyone. Anyone who knew me that well. Jeremy. Dorothy. Miss Grey hears a lot of my 'phone calls, I'm sure – she might be doing it, but that seems a stretch of the imagination. Steven Foster. Even Brent, if your guess is right and I knew her before during one of my blank periods.'

'Why would any of these do such a thing?'

Philip dropped the knife on the floor. He bent to pick it up. His head was reeling and he was breathing rapidly – his heart hammered at his ribs. He could see that George thought he was insane. What would he do next? The important thing was to act natural, rational.

'Dorothy might be jealous of me. She might want to get even, to scare me.'

'So she plants a "Confession" on your desk every morning?'

'It sounds weak, doesn't it?'

'A jealous woman has done queerer things before. What about the others?'

'Jeremy has always resented my success – I suppose you know that. And Dorothy was his girl before she was mine.'

'And now you are making love to Brent?'

'Yes, that would give him a motive. But, if he's writing the "Confession", why should he *suggest* her to me?'

Matthews nodded his head. 'Steven Foster?' he asked.

'The old man has never welcomed me as a son-in-law. But his methods are more direct.'

'Your secretary?'

'She resents me, too. But I don't think she has the wits to arrive at such a scheme, let alone the drive and stick-to-it-iveness to carry it out.'

'In other words, you don't think that anyone but yourself could be doing it.'

Philip tried to smile. 'I'm afraid that about sizes it up.'

Matthews knocked out his pipe. 'If you are writing the "Confession", we can regard it as a symptom. If you aren't of course, it might be a matter for the police. But since you and I both come to the same conclusion about it, I think we can look upon it as part of your syndrome.'

Philip had taken his hand from his pocket. His shirt sleeve was pushed back by the movement, revealing the soiled bandage about his wrist. Dr Matthews now saw his friend's bandaged wrist for the first time. 'Have you hurt yourself, Philip?' he asked casually.

Matthews had not considered this an important question. His only reason for asking it, beyond that of natural curiosity, was to break the tension his last remarks had created in Philip. He knew that an irrelevant question which shows human interest can often put a patient at ease during a difficult interview. But Philip responded quite differently from what Matthews had expected. He became highly excited, all but hysterical.

He jumped to his feet, clutching his injured wrist. 'I don't know, George, I don't know!' He held his wrist up to his mouth, sucking at it as a small child might do. 'I must have hurt myself the other night. But I can't remember. When I woke up yesterday morning, it was bandaged. I don't know how I did it.' His voice had become petulant, a child's voice. He whined rather than spoke and tears appeared in his eyes. Matthews saw that his pupils had dilated with anxiety. 'I can't remember a thing,' he said piteously.

'You found your wrist hurt the same morning that you found the first part of the "Confession" – is that right?' Matthews asked.

Philip gulped and nodded his head. 'And when I left the office to go downtown, I was nearly run over. A truck came out of a side street – I didn't see it coming. I think the driver swerved to hit me, although I could be mistaken. It might have been an accident. But then later, in the elevator, I was nearly crushed between the doors.' And he told Matthews about the large man, whose face he had not glimpsed, who knocked him off balance as the elevator's safety doors were closing.

Dr Matthews listened, but he made no comment. Philip gradually calmed. He realized that he had become abnormally excited – the blood was still pounding in his temples. Suddenly, it had seemed to him that everyone, everyone in the world, was against him and persecuting him. When Matthews opened a package of cigarettes and offered him one, he took it gratefully.

'Do you think that these "accidents" – both the ones you remember and the one you don't – could be part of a plot against you, Philip? Is that the way you feel?' Matthews asked.

Philip hesitated. 'Sometimes, I think so. Other times, I think that something's wrong with me – that I am trying to kill myself.'

'You mean that you are afraid that you might have slashed your own wrist while drunk? That you might have stepped into the path of the onrushing truck? That you bumped into the man in the elevator and threw yourself off balance?'

Philip nodded his head.

'You're highly disturbed emotionally, Philip. I prescribe a good, long rest in some quiet place where you can get the proper medical attention. Once you have tapered off on your drinking, your other symptoms may disappear. Why don't you come around to my office now and let me make the necessary arrangements?'

Philip had again become more and more uneasy as the conversation grew more clinical. Now he jumped to his feet. 'I'm sorry, George, but I've just remembered an appointment I must keep! I will come to see you though. I'll call you up and make an appointment.' And he began to walk away.

Matthews walked after him. There was little he could do, if Philip did not want to come with him. And he was uncertain as to his diagnosis. From Dorothy's evidence, and Philip's own admission, he did know that Philip had become an alcoholic. The first thing to do would be to treat his alcoholism; then – when he was less disturbed – would be time enough to attempt analysis. So when he caught up to Philip, who had been walking very fast, he had this to say: 'I don't want to alarm you, Phil, but you need a psychiatrist's care. If you don't want to come to me, I can give you the name of a good man . . .'

But Philip, smilingly, shook him off. 'I'm not as batty as you think, George. Just been working too hard, that's all. But I'll remember what you've said, and I'll come to see you some day.'

Then they shook hands and Philip hurried away. Matthews puffed at his pipe and looked at the check in his hand. He shrugged his shoulders, went over to the cashier and paid it.

As he walked back to his office, taking pleasure in the cool, clear light of the December sun and the cloudless blue of the winter sky, Matthews thought over Philip's peculiar story. And he grew more and more concerned about Philip. If his friend's neurosis were sufficiently advanced, he might worsen seriously before Matthews could persuade him to submit to treatment.

So when he reached his office, he gave his nurse Dorothy's name and the name of Steven Foster. 'Keep ringing both of them until you get them, and then tell whoever answers that I want to see them both tomorrow morning at Steven Foster's office.'

Later in the day, Miss Henry left a note on Dr Matthews' desk. It read: 'Unable to contact Dorothy Banter. You have an appointment with Mr Steven Foster at ten o'clock tomorrow morning.'

3

Jeremy and Brent had just finished breakfast and
Brent was washing the dishes, when the telephone rang.
Jeremy walked to the far end of the great loft room to
reach the instrument. He spoke into the receiver in a soft,
controlled voice, not because he felt the need to be
surreptitious, but because an announcer habitually
modulates the tone of his speech. When he realized that
it was Dorothy at the other end of the connection, he did
not speak more loudly. There was no need to, of course,
and the rush of water from the faucet would probably
have prevented Brent from hearing the conversation had
there been a need; but the fact was that Jeremy, if he
changed his manner of speech in the least, lowered his
voice as the dialogue progressed.

Dorothy wanted Jeremy to meet her for lunch. She
wanted to ask his advice on a matter of importance. When
he began an embarrassed apology for his impulsive act
of the previous evening, she cut him short with a pleasan-
try. She told him that she had not been aware until that
night of how much Philip and she had missed him. She
emphasized Philip's name when she said this, as if she
feared that Jeremy might otherwise infer that she, alone,
had appreciated his company. 'You must come to see us
more often, Jerry dear,' she went on. 'And you must bring
Brent along.' This time she emphasized Brent's name, as
if it were her particular caution not too imply too much.
'She is such an interesting girl, so intelligent – with such
verve!'

As Jeremy said less and less, Dorothy's voice rushed
forward. 'But about today, Jerry. You would be doing me

such a favour if you could have lunch with me. I know it's an imposition – please don't say it isn't, I know it is. But I really feel I must see you. Yes, it is important. No, it would be difficult over the 'phone. Yes, it's confidential, but that's not the only reason. Well, darling, you see it's so involved. I wouldn't know where to begin, but at lunch I can just talk at you and let it all come out. You can sort out and pick up the pieces, and then, perhaps, you'll tell me what you would do. Oh, Jerry, you are a dear!'

Jeremy hung up the telephone and walked to the long windows that overlooked the street. He did not stand too close to their sills, even though they were shut tight, because these sills were flush with the floor and this always made him dizzy and filled him with the crazy urge to jump. At the moment he was especially upset. Why had he found Dorothy's request so disquieting? And why did he feel he was being dishonest by accepting her invitation and not letting Brent know about it? Of course, he could tell Brent. No harm would be done, but it would do no good either. Not that he thought Brent was jealous of Dorothy – she had said she was not – but only curious about her. Nor was there any cause for jealousy on Brent's part, he was sure. If once he had been deeply in love with Dorothy, and had continued to love her even after she had married Philip, he no longer cared for her. A year's absence had effected that. Last night, a fugitive impulse had forced him to embrace her; it had been a childish passion and a wholly irresponsible one. He knew – he was certain he knew – that it had been only an incident, an inconsequential by-product of a dull evening. Nothing would come of it, because he did not want anything to come of it.

Or did he? As he stood at the window looking down on, but not seeing, the busy street – in his own apartment with the woman he told himself he loved, and with whom he had spent the night, only a few paces away – suddenly, he was a part of another reality, intensely aware of another presence. Now Dorothy stood between him and the window; Dorothy's aura, a combination of fond memories and the actual, physical pressure and warmth of her body as he had held her to himself the night before, surrounded him and overwhelmed him. Her scent was in his nostrils; her dark hair brushed lightly against his brow, cobwebby, enticing . . .

He stiffened and forced himself to withdraw from the dream that had seized him. Had Dorothy had a similar experience that morning? Was this why she had telephoned him and insisted that he spend an hour or two with her? Jeremy was afraid this was so. Faced with the possibility that Dorothy might desire to renew their love, he was not nearly as sure that he would be able to will it otherwise as he had been an instant before. Then he had thought of his action the previous night only in terms of his own wayward, selfish impulse. Would he be able to stand up against her longing as well as his own?

A sound made him turn quickly about to stare at the other end of the room. Brent had just come from the sink and was wiping her hands on her apron; her face was flushed with the heat of the water she had been using, and this unnatural colouring heightened the sensuality of her wide mouth and her brooding, changeable eyes. As he regarded her, he knew that for him Brent, too, was very desirable.

He continued to stare at her while she walked to the sofa, which the sheets and blankets still disguised, took a cigarette from the pack lying open on the end-table, lighted it and with a sigh of satisfaction bent over to unmake the bed. He watched her work, rapidly and efficiently peeling the sheets off, folding them, unmasking the pillows and fluffing out the dents made by their heads in the night. He felt a lump rise in his throat, and thought himself a sentimental fool.

'That was the studio,' he said.

'Again?'

'Joe's still sick. He has four shows this afternoon.'

'And they want you to work them? Jeremy, when are

we going to have some time to ourselves?' She straightened up and let a pillow drop to the floor. He could see that she took his words at their face value, and did not suspect that the call might not have been from the studio. But then, why should she? He had never lied to her before.

He looked at his wrist-watch. 'I'll have to be there inside a few minutes. The first show's at noon and I'll have to work it up.'

Brent had returned to her work. 'When will you be back?'

'This evening. They'll have to get someone else for tonight. I'm as tired of this as you.'

She did not answer him. He went to the closet for his hat and coat. As he was leaving, he asked, 'Will you stay here this afternoon?'

Brent looked up again, and smiled. Jeremy wondered if the guilt he felt had expressed itself in his voice. But if it had, Brent said nothing to indicate it. 'I may try to write this afternoon,' she said. 'If I do, I'll go home since I can never get into the mood here. If I'm not here when you get back, you can give me a ring.'

Jeremy shut the door and went down the stairs. Now that he had actually left the apartment, he felt he was making a mistake. He stood outside the building, hesitating. He could telephone Dorothy from the drugstore on the corner and make some excuse for not keeping his appointment, and then return to the apartment and Brent. But if he did that, he would have difficulty explaining why he had decided not to go to the studio. Or he could go back and tell Brent that he had lied, and that instead of going to the studio he was meeting Dorothy for lunch. Brent would be jealous of Dorothy if he did that, though, and angry at him for lying to her. The simplest thing to do was to keep his appointment. So, having reached this decision, he set off down the street, walking a little faster and with a little more determination than usual.

*

As soon as Jeremy had left the apartment, Brent had gone to the windows. By opening one of them, steadying herself on the ledge and leaning out a bit, she saw Jeremy leave the house and then pause momentarily as if he had not made up his mind which way to go. Brent watched him intently, her face strained with quick anger. Only when he began to walk up the street did she turn and go back into the room. She went over to the couch and lay on it and tried to cry.

Many times in past months Dorothy had thought of Jeremy, and had remembered his boyish, open face, his quick enthusiasms, with an uncomfortable nostalgia. Finally, she had called him and asked him to dinner. He had tried to refuse her invitation – she knew this was because he had been hurt by Philip's neglectfulness – by saying he had a date that evening and would be busy every other night that week. He had described Brent to her over the telephone, and Dorothy had insisted that he bring Brent along. Once done, she had delayed telling Philip that she had invited Jeremy and Brent, had delayed so long that she realized she did not want to tell him . . . that she feared his meeting Brent. She had not told him until the evening before, and she had been frightened by the effect her news had had on him. But she soon forgot this in her joy of meeting Jeremy again. All evening she had been afraid Philip would notice that she could not keep her eyes off her old friend. But what difference would it have made if Philip had noticed?

Dorothy knew that she had made a mistake by marrying Philip instead of Jeremy. Not that she had been unhappy with Philip during the first years of their married life. No, then, she had been almost unreasonably happy. But later, especially in the last year, she had felt Philip eluding her – slipping from her grasp. Philip was so relentless. He always had objectives he was working towards, but he seldom made them known to her. Frequently, she guessed them. Many times she had been angry, but it was a kind of ingrown anger that she could not express. 'I am as much to blame for my husband's immorality as he is,' she told herself. 'Yet this self-shame makes me hate him. But would life with Jeremy, if I had married him instead of Philip, have been so different?'

Dorothy was enough of a realist to sense that it might have been much the same. Any good-looking man flirts. Yet she felt Jeremy had a straightness in his character that was alien to Philip, a kind of self-restraint that recognized a law that had been freely accepted and cleaved to it. Besides, Jeremy was friendly; he liked people for what they were, not for what they were worth. Jeremy had loved her, while Philip had only recognized her value to him ... and had set about to obtain it and her.

When she thought of Philip and Jeremy, Dorothy also thought of her father. He, too, was a handsome man, erect and tawny even in his old age. As a child, her father had been a god, a bronzed, golden-haired image of majesty. She had seen him usually at a distance: at the foot of the table when she was allowed to dine with him, on the polo field at the championship matches which she had observed from the grandstand, standing by the fire-place, tall and unbending, when nurse brought her in to say good-night. To this day she perceived her father through the wrong end of an imaginary telescope; there was a barrier to scale or a distance to span between them at all times. Of course, she knew, it had not always been so. There had been times when her father had taken her in his arms and held her, one of them as recent as her wedding. But this was a memory that her consciousness usually denied, a holy thing to be kept in a safe place and reverenced, not a well-worn pocket-piece to be fondled at odd moments and perhaps mislaid. Only in the stillness of calm and peace or at the height of euphoria, did she ever think of that wedding-day embrace. Her father, rigid in his dignity, had closed her into his arms with inexorable strength and had kissed her acceptant mouth with lips and tongue; there had been greed in his ardour and immeasurable satisfaction. Philip's husband kiss, a breathless moment later, had been father-like.

This was the way Dorothy thought – compulsively, circularly – about her life and Philip. And each time her thoughts reached the same, questioning *impasse*: would Jeremy have been different? Then, the night before, she had seen him, talked to him, and had grown jealous of Brent. Jeremy was just the same as he had always been, a little effusive, perhaps, and getting slightly stout – but good-hearted and still youthful. When Philip had passed the time by being impolite to Jeremy and paying court to Brent, Dorothy had at last decided that she had had enough. As Jeremy was leaving, she followed him into the hall, interposed herself between him and the door, and smiled and waited. He had kissed her and held her in his arms while she whispered in his ear. Later, she had to leave the house, to get out on the streets and feel the cold wind on her face. She had not returned until late in the night, and she had not been surprised to find that Philip's bed was unoccupied. She had waited until the middle of the morning, suffering a kind of dry-mouthed terror, before she had picked up the telephone and dialled the number of Philip's office. She intended to speak to him of her feelings, tell him that she doubted her love for him and that she wanted to leave him. It had come to that; which is not to say it was easy for her to do. Her pulse pounded in her ear while she waited for the connection to be completed, and she gasped with great relief when the switchboard girl told her that Philip had left and had not said when he would be back. But, as soon as she had hung up, she was alone again and miserable. She went over to the piano and played a little Mozart, but this did no good either. She lighted a cigarette, and then let it go out. Finally, she went back to the telephone and called Jeremy. When he answered, she spoke brightly, affectedly, begging him to have lunch with her. She would tell him about Philip and ask his advice – it would be the sensible way to let him know that she now considered herself free and unencumbered. Philip would not mind if she had an affair with Jeremy. The thought of Philip's minding made her smile bitterly to herself. The chances were he might even be pleased.

Dorothy had told Jeremy to meet her at the Three Griffins. This was a small café that Philip and she had visited often during the first months of their marriage, and she felt it somehow fitting that she should go there on the day she had decided that she must end their relationship. She put on her silliest hat, a tiny perky affair with a wild-eyed peacock's feather stuck in it, and daubed her fingernails with a gaudy polish that she had bought once when she was feeling gay and had never dared to use. She spent an inordinate amount of time dressing: taking a long, long bath, brushing her hair for many minutes before her mirror, carefully painting her mouth with lipstick that matched her nails; so, of course, she was late to her appointment.

Jeremy was sitting in a booth at the rear of the long, narrow, dimly lighted café glumly considering a martini. He did not see Dorothy until she was standing beside him, then he jumped to his feet and smiled quickly. Dorothy was suddenly nervous. She dropped her purse as she sat down; Jeremy stooped for it at the same time she did, and their heads bumped resoundingly. The mutual, ridiculous pain established a bond; by the time Jeremy had ordered a martini for Dorothy, and the waiter had brought it, a warm feeling existed between them and Jeremy's hand was groping for hers beneath the table. They talked about small, topical things at first: the weather, Dorothy's hat, the fact that the martinis were rather good – at this point they ordered two more – gossip about a mutual friend, the latest shows they had seen. Then Jeremy remembered a Gershwin show and Dorothy hummed its tunes, her head tilted back, her dark eyes glinting; and Jeremy's hand became bolder.

They had seen that show together on a weekend in New York when they had happened to meet; it had been a rainy, miserable day and they both had been unhappy about a party that had been a frost the night before. Now, that day came to life again and with it the Thirties. Jeremy remembered the words of a Cole Porter song, and Dorothy reminded him of a dance they had gone to together at which another mutual friend had gotten very drunk and made a scene. It was all of a piece, a mood that owed much to the martinis – they were now drinking the third round – and to that queer feeling of opportunities missed and illusions mislaid that comes upon us all when we try to remember. It was very inappropriate, too, they both realized, for what they were doing in actuality was endeavouring to escape the cage of the present by admiring and reconstructing the bars that had made the cages of the past. Neither of them mentioned Philip or Brent; Dorothy delayed because she was not at all sure that now was just the time, and Jeremy forgot on impulse because it was pleasant for the moment and he was confident that this hour would never influence the future. At last, they ordered lunch, although they were not hungry; Jeremy came around to Dorothy's side of the table and they ate off each other's plates – soon she was in his arms and he was kissing her, and getting the tulle from her hat in his mouth and her mouth, and feeling her warm form go soft and supple in his grasp.

He stiffened. 'Dorothy, I don't think we should.'

She did not answer, but only looked at him and then dropped her head. He glanced down at her bowed head and was taken by surprise by the whiteness of her part. It was difficult to speak. 'I'm not a prude, Dorothy. But I don't think we really should.' (All the while staring at her dark and complaisant head, feeling the vague outline of her soft warmth.) 'We are older now, mature, with responsibilities to think of. Don't you see, Dorothy, it's really not the same?'

Dorothy did not understand herself what had come

over her, except that she felt that Jeremy welcomed her and wanted her, in a way that Philip never did. She inched closer to him and laid her head on his shoulder. Her voice crooned softly to him in a broken, murmuring sing-song. 'It is the same . . . that's why I had to see you. You see, he's been so strange . . . so distant . . . he never looks at me any more . . . he never comes to me. I'm used up . . . no good . . . a formality. I tried to tell him . . . today . . . before I called you. He wasn't in. I thought that it mattered that I tell him first . . . but it doesn't . . . no, it doesn't. It's you I must tell. You're the one who has to know . . . before it's too late . . .'

She pressed her mouth against his, her tears dampening his cheeks. He saw the shielded lamp on the wall through the diffusion of her dark hair. He felt the points of her breasts against his chest and the oblique pressure of her thigh across his hip. Brent, he thought, Brent. He tried to remember her face, the soft slur of her voice. But Dorothy was whispering again. 'Hurry, darling . . . let's go some place . . . away from here . . . oh, dear!'

4

Philip was afraid. He tried not to think about what
George Matthews had said, tried to distract himself by
carrying on the small matters of life just as if nothing had
happened. Since he had slept in his clothes, and badly,
he stopped by a barber shop for a shave and a facial. The
barber talked monotonously while he kneaded his face
and applied hot towels; Philip tried to concentrate on the
barber's patter, but it was no use. His mind kept reverting
to its central problem: who was writing the 'Confession'?
He remembered the dream with which he had awakened
and saw again the faces of Dorothy, Brent and Jeremy
ringed around him pointing accusing fingers. He began
to tremble. Soon he was shaking uncontrollably. The
barber put his hand on his forehead, but said nothing –
Philip was grateful for the firm, cool fingers, yet he could
not help but wonder what the fellow was thinking. He
might have decided that this particular customer was
recovering from a binge – what would he say if he knew
what was really wrong? Had he looked out of his mind
when he entered the shop? Was his confusion so readily
perceptible?

What was it that distinguished the aspect of the sane
from that of the insane? Surely there was a difference. He
knew that many times in his life he had encountered
psychotics, casually, in buses or on the subway, on the
street, almost any place. They were not all locked up
by any means. Some he had known by their peculiar
attire, such as the man who was in the habit of making
incoherent speeches at Columbus Circle wrapped in the
flags of the United Nations; others had a compulsive

gesture or an eccentric characteristic: they jerked or swayed, they shouted strange sounds, they talked continuously to themselves. He doubted if he had acquired suddenly any of these symptoms. But hadn't he occasionally identified madness in others by some other, subtler sign? Yes, he remembered a reporter who used to work next to him in the city room of the *Herald-Post,* a quiet, sensible chap who had a pretty wife and a bright little boy. He had gone queer overnight. They had all noticed it, and had talked it over amongst themselves – Philip and the other reporters and the men at the desk – so it had not been his imagination. Yet there had been nothing obviously wrong with this fellow, except that those characteristics that had always been his had asserted themselves to a greater and greater degree: he had been quiet to begin with – he grew quieter; he had been affable and polite – he grew extraordinarily apologetic; he had frequently paused in his work to gaze out the window – he got so that he did little else. Then, one night after work was over, he went down to the Lexington Avenue Subway and stepped off the platform in front of an express.

Philip had known that something had gone badly wrong with him, and so had everyone. There had been a blank look about the fellow's face. His eyes had seemed dead and lack-lustre. His movements had been slow and listless. Now Philip wondered if the barber who kept talking such drivel had seen the same things in himself. Was he actually frightened of him? Was this why he kept talking so much, and why he had made no remark when Philip began to shake?

He waited anxiously for the massage to be over. As soon as he was out of the chair, he darted a quick glance at himself in the mirror. He seemed the same; if anything he looked healthier than usual as his skin was fresh and pink from the hot towels and the massage. But then he would not recognize any change in himself if there were one, would he? Wouldn't it be a part of the disorder to seem unchanged even as one changed, particularly to oneself?

145

He paid the barber, tipped the man a dollar and walked rapidly from the shop. As he went down the street he felt as if everyone were looking at him. Several times he was on the verge of stopping to turn around and see if he were being followed, but each time he assured himself that he was only nervous and upset from his strange experiences and the disquieting talk with Dr Matthews. Yet he walked from 50th Street and Madison Avenue to Times Square without knowing where he was going or why, and he might have kept walking indefinitely in this aimless fashion if he had not glimpsed out of the tail of his eye a gigantic purplish hand. It had a cluster of huge, misshapen fingers and the thickest, longest finger was pointing directly at him. He stopped dead in his tracks, rigid with terror, unaware of the other pedestrians who kept pushing and shoving their way past him, too panic-stricken to face the tremendous symbol of guilt that had sought him out.

Philip first thought that he did not know where he was. He had been walking, thinking about and reconsidering everything that had happened to him in the past two days, wholly unconscious of his surroundings except that he had known that he was out on the streets of midtown Manhattan. Now he was isolated in his terror and acutely conscious of the fact that just behind him – without moving he could see it darkly – a hellish finger designated him, silently accused him – of what? A terrible idea arose in his mind, an idea that was in itself the configuration of evil: had he crossed the threshold that divided the appearances of sanity from the misapprehensions of insanity – had he literally *walked* into a madman's world? Was this thing that lurked behind him the first, weird landmark of the distorted landscape which would be his natural environment henceforward? Great waves of fear battered him, his tongue grew dry and felt like cloth in his mouth, his legs threatened to collapse. He seemed to be shrinking, gradually losing weight and stature, dissolving into a mammoth lake of terror. Yet a shred of reason, a grain of scepticism, remained in the welter of his emotions like

146

flotsam adrift in the surf. Before he gave up, before he surrendered entirely, wasn't he capable of turning around to stand full face with this apparition that had descended upon him? He fought to turn, finding that to perform this simple manoeuvre he had to assert all his strength as if he were defying gravity or forcing his way through an almost impenetrable obstruction; he moved slowly, somnambulistically, until he stared directly at the giant, pointing finger that soundlessly menaced him.

As he stared, he became aware again of light . . . of people . . . of shining chromium . . . and glittering glass. He saw that the great hand and menacing finger were not flesh and blood, but were *papier-mâché* and part of a motion picture theatre's lobby exhibit. A large sign hung above the monster that read: 'See *Man Alone* - A Tale of A Man Fighting Against Desperate Odds - And As You See it, Remember, It Could Have Happened To *You*!'

Philip walked around the dummy hand, examining it carefully and shaking his head, still doubting his eyes. He must have walked past the theatre front without knowing and have seen this advertising come-on with only the lesser part of his senses: what his eyes had seen communicated itself to his mind, which had been busily debating the question of his sanity - thus the theatre eye-catcher had been neurotically garbled and magnified into evidence of lunacy by his overwrought intelligence. He felt like laughing, like crying aloud his joy at discovering the mistake he had made. He did chuckle, and then grinned, and finally went up to the box-office and bought a ticket to *Man Alone*. Although he had not planned on seeing a show it was as good a way as any of wasting time and it was also a form of activity that had not been predicted by the 'Confession'. He was still smiling to himself as he selected a seat in the welcome darkness of the balcony and fastened his eyes on the screen.

Philip, willingly surrendering his objectivity as he centred his attention on the motion picture, saw first the

147

back of a tall man walking away from him. He was immediately struck by the fact that something about the scene was extremely familiar to him, but he was not allowed time to follow this thought to its conclusion since his mind was registering the images seen and the sounds heard, to extract their meaning. He had entered the theatre after the feature picture had begun, which meant that he did not know what action had transpired before. He saw a man walking down a busy street, a New York street, in fact (he realized this with a shock that was strangely unpleasant), a street he had walked himself only a few minutes ago! Before he could consider the full meaning of this coincidence, something else happened on the screen: a girl, a beautiful, dark-haired girl, stepped out of a doorway and smiled at the man – who still presented only his back to Philip – welcomed him without words. The man stopped walking and his back grew larger until it forced itself, obtruded itself, to the very edges of the screen. All Philip could see were the man's back and, over his shoulder, the smiling eyes of the girl which, as he watched, ceased smiling and became dull with fright. A scream shrilled in Philip's ears and the monster's back and shoulders began to rock to and fro, the eyes dangled and jumped and shook – again the scream shrilled, then formed itself into terror-stricken words: 'Oh, don't, Phil, don't! I never told on you. I swear it. He lied! He lied!'

Philip was charged with anger. He leaned forward until his chin rested on the seat in front of him – he did not feel the prickle of the upholstery since it was a part of the reality he rejected when he looked at the screen. His fingers clenched and closed spasmodically as the scene changed: now he, Philip (or was it the shadow-Philip?), found himself in a night club. The place was dark except for a single spotlight that picked out the figure of a girl, a beautiful blonde, who was singing a blues song into a chromium-plated microphone. As she sang, she bobbed and minced in time to the thud-ting, thud-ting of the hidden orchestra.

Philip picked his way to a table. When her number was finished and the lights went up to show a large, circular room with a dance floor of black plastic that shone like a mirror, she saw his inquiring eyes and came to his table and sat opposite him. Philip questioned her in low, threatening tones spoken out of the corner of his mouth, and when she refused to answer he clamped his fingers on her wrist and began to turn it slowly, torturously until she cried in pain. Then he slapped her face and walked out of the night club . . .

It was a grade-B movie he had stumbled on, and one that was in no way distinguished except that its principal character happened to be named Philip. Philip had often seen plays or movies where he shared his name with one of the characters involved in the drama. But this time, coming in when he did as the murderer was strangling his first victim, the familiar magic worked too well. The narrative continued on the screen – as the man who had escaped from prison killed his first victim and went on to kill another and another, all the time searching for the man who 'sent him up' – and each time Philip performed, partly in his mind and partly in elaborate, unconscious pantomime, each of the killer's actions. In the climactic moments of the movie, the detective, who had been following the murderer from city to city and murder to murder, at last caught up with him and killed him just as he had found and was about to kill the man for whom he had been searching.

Philip had long since lost all track of reality. The action on the screen was his action, he was the murderer – and each time the girl who was murdered was Brent. He killed her again and again, every time a different way: by slow strangulation, by poison, by shooting and once by pushing her from a high window. He was a hunted man, even though his actions were not his actions but the fictional acts of the shadow he watched – still they were real to him to a greater extent than the giant finger had been real to him, and they carried with them a sense of guilt that

149

was overwhelming. The sounds and shadows which he watched, the shape and darkness of the theatre, the actual sensations of breathing and contact with the material world, all became merged into an amorphous, phantasmagoric delusion. Philip killed, felt remorse, anger, jealousy, lust; he drank, ran, strangled, sweated, feared; he heard jazz bands, saw the other shadows as he had seen Brent and confused them with her, enacted crimes with the ease of any of a hundred odd actions in his normal life. The climax of the picture left him hysterical. He sat and sobbed through the news-reel, the Mickey Mouse and the Coming Attractions. These short subjects, instead of breaking the continuity of his delusion, served to confuse him more than ever so that the second time he saw *Man Alone* his experience was even more terrible.

About six o'clock the balcony began to fill up. A woman sat next to Philip for a little while and then went to an usher and complained. 'There's a man up there who keeps grunting and tearing at his seat like an animal. I won't sit beside him!' The usher investigated. He had to shake Philip to bring him to his senses, and he insisted that Philip must leave.

Not until he reached the street – as he groped his way down the stairs and walked through the ornate lobby, he still felt he had done some heinous wrong for which he was being pursued – did Philip begin to understand how extraordinarily he had acted in the theatre.

Then he went across the street to a bar and had a drink.

The bar was small and unpretentious, and it was not crowded. This was the kind of bar Philip liked. He usually drank at a table – he would find the table or booth farthest from the door, the one least exposed to view, and then sit at it in the most inconspicuous position. There was no conscious reason behind this habit; in fact he was not aware of his preference for privacy when drinking. Today, however, he sat at the bar. He wanted to be near people and he was eager to start a conversation. If he could talk to someone, he thought he might get his mind off his fear.

He drank three double bourbons in rapid succession and felt much better immediately. He had been acting the fool's part all along – he saw that now. Yesterday, when he had read the first instalment of the 'Confession', he should have made no secret of it. He should have questioned Miss Grey thoroughly, as well as every other person in the office who might have had the least thing to do with it. He should have told his wife about the 'Confession', too, if for no other reason than to judge her reaction. During the evening with Jeremy and Brent, he might have joked about it. Certainly one of these persons, Miss Grey or Dorothy or Brent, had written it. Or himself.

He had made another mistake at the same time. He had allowed himself to forget about the manuscript from the time he had first read it until Dorothy told him that they were having friends for dinner. As a result he was unprepared for the shock of having the 'Confession's' predictions come true. He had grown nervous and withdrawn, and he had either thought too much or not at all about every word he said, everything he did. If someone had written the strange prophecy with an aim to get him to follow a particular course of action, he could not have done more to help this person's plans or to hurt himself. He had walked into every trap that had been set for him – if, indeed, traps had been set for him at all. Now, what he should have done . . .

'Have a drink on me?'

A deeply tanned face was looking into his, a young man's face. But this face, though still recognizably young, was fleshed so tightly that the cheekbones seemed drumheads and the thin, smiling lips were as worn and polished as an old coin. He was a soldier and the service ribbons of three theatres of war were displayed on his breast. Apparently, Philip did not answer him as quickly as he expected, for the smile left his lips and the eyelids closed down on his dun-coloured eyes. He no longer seemed friendly, only lonely, and disheartened and grim. 'Yes, thank you,' said Philip, and he added quickly, 'if you'll have one on me.'

The boy – for Philip saw he was very young despite his grizzled look – whistled at the bartender and ordered drinks. He ducked his head in Philip's direction. 'I'm celebrating my release.'

'Have you been in the Army a long time?'

'Four years.'

'That is a long time.'

'It's all my life.'

Philip did not understand. The drinks came and he reached for and fingered his glass. He wanted to ask the youth what he meant by his remark, but he desisted.

'Do you like it here?' the soldier asked.

Philip glanced around him. 'It's all right as these places go. I've been in worse.'

The soldier shook his head. 'Not *here*,' he said. He made a wide, sweeping motion with his hand, an all-embracing gesture. 'I mean all around.'

Philip felt put off by his terse way of talking. 'Do you mean New York?' he asked.

The boy grimaced. 'New York, Chicago, 'Frisco, all the places I've been State-side.'

'I like New York,' Philip said.

The soldier looked him unblinkingly in the face. He might stare at me like this if he wanted to start a fight, Philip thought. But he is not belligerent. What is wrong?

'Does it seem real to you?' the soldier asked.

'New York?'

'Yeah. New York, Chicago, any place here.'

'Of course it seems real to me. It is real.' Then he remembered his bewildering afternoon. 'Although, at times, it can seem very unreal.'

The soldier's eyelids unshuttered his eyes and a thin smile lurked on his die-cast lips. His next question was put forward eagerly. 'Does it sometimes seem to you like this' – he waved his hand again – 'is not here, that you are not here, that you are only dreaming it?'

Philip did not answer. Yet, because he did not want to seem unfriendly, he smiled.

The boy had not noticed that Philip had failed to understand him. 'It's like that all the time with me. I look at a building, I crane my neck up at it and I laugh. It ain't real, and I know it ain't real. It stretches way up to there' – and he pointed upwards with his hand, causing Philip to look up with him – 'and down to here' – and he pointed downwards, Philip's eyes following – 'and yet it isn't. If I weren't looking at it, it wouldn't be.'

Philip nodded his head. Now he thought he understood what the boy was driving at and he became interested. Had he read Plato or had he thought this all out for himself?

'You mean,' Philip said, 'that you doubt the verifiability of the existence of things. You can only be sure of their appearance, the way they seem to you. Is that what you are saying?'

'Here,' said the soldier.

'Here? What do you mean by "here"?'

'Things ain't real here. Chicago, New York, all the places I've been here, ain't real.'

'Are they any more real anywhere else?'

This question had an effect on the young soldier. He began to glower, his face was torturously twisted and a tic developed in his cheek. 'All I have to do is shut my eyes and' – he waved his hand – 'all this crumbles.'

Philip threw his drink down his throat. His entire system had by now been invaded by the fire set by the liquor and he felt well and strong. But he did not like what his companion was saying. It horrified him.

The soldier had shut his eyes to test and prove his statement. 'The sun is everywhere. It glimmers and shakes in front of me. The canvas of my tent stinks. The water I am drinking stinks. The coke and beer I get at the P.X. stinks. I call it the sun stink. Can't you smell it?'

'No,' said Philip.

'I can. That's real. That won't crumble. It'll always be

here.' He opened his eyes and tapped his forehead. Philip saw that two of the fingers of his right hand were gone, and in their place was a badly healed scar. The soldier saw him looking at it. 'That's real, too,' he said. 'Jungle rot got in it. That won't crumble.'

'I don't understand you,' Philip said slowly. 'I thought I did at first, but now I'm not sure I do. Do you mean that you think you're not in New York?'

'It don't matter what you call it,' the boy said roughly. 'It ain't real. It will crumble.'

Philip was fascinated. He decided to tell his companion about what had happened to him that afternoon. He wanted to see what would happen when he told it. Before he told anyone else, he wanted to try it out on someone he did not know. He began at the barber-shop and told him about the giant finger that he had thought had been following him and pointing at him. He told him about his fear of losing his mind and of the queer, dream-like incoherence of his experience at the movie. When he had finished he was at once afraid that he had gone too far. He ordered another round of drinks for himself and the soldier.

'Does it come back to you when you shut your eyes?' the soldier asked. 'Can you shut your eyes and step right into it? Then it's real. Then you see the same thing I do. The stink – ain't it hell ? – the stinking sun!'

Philip shut his eyes. He did see the monstrous finger. It was pointing directly at him. But, he told himself, this is only because you are thinking about it, remembering it. Then he saw Brent's face the way it had looked when she had asked him to leave her apartment. And he heard Dorothy's voice saying, 'I'm going to leave you, Philip.' And Jeremy was saying, 'Good old Phil, always the life of the party!' He opened his eyes. The bar room did look unreal, his face in the mirror looked unreal, the soldier's voice droning on about 'the stink' was unreal. Nothing existed.

He ordered another drink for himself and the soldier.

'I was in Greenland,' the soldier said, 'and then North Africa and Normandy. I was wounded at Caen and invalided home, and then, after a delay in route, they shipped me to the Pacific. We were stationed on an atoll that didn't have a name, only a number. The war had passed it by; we were guarding ammunition and an airstrip that was never used. A dozen bull-dozers and a couple of excavators were rotting in the sun – we were supposed to keep them in working order. They were covered by canvas and we oiled them regularly, painted their metal, polished, scraped. Every week we'd hack the jungle back, burn the vines, make a little clearing around them.

'The rest of the time we sat around, or, when the C.O. got worried about us, we drilled in the sun. The sun was everywhere. It got inside your skull and beat at your brains. It was like prying fingers inside your skin, always moving, always hot, always tormenting you. We got so we hated each other. One of my buddies would say something to me – something like "Have you got a match?" – or "Hell, ain't it hot?" – and I'd want to kill him. We all got so we never said an unnecessary word. We just sat around and thought and sweated.

'It was then I thought of home' – he waved his hand – 'of here. I'd shut my eyes and try to see it the way I remembered it, and sometimes I would see it. But most of the time all I could ever see was a dull, red glare – the stinking sun. It got so that even at night, when I shut my eyes, I'd see that red glare – sometimes I'd even see it in my sleep.

'I kept telling myself that the day would come when I'd go home, leave the island for good, and then finally, the day would come when I wouldn't even remember what it was like. I kept telling myself that the day would come when I'd shut my eyes and try to see the tent and the goddam, stinking sun – and I wouldn't be able to! If I hadn't kept telling myself that I'da gone nuts!'

The soldier talked on and on. Philip bought round after round of drinks and sat with his eyes shut while the soldier talked. He said the same things over and over again. When he had been in the Pacific, he had tried to dream of home and only rarely had he succeeded – home had been distant, unreal, the blinding sun had stood between him and his dream. He had consoled himself with the thought that the time would come when he would not be able to recall the atoll, and the sun would be eternally vanquished. But this had not happened. Now that he was in the United States, he could not believe that the world he saw and the experiences he had were real. All he had to do at any time was to close his eyes, and he was back on the atoll facing the shimmering, relentless sun. He had convinced himself that his reality lay in his mind's picture of this past experience, that he was dreaming when he saw New York but not dreaming when he saw the high Pacific sun, that the drinks he was having in this bar – even his conversation with Philip – did not exist.

Philip did not try to shake his conviction. On the contrary, every word the obsessed soldier spoke strengthened a conviction of his own that he was no longer able to discriminate between real and mental images. By now, when he shut his eyes, Philip saw many different scenes. He lived over again all the events of the past day and a half, and he was freshly horrified by their import. He remembered, or thought he did, each word and phrase of the two instalments of the 'Confession', and he saw in his mind's eye each of the scenes depicted in it – including some that had not happened, some that had partly happened and some that had not happened yet. His memory confused these scenes with the actualities of the previous night and that afternoon, just as on the street and in the theatre he had misinterpreted and jumbled together real perceptions and imagined ones. As the soldier's voice buzzed on, compulsively reiterating his distorted version of reality, Philip grew more and more frenzied. His pulse pounded. His fingers were numb and it became increasingly difficult for him to pick up the jiggers of whisky that followed each other incessantly across the bar. Finally, it seemed to him that he was not sitting at a bar, but rather that he was placed beside an endless conveyor belt that kept moving past him. On the belt were glass after glass of whisky. It was his task to pick up each glass and drain it, and throw a half a dollar after it, before the next one came along. He had been doing this for years, it seemed, and so far he had been able to keep up – but now they were speeding up the belt. He could not continue . . . he could not . . .

He turned around to ask the soldier to help him, but the boy was no longer there. He looked around him. There was no one in the place (as he stared groggily, the room gradually assumed normal proportions, although it kept wavering and fading before his eyes), except for a man in a long, white apron who was doing something to the door. Now, the man was beckoning to him, saying something to him in a loud, harsh voice that was wholly incoherent. He stood unsteadily and walked towards the man and the door. As he reached them, he put his hand out to support himself (he felt as if the room were listing badly, as if the floor were slipping out from under his feet). But his hand met with no substance; the lights about him dulled and went out. His hand groped forward, still expecting to find a door, and he followed it, uncertainly, slowly, with exaggerated care. And then he saw a street lamp shining on a green and yellow taxi – was it real? – and he guessed that the scene had changed again.

The cab-driver saw a well-dressed drunk stagger out of the bar. He opened the door to his cab and the drunk stumbled into it – 'as if there'd been a magnet in there that drew him to it,' as the cabby explained to a friend later. He knocked down the flag on his meter, eyed his customer for a moment – he wasn't a bad-looking fellow – and asked him where he wanted to go.

'Home to Dorothy,' said Philip. 'Home to my lovin' lil' wife.' And he gave an address on Jones Street.

5

Tom Jamison and Alice Grey had been to a movie and now they were sitting in the Times Square Child's. Jamison's face was especially glum and Alice, while she ate her sandwich, kept glancing at him. He paid no attention.

'You haven't said a word in ten minutes, Tom,' she said.

He looked at her and smiled slightly.

'What's wrong?'

'You lied to me this afternoon.'

Her face flushed. 'But, Tom, I didn't.'

'Do you have to lie again?'

She laid her sandwich down. 'Tom, what did I say that you thought was untrue? Tell me, Tom! I want to know.'

'You said you didn't meet anyone the other night when I was late in calling you.'

She looked at him defiantly. 'Well, what if I did? What's wrong in meeting someone else?'

He stared at her, then dropped his eyes. 'It was a man, wasn't it?' His voice was cold.

'What if it was?'

'Who was he?' Anger made his voice squeak.

'Why should I tell you that? I don't have to.'

Tom was silent. He took a cigarette from his pocket and lighted it without offering her one. 'No, you don't have to tell,' he said.

'It was an accident.'

He did not speak.

'I just happened to meet him. He came into the bar

while I was having a drink. He spoke to me and I had to speak to him. I couldn't ignore him. He asked me to have a drink with him. I was angry with you and I did. It was awful. He told me the story of his life. He's so queer, Tom.'

Jamison was now paying close attention. 'Who are you talking about?' he asked quietly.

'Philip Banter,' she said. 'I met him in the bar. He sat and talked to me for an hour or more. He told me about his wife and how he was unfaithful to her. He told me about his mother and how he had never obeyed her – though what that had to do with his wife, I don't know. He kept telling me there was evil in him and he knew it. I tried to kid him out of it, but he got awfully excited. Then he did the strangest thing!'

'Why didn't you tell me this before?'

'I was afraid to tell you. But let me tell you what he did –'

Jamison shrugged his shoulders. 'Go ahead.'

'Philip kept saying there was a devil in him – that he was possessed with evil. I told him that I did not believe in devils, that it was childish for a grown man like him to talk like that. Then he got awfully excited. He said there were things he did that were so terrible that he could not even remember doing them. His eyes grew wild and crazy-looking. He said that he could tell when he was going to do evil. He said the lights grew dim; he said that he heard a tiny bell tinkling in his ear and a voice – his own voice, he said – would speak to him. That was when he was going to do something bad.' Miss Grey had been speaking rapidly and quietly. Now her voice was suddenly louder. 'Then he did the craziest thing, Tom! He stood up and reached across the table at me – we had left the bar and were sitting at a table in the rear – he started to claw at me. I don't know if he meant any harm, but he scared me. I picked up a seltzer bottle and hit at him. The bottle broke on his wrist – it cut him badly. When I saw the blood, I ran. I ran right out of the bar and I didn't stop until I climbed on a bus!'

Jamison shook his head. 'Do you mean that after all this had happened the night before, you were foolish enough to take that money the next morning – and put that thing on his desk?'

'Yes. I was mad at him.'

'But hasn't he ever referred to what happened?' Tom asked.

'Not a word. He had a bandage on his wrist though. I saw him looking at it.'

Jamison leaned forward and spoke earnestly. 'Look, Alice, you're getting deeper and deeper in this. If you don't watch out, something will happen and you'll be blamed for it. The best thing for you to do is to tell him you're quitting. If he ever remembers what he told you that night, he'll fire you anyway.'

'I had thought of that. But, Tom, I don't want to give up my job. We need the money.'

He held her hand in his. 'You can get another job – maybe a better one. You know as well as I do that something very queer is going on in that office. And you've had a hand in it. If you get out now, you won't be implicated. But if you hang around, you'll only be courting trouble.'

'When do you think I should give notice?'

'Tomorrow morning. The first thing. Don't lose any time doing it.'

'All right, Tom, if you say so. But I don't see why you're so alarmed.' Alice Grey smiled. She would like telling Philip Banter that she would not work for him any longer. It would be satisfying.

At about the same time, in her apartment on Jones Street, Brent had nearly finished the writing she had been doing all afternoon. After Jeremy had left her to keep his appointment with Dorothy, she had returned to her apartment. She had written the rest of the afternoon and evening and now it was close to midnight. Her eyes were tired from the continued effort and her back ached in that inconvenient place under the shoulders which she could never reach to rub or soothe. As she completed the last page of what she was typing, she ripped the sheet of paper from the platen of her typewriter and let the lid fall on the portable with a triumphant bang. She pushed her chair back, stood up – her hand pressed to her forehead, her manner dejected. Wearily, she crossed the small room to the telephone and slumped down beside it on the sofa. She stared at the instrument several minutes before she began to dial.

She was calling Jeremy's place again. Since six o'clock she had been trying to get him, but the only response had been the familiar sound of persistent ringing. He had said that he was not working that night, still she had called the studio once just to see if he might have changed his mind. But he was not there and the night operator could not tell her whether he had been there at all that day. Brent had doubted him when he had told her that morning that he was going to work; there had been something about the way he said this, a hesitancy, perhaps, that had informed her that he lied. She suspected that the telephone call he had received had been from Dorothy, and that he had left to meet her. He was probably with Dorothy now.

But each time Brent came to this conclusion, she rejected it. She did not want to believe that Jeremy had lied to her about Dorothy, especially since she had no evidence to support her suspicion. You resent Dorothy only because she knew him first and because he loved her before he loved you, she told herself. You are insecure in your relationship with him as you have been insecure in your relationship with all men since your childhood. You never let yourself forget your father, his glib tongue and his dark negligence – do you? You can always remember, without half an effort, that first night alone after your mother's death, when your father had gone out saying he would return, and he did not – can't you? That loneliness, that horror of moving shadows and unexplained sounds, that shriek that has been caught and held and never uttered in all these years – they are always there waiting for the unguarded moment, the flickering instant when restraint is loosened and the walls of reason crumble – aren't they? This implacable, childish terror (it has grown strong despite its fetters) was swallowed when your father at last returned, after a day and night of your vigil, somehow shrunken and dishevelled by his absence, swaying on his feet, clutching at you avidly while you eluded his drunken advances and shut your ears to his mutterings – it was swallowed then, but never digested – wasn't it? 'Yes,' she said aloud, as if hearing her own voice speak the words would render their truth harmless, 'it has remained a part of me, yet apart from me. It arises again and again and I re-swallow it as I might my heart's bile. I must continue to try to reclaim that which I can never assimilate.' (Except by wild rationalizations, by catch-as-catch-can plausibilities, by the butterfly nets of reason, her conscience added.)

Each time she had beaten back her suspicion in this way, had paced the floor and wrung her hands, had argued back and forth with herself, and each time she had returned to the typewriter to lose herself and her fear of losing Jeremy in her work. But now work was done for the night. The stream of words was stopped, the complex of thoughts and fingers, of words and ribboned ink and metal keys, was inaccessible to her. She was written out, and she would have to sleep another night and live another day before that escape would be possible again. Yet she knew that she could not sleep, that there was no use in lying down or trying to invite it in any of the usual ways for it would not come to her until she had heard Jeremy's voice and listened to him excuse his absence. If this did not happen, dawn would find her still alone with the ghost of her childhood . . .

The doorbell jangle broke in upon her self-torment. She stood stock still and listened to its dying vibrations. Was it Jeremy? She made no move to answer. It rang again, this time a prolonged signal that forced her to press the buzzer button in response. Then, her weight thrown against the door as if to ward off the visitor, she listened for the footfalls on the stairs. When they came they were heavy . . . hesitant . . . not Jeremy's.

Suddenly, she was a child again, the same child that had listened and waited for her father. The room became the hall-bedroom of a St Louis boarding-house – she could feel the brush of pig-tails on her back and her hand felt spontaneously for the golden locket, that had clasped a strand of her mother's hair, which she had always used to wear about her neck. The empty yearning that belongs to children was hers again, and with it the fear of the un-known – the yet to be – which as an adult she had learned to forget. She fought against the foolish dread that accompanied this throwback to the past, chided herself for harbouring such a silly fear. Yet the hammering on her heart prevailed against all reassurances, insisting that her senses were right: that the lumbering footsteps she heard were her father's . . . even though she knew him long since dead!

The sound of a large man walking uncertainly con-tinued up to her door. There was a silence, and then a fumbling and scratching – as if whoever it was was trying to fit a key into the keyhole – and a belched curse.

Brent pushed as hard as she could against the door. Her body was shaking with fright and her mouth was open and moaning. She wanted to cry out, to scream and end this nightmare (for one distraught moment she managed to convince herself that it was not happening, that she was only dreaming and, if she fought a little more desperately, she would succeed in awakening) – but the same thing in her that had held back any cry of protest as a girl, forced her to bite her lip and quiet her whimpering now. The scratching continued and with it the sound of harsh, whistling breaths.

Then she heard a tinkle, followed by another curse. He's dropped his key just as he used to do! she thought. But then something even more terrible happened. There was

163

a heavy, slumping thud – a scrambling sound of cloth and leather on polished wood. And then a gurgling retching . . .

When Brent finally dared to open the door, she did not find her father there. Philip's limp body sprawled in upon her feet. He was not dead, only very drunk. And he had been sick in the hallway.

The Third Instalment

1

It had come to pass. Philip awakened with this conviction – he knew *where* he was, in the moment before he
opened his eyes, even if he did not know *how* he happened
to be there. He was in Brent's apartment and in Brent's
bed. Somehow, in some way, he had betrayed himself.
The 'Confession' had triumphed again.

When he opened his eyes, he saw the same small room
that he had visited once before, the same cheap maple
furniture. He was lying on the studio couch and across the
room on a chair lay his brown tweed suit, his brown snap-
brim felt hat and his brown brogues. But the suit he had
been wearing the night before was his grey urquhart plaid,
his hat had been grey and his shoes black! If this were
Brent's apartment – and he was sure it was – how did a
change of clothes happen to be ready for him? He sat up,
clutching the blanket about himself. A sound of dishes
being rattled in the next room prompted him to call
Brent's name.

'So you're up?' she answered matter-of-factly. 'The
bathroom is across the hall. I put a towel out for
you.'

Philip pulled on his trousers. 'How did I get here?' he
asked.

'That was one of the things I was going to ask you.'

Philip tried to remember the events of the previous
night. What had happened during the afternoon, especially
his nightmarish experience in the theatre, came back to
him with great clarity and a sense of immediacy – as if it
had just occurred. He could also remember leaving the
theatre and going into a bar to have a few drinks. He had

met a soldier who had talked very queerly . . . but what had happened after that?

'I don't remember,' he admitted. 'Was I drunk?'

Brent came out of the kitchen alcove. She was wearing a house dress and her dark hair was done up on top of her head like a little girl's. But her eyes were not those of a child's; they flashed with suppressed rage. 'You were drunk,' she said flatly. 'You rang my doorbell and you managed to get up the stairs. I found you in the hall. You were being very sick all over yourself.'

Philip blushed. He looked away from Brent and, as he did, he felt a wave of nausea rise inside him. He fought to keep it down, swallowing desperately. Then he rushed out of the door and across the hall to the bathroom. He thought he could hear Brent laughing.

Later, after he had finished dressing, he went into the small kitchen. Brent was having breakfast; she poured him some black coffee and offered him some toast. Philip drank a little of the coffee. 'I'm afraid you've been terribly inconvenienced,' he said.

'That is an understatement,' she said coldly.

'I don't know what made me do it.'

'The only reason I did not call the police when I found you in the hall is because I did not want the neighbours to know what had happened. I took you in, put you on the couch and took your keys from your pocket. You had ruined your clothes, so I went to your apartment – letting myself in with your key – and got you a change. When I came back here, you had managed to undress yourself and get into bed. I had to sleep on the floor.'

'What can I do by way of apology?'

'Nothing.'

Philip had never before experienced so thoroughgoing a rebuff. Brent's contempt was coldly magnificent. She regarded him steadily with concentrated animosity that was almost warlike.

'I want you to understand something, Philip,' she said.

'I never want to see you again. What I did last night, I did in my own interests. I should have called the police, but had I done that I would have awakened the house. Everyone would have known that a man had tried to force his way into my apartment, a besotted fool who could not even hold his liquor. So I took you in, and what I did you might mistake for kindness, Philip. It was not kindness. If I got you fresh clothes, it was only to keep some of my friends from seeing you leave my apartment the way you would have looked in those rags.' She pointed to a bundle that lay next to the refrigerator. Philip recognized the suit he had been wearing the day before. It was badly stained and still odorous.

Brent had not finished. 'When you are through with your coffee, I want you to leave. I want you to take that with you. I do not know where you got the idea that you could act this way with me. I do not care to listen to any excuse you might make or any apology you might offer. I only want you to get out of my house. And, please, stay away from me hereafter!'

Philip stood up. His action was automatic, a will-less response. He felt inert and nerveless, as if he were a thing, not a person. Brent's anger had turned to quiet tears. Her face was pale with emotion and her lips trembled.

Philip picked up the bundle of clothes and left the apartment. When he reached the street, he threw it in the nearest trash can. He began to walk uptown. After he had gone a few blocks, he realized that, although Brent had said that she had visited his apartment in the middle of the night, she had not mentioned seeing Dorothy. Did that mean that Dorothy had not been at home? Philip searched his pockets for a nickel to make a telephone call. In the last pocket he found a nickel and a dime. He would make a telephone call with the nickel and use the dime to pay his bus fare uptown.

He went into the first drugstore he encountered to telephone Dorothy. There was no response. He hung up and dialled the same number again, thinking that in his haste he might have made a mistake. But there was still no answer. He looked at his watch. It was not yet nine o'clock. Knowing Dorothy's liking for sleeping late, he found it probable that she had been out all night and had not yet returned.

He left the drugstore and walked along twisting Village streets to Fifth Avenue. He hailed an open-deck bus and climbed the stairs to the top deck. It was a beautiful morning. The sky was wholly clear of clouds and of the deepest blue. The sun was strong for December, and it was even unseasonably warm. Yet Philip noticed none of these things. His mind was on the many-faceted problem he faced and which he seemed impotent to solve. If Dorothy had not spent the night at home, where had she been? Had she already left him? Wouldn't he be given a chance to explain his actions?

But one question, of far greater significance than any of the others, was present continually, was, in fact, so well known to him that he scarcely needed to formulate it. When he reached the office, would he find another instalment of the 'Confession'? And if he did, what would it predict this time?

Philip descended from the bus at Fiftieth Street and went to his bank in Radio City to a cash a cheque. Then he had another cup of coffee at a Whelan's. He smoked several cigarettes and contemplated not going to the office, so intense was his desire to avoid finding a third section of the 'Confession' on his desk. But, in the end, some part of his will remained to make him face up to what he had come to consider his fate. He left the drugstore and, walking slowly and with great hesitance, headed for Madison Avenue.

The desperate confusion that had marked all of his actions of the day before had passed away; in its place was a superficial calm. The despair he felt no longer showed itself in his actions, except, perhaps, in the subdued unsteadiness of his gait. To the casual eye, if it had paused to inspect him, he might have seemed to have been suffering from a bad hangover – which, of course, he was. A more critical appraisal, such as George Matthews might have made had he met him at this time, would have considered his state an exaggeratedly neurotic and depressed condition. Philip, when he entered the lobby of his building, was walking with the measured, yet sometimes faltering, strides of a condemned man marching to the place of his execution.

Sadie, the elevator operator, did not say good morning to him, although they were alone in the car. She kept her eyes fixed on the ruby lights of the indicator so that all Philip saw of her was her back. He took this as an omen, deriding himself for being superstitious even as the thought occurred to him. Something was badly wrong about him – this he was sure of by now – if a girl who had always been flirtatious and friendly in the past should now make a point of snubbing him. As the elevator doors opened at his floor, he tried to catch her eye. If she would only smile at me, he thought, it would be encouraging! But, whether her indifference was due to a change in himself or not, he did not succeed. Sadie paid no attention to his wink.

It was the same with the receptionist. Her smile, and her way of saying good morning, had always affected Philip adversely; but this time her mien was so bleak as to be frightening. He felt that she must have discovered some part of what was going on and had grown thoroughly contemptuous of him because of it. As he walked down the corridor to his own office and Miss Grey, it seemed to him that all the girls in the office were watching him, pointing at him behind his back and saying things to each other about him. With his hand on the knob of his door, he stopped and tried to make himself turn around to face their derision; but he did not have the courage. He opened the door and went through it hurriedly.

'Good morning, Miss Grey,' he said as soon as he was

inside the door and before he had looked at her. She was seated at her desk, her pocketbook lying open on her typewriter, busily filing her nails. She barely nodded to him.

'Good morning, Miss Grey,' he snapped again. He was not going to allow such impertinence.

She glanced up at him. 'Good morning,' she said, and she smiled briefly. But she went on filing her nails.

Philip hesitated. His anger had flared momentarily, but now he was unsure of himself. Miss Grey was the one person in the office who was closest to him – the person who might logically know most about the 'Confession'. She could have seen it on his desk on the other two mornings. She undoubtedly knew what was on his desk now. Was it because she had read the latest chapter of the 'Confession', that she acted so casually indifferent to him as he stood before her? Was she secretly smiling and waiting to see what he would do when he went into his office and read it himself? Philip turned his back on her and opened the other door. His heart was pounding violently . . .

At first he thought there was nothing on his desk. His typewriter was not open on it. There was no neat pile of manuscript. He sighed and hung up his hat. Then he walked around and sat down. He checked all the articles that belonged on his desk top: the blotter, the fountain-pen set, the calendar, the file boxes, the clock, the buzzer buttons. He saw that he had been wrong, that there was one new thing lying on his desk – a blank piece of paper.

He picked it up in his hands and stared at it. Good bond paper, he noted, watermarked. He turned it over, held it up to the light. No, there was no marking on it whatsoever. He might have left it here himself the day before. Or it might have been here a long time and he had not noticed it. He laid it down again. A blank piece of paper signified nothing. The main thing to remember was that there was no manuscript on his desk. Which meant, of course – he was absolutely sure of it! that what had been happening to him had come to an end. He leaned far back in his swivel chair and laughed loudly, so great was his relief.

'Mr Banter?'

Philip had swerved around in his chair so that he faced the window. Now Miss Grey's voice cut his laugh short. He turned around and saw that she was standing in the doorway that connected their offices. She had her hat and coat on.

'What is it?'

'I wanted to tell you, Mr Banter, that I'm leaving. I've got another job. I've already told Miss Rossiter.' (Miss Rossiter was the assistant cashier who also acted as supervisor over the secretaries and stenographers in the office.)

Philip gaped. The girl was smiling at him, openly showing her pleasure at being able to speak these words. All Philip could say was, 'B-but I-I thought you were ha-happy here?' And he cursed himself silently for stammering.

Miss Grey looked down. She fiddled with her gloves for a moment before she answered. When she did, she looked up, her eyes wide, her mouth trembling. 'I didn't want to tell you my real reason, Mr Banter. I thought I might hurt your feelings, and I know how sensitive you are – I didn't want to make you feel bad.'

She paused, Philip waited quietly. She is going to tell me that she has read the 'Confession', he thought.

'You've been so queer lately, Mr Banter. You look at me in such a funny way, when you look at me at all. It's as if you weren't seeing me, as if you were looking through me at something behind me. Then you get angry at the least thing – like the other day when you implied that I had been using your typewriter. You make me feel uncomfortable all the time.'

Philip did not know what to say. She was embarrassed, too, and stood twisting a glove that was half-off one of her hands. Then Philip remembered that he had promised himself to ask her some questions the next time he saw her.

'I'm sorry you feel that way, Miss Grey,' he began. 'But if you're not happy here, you had better leave. Before you go – since you have referred to the episode of the typewriter – I would like to ask you a few questions.'

Miss Grey stripped her gloves from her hands. 'I'll answer what I can,' she said.

'Both yesterday and the day before, when I came into my office I found my typewriter open on my desk. But that's not all.' He stooped and fitted the key to the bottom drawer of his desk into the lock, opened the drawer and withdrew the two sections of the 'Confession'. 'I also found these manuscripts on my desk, Miss Grey. Have you any idea who put them there?'

The girl did not step forward to inspect the thick sheaf of manuscripts Philip held. Instead, she put her hand to her mouth and began to whimper. 'I don't know anything about it. You keep accusing me of things I didn't do. I don't know.'

Philip shook his head. 'I'm not accusing you of anything. I'm simply asking you for information. Do you know how these manuscripts could have gotten on my desk? Could they have been put there at night – or early in the morning before anyone's at work? Is the main door to the office kept closed and locked, and, if so, who has a key?'

Miss Grey leaned against the jamb of the door. Philip could see she was frightened. Good God, did he have this effect on everybody? What was the matter with him?

'I don't know who put those papers on your desk, Mr Banter,' the girl said weakly. 'I'm sure I didn't. And I don't think anyone in the office did. Are you sure you didn't put them there yourself, and then forget about it?'

'I am certain I did nothing of the sort,' Philip said.

'Well, the door to the office is left open for the cleaning women. They're supposed to lock it, and they usually do. Although some of the girls who get here earliest say that on some mornings the door is unlocked. We all have keys, of course.'

'What would I do if I wanted to get into the building late at night, and I had forgotten my key?'

'You could ask the watchman for one. You'd have to sign the register, but he'd lend you one.'

'So anyone could procure a key to our offices and walk right in and steal anything, I suppose?' Philip asked sarcastically.

Miss Grey shook her head. 'The watchman wouldn't give just anyone a key. He would have to know you.'

'I suppose the watchman knows all the tenants of this building?' Again Philip's voice was heavy with sarcasm. Miss Grey began to cry. 'Oh, I don't know, Mr Banter – I just don't know. I don't see why you keep after me like this. I didn't put those old papers on your desk!'

Philip realized that he was not succeeding. He sat down and regarded the pile of manuscript bitterly. Miss Grey started to speak, then thought better of it. Still sniffling, she left the room.

Philip continued to stare at the sheaf of papers. Until now he had been looking at it, not reading it. But, without being fully aware of what he was doing, he began to read it. He started reading about the middle of the first page.

Dermo not only cleanses clothes faster – people tell us a day's laundry takes only half a day when they use Dermo – but it actually makes clothes brighter, cleaner, than old-fashioned bar soaps. Dermo – spelled D-E-R-M-O – is the modern way of washing clothes, the economical way. Ask your grocer for the big, family-size today. Don't forget, get Dermo – spelled D-E-R-M-O – today!

Philip looked at the next page. What he read was also part of a radio script for one of his clients – a script for which he had written the commercials weeks ago. Quickly he thumbed through the entire pile of paper. They were all the same! He threw them on the floor in disgust.

He jerked the bottom drawer of his desk out and shuffled through its contents. He did not find the 'Confession'.

He pulled out all the other drawers of his desk and searched them all. Still he did not find it. He went to the file cabinet and spent a good fifteen minutes disrupting its orderly rows of folders – without success. Finally, he had to admit the fact that the 'Confession' was gone.

Had it ever existed? Philip sat and stared at the blank piece of paper that he had found on the top of his desk that morning. There was no doubting the reality of this – he was touching it, he could feel it – although he could doubt its significance. Well, there was one good use for it. He took a pen from the stand and began to scribble on it. He put down all of the events of the past two days from the moment he walked into his office and found (or thought he found) the 'Confession' on his desk until a short time before when he had discovered its theft and the substitution of several old scripts in its place. Or had he discovered only that he had been deluding himself?

By the time he had finished writing, he had covered both sides of the sheet of paper with fine writing. He had it all down on paper, concisely – and yet the puzzle remained. Who was writing the 'Confession'? Who had placed that sheet of blank paper on his desk?

He opened his drawer and withdrew another sheet of paper. He held it up to the light and matched its watermark with that of one he had found. The marks were the same. He took his pen again and wrote down these names:

Steven Foster
Miss Grey
Dorothy Banter
Jeremy Foulkes

He studied them for many minutes, then read both sides of the other sheet of paper again. Then he underlined the last name on the list like this:

Jeremy Foulkes

2

Dorothy and Jeremy had attempted to recapture their
past, and had failed. The irresponsible holiday, that
had begun the day before at lunch in the Three Griffins
and had continued with a drive up the Hudson, dinner at a
roadside inn and a night together in one of the inn's
upstairs rooms, was ending gloomily with each feeling
dislike for the other. Yesterday, their high spirits had
scarcely outlasted the effects of the martinis they had
drunk at lunch. The stiff river breeze – the only car
Jeremy had been able to rent was a shabby, well-ventilated
convertible coupé – had been sobering. They had first
quarrelled about where to stop, Jeremy being all for
pushing on to the next place, and the next, while Dorothy
felt headachy and hungry and favoured each roadhouse
they encountered. When they did drive up to an inn, it
was late and the dinner they were served was bad. They
ate cold ham, canned peas and soggy boiled potatoes and
drank lukewarm coffee. After dinner they managed to
patch up their injured feelings briefly, taking a walk along
the wooded cliffs that overlooked the river until the gale
forced them back inside. They went up to their room as a
last resort and played at being lovers like actors reading
their parts for the first time, each aware of the other's
fumblings as well as his own inadequacy.

The inconvenience of the room contributed to their
disillusionment. The brass bed was lumpy, the bath was at
the wrong end of the dark corridor, the light bulbs were
bald and over-brilliant, the linen had been used before.
Jeremy, in pyjamas, could not hide the soft roll of fat that
had enveloped his stomach; their intimacy was curt and

conventional. Afterwards, neither had been able to sleep for the unfamiliar creakings of the old house and the sighing wind in the pines. But they had both feigned sleep to avoid the pitfalls of nocturnal conversation, and had lain stiff and tense listening to the other's breathing and uncomfortably aware of the absurdity of their situation.

The truth was that Jeremy had found himself thinking more and more of Brent as the day had darkened into night, and increasingly conscious of his disloyalty to her. There had been no reason for it. He had drunk too much at lunch and felt an appetite for a woman he had once loved; but she was no longer the person he remembered fondly; she was, in fact, a stranger. He had told Brent that he would return to her that night, yet when he had visited his loft apartment to pack a bag, he had not left her a note or telephoned her. He could only guess what she would make of his behaviour. By the time he was having dinner with Dorothy, he wanted more than anything else to drive back to town, to return to Brent. But there was Dorothy to consider. He had accepted her advances and had responded to them, had acted as a lover. Now they were alone together and the scene demanded to be played out. To have declared his feelings, would have been to scorn her. So Jeremy continued to pretend ardour, although he lacked desire.

Dorothy's attitude was more complex. She had reached out for Jeremy because she felt she had lost Philip. Jeremy was to be a test, a way of proving to herself that Philip had lost interest in his marriage for some cause other than her own inadequacy. Jeremy had wanted to marry her once, and she had chosen Philip instead; now she tried to use Jeremy to substitute for Philip, in the absence of his love, as she might have worn a charm about her wrist to substitute for him, in his physical absence. Either way Jeremy's value to her derived from Philip: she felt that if she could win Jeremy's affection away from Brent, then Philip's dereliction would not be due to any fault or lack of her own; and she felt that, having lost Philip, if she could gain Jeremy, she would be choosing again as she had chosen before.

This expedition along the Hudson had been to Dorothy an unusual experience which she understood, if at all, only on the level of her emotions. She partly knew that when she looked at Jeremy she was seeing Philip, and also her father before Philip. Unconsciously, and this she did not realize, she was re-staging the rejection scene that had shaped her personality and made her life. If Jeremy, as they drove farther and farther along the Hudson at first disagreeing and then openly quarrelling as to where to stop, thought more about Brent and less about Dorothy, it was not accidental. Dorothy was that unfortunate type that must always cast experience in the same rigid mould: she forced Jeremy to think of Brent, even when she tried to attract him. There was that in her that made her circumvent her ends.

So when the night ended and there was an excuse for breakfast, Jeremy's infatuation with Dorothy, that had lasted a number of years, was finished. They spoke to one another in monosyllables at breakfast, and on the trip back into town did not break the silence for miles at a time. They had not spoken for many minutes when Jeremy turned off Riverside Drive and headed for the midtown area, and he was the one to speak then.

'Do you mind if I stop off at your place for a moment?' he asked. 'I want to make a 'phone call before I go home.'

'Why shouldn't you?' Dorothy asked, shielding her eyes against the morning sun that suddenly confronted them as they drove East.

'I thought Philip might be there.'

Dorothy considered this. She dropped her hand and stared at the sun until the glare caused her eyes to glisten. 'Philip won't be there,' she said.

She spoke quietly, with resignation and sadness. Her manner disturbed Jeremy and made him turn to look at her. He saw that the lines of her beautiful face were set

179

and her eyes stared forward blindly. He sensed that
something was about to happen . . . that Dorothy was
allowing herself to be drawn to crisis as iron is drawn to a
lodestone.

After Philip left, Brent finished her breakfast unhur-
riedly and then passed the next hour tidying the apartment. She went to the phone and began to dial Jeremy's
number several times during this hour, but each time she
broke off before the connection could be completed.
When there was no more to do about the house, she curled
up on the couch and tried to read. After a few minutes of
this, however, she tossed the book aside and returned to
the telephone. This time she waited until the sound of
persistent ringing had lasted for several minutes, long
enough to prove without doubt that there was either no
one at home or whoever was there was not answering.
Slamming the receiver down in exasperation, she took a
hat and coat from the closet and left the apartment. When
she reached the street, she walked to the corner, hailed a
taxi and gave the driver Jeremy's address.

She did not expect to find him home, yet after she had
paid the driver off and was climbing the steep stairs to the
loft she could not escape the fear that she might. If he were
in, Dorothy would be with him; if he weren't in, he might
possibly have spent the night with other friends – or so
Brent reasoned. She knew that this line of thought was
little better than an incantation with which she attempted
to ward off the catastrophe she was certain had befallen
her. Nevertheless, she was relieved when she found the
wide door of the loft ajar, and walked into the barn-like
room to see that, in actuality, Jeremy was not there.

She took off her hat and coat and, womanlike, began to
do the same things in this place that she had been doing
in her own. She swept the floors, dusted the furniture,
mopped the kitchen floor, rearranged the dishes in the
cupboard. Even so, she soon had exhausted the house-
wifely tasks the loft had to offer since most of its cavernous

depth had never been properly domesticated – Jeremy lived in the corners of the great room – and there was no point in trying to straighten and clean the piles of ruck he had let accumulate in the disused portions. At last, she was reduced again to the couch and a book, albeit a different couch and –

While stretching for a novel that rested on top of the end table, Brent noticed a pile of paper that lay beside it. How did I overlook that when I was dusting? she wondered. She picked it up, instead of the novel, and began to read it. Her interest quickened when she saw that on the first page of what appeared to be a typewritten manuscript was the name and address of Philip Banter and the one word, 'Confession'. She continued to read; by the time she had finished the first few pages her interest was consuming.

A half-hour later, a moment after she had read the last page, the doorbell rang. Laying the manuscript down on the couch, she walked to the door and pressed the buzzer button – most of her thoughts were occupied with what she had just been reading. If she thought at all about who was ringing the bell, she decided that it was Jeremy and he had lost his key again.

It was quite a shock to her when she opened the door and Philip walked into the room.

3

Miss Grey had come back into Philip's office shortly after he had decided who was the most likely author of the 'Confession'. She was still wearing her hat and coat and her eyes were red-rimmed. Philip had thought she had left, and he showed his surprise at seeing her.

'I have something to tell you,' she said. She put out her hand to steady herself – she was swaying noticeably – and it came to rest on the edge of Philip's desk. He got her a chair.

'I lied to you this morning,' she continued. She spoke hesitantly and in broken phrases. Her hands constantly fretted with her gloves. 'I do know something about the manuscript you found yesterday morning . . . and the morning before that . . . I put it there.'

'What!' Philip exploded.

'When I came into the office day before yesterday . . . there was a messenger waiting for me. He had a package . . . and a note. The note was addressed to me. It was typewritten . . . but it wasn't signed. With it was a hundred dollar bill.' The girl paused. Her face was grey and contorted. She forced the next words out. 'The note asked me to put the manuscript . . . that was in the package . . . on your desk. It said you would be expecting it . . . but that the contents were confidential . . . that I must never speak to anyone about it . . . not even you. Even if you asked me directly . . . I was to say nothing.'

Now that it was coming out, Philip was surprised at his own calm. He stared at the girl, who had caused him so much annoyance in the past, as he might have regarded a convicted murderer. 'And you believed that?' he asked.

The girl nodded her head. She sobbed histrionically. 'I know I should have told you. I know it was wrong. But I'd never had a hundred dollars before in my life . . . and you had been bawling me out all the time. I had come to hate you!' She said these last words not defensively, in justification of her offence, but defiantly, accusingly. Philip felt himself shrink inside.

'So when you asked me who had been using your type-writer . . . I told you the truth . . . that you had used it yourself the night before . . . and hadn't put it away. I knew what you were hinting at . . . but I couldn't let you know I knew . . . I didn't want to . . . and I had been told not to . . .'

'What about yesterday morning?' Philip asked. 'What happened then?'

'When I came in the messenger was waiting for me again . . . this time I asked who sent him . . . he had a uniform on and I thought he might tell me . . . but he had been instructed not to tell. He left another package . . . and another envelope with a note . . . and a hundred dollars. The note read, "Do as you did before." I did. But when I saw you asleep slumped over on your desk, I was scared. At first I thought . . . you were dead . . . but then when I came closer . . . I saw you were all right. I put the manuscript down beside you . . . and then I awakened you.'

'Do you know the name of the company for which the messenger worked? You said he wore a uniform.'

'I noticed that particularly. It was the Zephyr Fast Delivery Service.'

Philip picked up the telephone and asked the switch-board operator to get him the messenger service Miss Grey had named. After a few minutes' wait the connection was completed and Philip explained to the voice on the other end of the wire that he had received two packages on each of the last two days and wanted very much to know who had sent them. The voice listened as he gave his name and address, and then asked him politely to wait a few minutes longer. Philip cradled the receiver between his head and his shoulder and returned his attention to Miss Grey.

'How did my typewriter come to be open on my desk yesterday morning, too?' he asked. 'I know I did not leave it open a second time.'

'I put it there,' the girl said. 'While I was deciding whether or not to wake you up.' She looked away from Philip's steady gaze.

'Did the note tell you to do that?'

Miss Grey shook her head.

'Then why did you do it?'

'I was angry at you . . . you had scolded me for not putting it away. I had made up my mind to quit . . . and I felt like being nasty. I know I shouldn't have done it . . . but I don't care. I can get another job.'

Philip nodded his head and listened for a moment to the crackling sounds that came out of the telephone. 'Then what happened this morning? Did you find a messenger waiting for you when you came to work?'

The girl shook her head again.

Philip leaned forward. 'I put the manuscripts contained in those packages in the bottom drawer of my desk, Miss Grey. And I locked that drawer. When I opened it this morning, they were gone. Do you know anything about that?'

Miss Grey reached into her purse for her handkerchief and began to dab at her eyes. At the same time she nodded her head violently. 'When I came in this morning, your chair was pushed way over to the window. The drawers of your desk were pulled out. The papers in the bottom drawer were in a mess. I was afraid . . . I thought you'd accuse me of being careless. I rearranged the papers in the bottom drawer to make them look as if nothing had been disturbed. When I did this I saw that the lock had been forced. It still works . . . but it will unlock if you pull hard on the drawer. There are scratches on the varnish . . . as if somebody had used a knife on it.'

Philip glanced down at the bottom drawer. There were scratches around the lock all right. Why hadn't he noticed them before? He was reaching for his key to try it in the lock, when the phone that he had been cradling next to his ear came to life. 'Mr Banter?' the voice said. 'So sorry to keep you waiting, Mr Banter. I have the information you requested on those two deliveries. You sent us a letter earlier this week enclosing two one hundred dollar bills and accompanying a package containing a manuscript. Your letter instructed us to deliver the manuscript and the note with one of the bills to your secretary, a Miss Grey, at your office on the morning of the first of December. Your letter also stated that another manuscript, together with another note, would be sent to us the next day. You asked us to follow the same procedure then, enclosing the second bill with the note and delivering the manuscript to Miss Grey. Both deliveries were completed as requested and I have a record of Miss Grey's signature on the receipts. Is there anything wrong, Mr Banter?'

'No,' said Philip, 'everything is quite satisfactory. I just wanted a check-up. Thank you.' He hung up. He looked at Miss Grey and wondered if she could possibly have heard. If she had, she was not letting him know. She had her purse open and was fumbling in it. As he watched, she withdrew two crumpled one hundred dollar bills. She laid them on his desk.

'I know I shouldn't have taken them, Mr Banter.' She gulped and looked away. Her voice had fallen to a whisper. 'But I had never seen that much money before . . .'

Philip stared at her pimply face, her straggly, mouse-coloured hair that was always either all over her face or tightly curled in disgusting little spiral knots. 'You can keep it,' he said. 'And you can forget about everything that has happened this week. It was all a mistake.'

Miss Grey stood up. She picked the bills from the desk hesitantly, and looked at Philip and tried to smile. Slowly, she put the bills into her purse and snapped it shut. She waited a moment longer – plainly expecting Philip to change his mind – then began to inch towards the door.

Philip turned his back on her and went to the window. He stood looking out at the buildings across the street, his mind blank and purposeless. When he heard the door shut behind him and knew that the girl had left the room, he went back and sat in his chair. For a long time he did nothing at all.

And then, he decided to visit Jeremy.

4

Dr Matthews arrived promptly at ten o'clock at the offices of Brown and Foster, and he was shown in at once to Steven Foster's office. 'Mr Foster will be with you in a few minutes, doctor,' the receptionist said, and went out closing the door softly behind her. Matthews was annoyed at this. He had cancelled several appointments to make this call because he had felt it important to talk to a member of Philip's family about his illness. But he had not expected to be kept waiting.

Steven Foster's office was large and luxuriously appointed. A broad mahogany desk commanded the room, but there were also several comfortable leather chairs, an imitation fireplace, books and paintings along the walls. Most of the books dealt with advertising and business, but one brightly-jacketed volume caught his eye: William Seabrook's *Witchcraft*. Matthews pulled it off the shelf, riffled its pages and then put it back – shrugging his shoulders. He had just finished lighting his pipe when Steven Foster belatedly entered the room.

He came forward and shook hands cordially with Matthews, but his eyes reflected no warmth and the lines of his face were as tense as before. 'I had not expected to see you so soon,' he said. 'Is it about Philip?' He waited until Matthews had sat down in one of the leather arm-chairs before he took his place behind his desk.

'Philip had lunch with me yesterday,' Matthews said. 'He is concerned about himself. He has some unusual symptoms.' And he went on to tell Foster everything Philip had told him about the 'Confession', the voice he heard and his other delusions.

Foster listened expressionlessly. He sat rigidly in his chair, his gaze fixed coldly on the doctor. When Matthews had finished, he said, 'What is your diagnosis?'

Matthews waved his hand. 'Philip is an alcoholic. Like any alcoholic his chronic drinking is a symptom of his disorder and not the disorder itself. However, it should be treated first. If Philip could visit a sanatorium I know in the Catskills, where he would be able to rest and get the best of care, we might be able to prevent a subsequent breakdown.'

Foster's eyes glinted and the corners of his mouth curled tightly. 'Then in your opinion he has not had a breakdown yet?'

'The line of demarcation between neuroses and psychoses is so slight as to be often imperceptible. In very few cases is there a definite point at which you can say, "This patient is now insane." Insanity encroaches. It bores from within gradually, seizing possession of the intellect. I could make tests, subject Philip to a complete mental and physical examination – this I would do anyway – but I doubt if my diagnosis would change until the alcoholism is cleared up. Then we may be able to say definitely whether Philip has had a break.'

Foster raised his eyebrows. 'I had not been prepared for so encouraging a statement from you, doctor. Frankly, I've been worried about Philip. I have watched my daughter lose her spirits and grow pale in the past few months. I have heard what she has had to say about the way her husband has treated her – we are very close, you know – and I had come to the conclusion that the man was both a rotter and crazy. He would have to be crazy to do some of the things he has done.

'Now you tell me about a "Confession". This is something I know nothing about, and I think I can say Dorothy also has not heard of it. Philip must be writing it himself, or else it is an elaborate excuse to explain away his other actions. I want to see him and talk to him about this!' And he reached for the telephone.

Matthews held up his hand. 'Before you call Philip in, I want you to know that the purpose of my visit today is to get help in persuading Philip to go to a sanatorium. You know, of course, that we must have Philip's consent or that of some member of his family. Dorothy could commit him, if that becomes necessary. But it is much better for him if he goes of his own free will. I spoke to him about it yesterday afternoon, and he suddenly invented an appointment that he must keep to get away from me. I thought if we both talked to him, he might see things differently.'

Foster nodded his head and reached for the telephone. He called Miss Grey and asked her to have Philip come into his office. When he replaced the instrument, he sighed and said, 'You know, just this morning I had one of the girls come in to tell me that she was leaving us. She has been with us several years and most of that time she has worked as my son-in-law's secretary. Recently, when his condition became obvious to me, I called Miss Grey aside and asked her to report to me anything that Philip did that seemed to her peculiar. She has done this faithfully and I have relied upon her. Yet she told me today that she is quitting, that she can't stand to work for Philip any longer. She says he is too strange, that he frightens her. I tried to persuade her not to leave us and told her that she did not have to work for Philip. As a matter of fact, I gave Philip notice yesterday afternoon, but I didn't want to tell her that. She said that she would think it over.' He spread his hands dramatically to indicate his confusion. 'So you see how Philip has affected Brown and Foster,' he said.

Matthews started to speak, but he heard the door open and turned around to see Philip enter the room. Philip's eyes were bloodshot and heavy lidded, his skin was pale and he held himself badly. When Matthews had seen him yesterday, he had been unshaven and his clothes had been slightly crumpled. Today his clothes were neat enough, but he looked ill.

'You wanted to see me?' Philip asked. He stood just inside the door which was still ajar, his hand on the knob.

'Come in, Philip,' Foster snapped. 'Dr Matthews is here to see you.'

Philip glanced at his friend. 'I told you that I'd call you and make an appointment,' he said sullenly.

'Sit down, Philip,' Foster commanded. 'What's this Dr Matthews tells me about a "Confession"?'

Philip had not expected this. Matthews could see him grow tense. He looked at him and said, 'I didn't think you'd tell everybody about that, George.' He spoke quietly but each word expressed his anger and disappointment.

'I have only told your father-in-law. I wanted to talk to Dorothy, but my nurse could not reach her yesterday afternoon. I thought that someone close to you should know how ill you are, Philip.' Matthews spoke quietly and kindly.

Philip looked at him coldly. 'You want to put me in a sanatorium, don't you? You think that I am losing my mind. And if I refuse to commit myself, you intend to persuade Steven or Dorothy to commit me.'

Old Foster pounded his fist on his desk. 'Dr Matthews has just been telling me why he did not think you were insane,' he snorted. 'If he wants you to go to a sanatorium, it's because he thinks it will cure your drinking. Not that I think that's all that is wrong with you!'

Philip smiled at his father-in-law's outburst. 'Suppose I told you that I now have evidence that I am not writing that "Confession", George?' He turned and looked at Matthews. 'And suppose I said that if you would give me the rest of the day to prove to you that someone else has been writing it, someone else who wants to drive me out of my senses – what would you say to that?'

Matthews regarded his pipe which had gone out. He did not look at Philip. 'I would still say that you need a good long rest. And a doctor's care.'

Foster sat rigidly, his eyes unswervingly on Philip, who went on speaking, hurriedly, anxiously.

'Well, this morning I came down to the office expecting to find another instalment of this "Confession". Although the last section had been wrong about many things, it had predicted that I would do a terrible thing last night – and I did. I was unnerved this morning. But when I got to my desk I found only a blank piece of paper waiting for me. I could have left it there myself for all I know, although I doubt it. I had told Miss Grey to clean up my desk every night before she left, and she said that she had not noticed this piece of paper.

'Then I looked in the drawer of my desk for the two previous instalments of the "Confession". They were gone. My desk drawer had been forced and its contents stolen. Now, I ask you, if I had been writing the "Confession", and then forgetting I had written it, why should I steal it from myself?' He looked at both Foster and Matthews and waited for them to answer.

Neither man spoke. Philip continued, 'Doesn't it seem likely that whoever was writing that manuscript, for whatever reason, wanted it back? Wasn't he afraid that I might do what I should have done in the first place, go to the police with it? So he came to the office last night or early this morning. He broke into my drawer and stole the manuscript. And by now he has destroyed it.

'But it won't do him any good. I know who he is, and why he has been doing this to me. He is a man who has hated me ever since I married Dorothy. He has resented my success, coveted my wife. He did not have the courage to attack me to my face. But, since he is a thwarted novelist, he conceived of the "Confession" as a subtle way of getting rid of me. He used Brent and me as pawns in a game – his only goal was to get Dorothy to divorce me. He did not care if I landed in an asylum or not. All he wanted was my wife.'

Philip stood up. He swayed on his feet, his eyes blazing. 'I am going to see Jeremy Foulkes, gentlemen,' he said.

'I am going to wring the truth out of him – and neither of you can stop me!'

Both Matthews and Foster were on their feet and approaching Philip. He backed towards the door. And as he did, he picked up a heavy leather chair and brandished it at them. They kept coming on – he kept backing. When he reached the door, he threw the chair. They both fell flat to avoid its crashing bulk. When they stood up, he was gone.

Foster was white with rage. 'I'm going after him!' he cried. 'Why, he'll kill somebody!'

Matthews was cooler. 'First, we have to find out where Jeremy Foulkes lives. I knew him in college, but I've lost track of him since. And then I want to call a friend of mine in the Police Department and ask him to stand by.'

But Foster already had his hat and coat on. 'Forget the police. We can handle this ourselves. And don't worry about finding Jeremy's address. I know where he is.' And he plunged out the door.

Matthews followed him, reluctantly. He was afraid this would develop into a wild-goose chase.

5

Philip was as shocked to see Brent, as Brent was to see Philip. They stood for a moment, each on his side of the threshold, frozen with consternation. Brent was the first to move; her hand crept to her mouth to cover her trembling lips. Then, without willing it, she stepped back a pace . . . and another . . . and another. Philip followed her, waiting for her to cry out, to scream – knowing that he should turn about and go away – but following her anyway. He was compelled to enter the room.

Brent never screamed. Instead, she managed to recover her poise and even smile. 'I wasn't expecting you,' she said.

Philip felt like laughing, but some inner decency prevented it. 'I'm afraid that's an understatement. I didn't expect to find you here, you know. I wouldn't have come if I had.'

Brent sank down on the couch, Philip remained standing. He had not even taken off his hat. 'You came to see Jeremy?' she asked.

Philip nodded his head. 'I wanted to talk to him.'

There was an unusually long silence. He kept waiting for her to speak to him the way she had earlier in the day, to order him out of the loft. She was trying to remember all she had just read in the 'Confession', to piece it together and to make sense out of it. And she was afraid . . .

'You aren't feeling well, are you, Philip?' Brent smiled and her changing eyes were unexpectedly soft and kind. 'You're confused, aren't you?'

Philip did not know what to make of her questions – he had expected an entirely different reaction. He had not as yet seen the manuscript that was lying on the sofa. All he could say was a wondering, 'You aren't angry with me?'

Brent tossed her head. 'I was this morning, Philip. Can you blame me? But I'm not now.'

Philip smiled. He took off his hat and coat and put them over the chair hesitantly. Despite her reassurance, he still expected her to revert to her previous attitude. He certainly did not expect what came next.

'Sit down, Philip. Make yourself comfortable,' she was saying. 'I want to talk to you about this. As a matter of fact, I'm glad you came.' And Brent picked up the 'Confession' and placed it on her lap, thumbing a page. Instantly, Philip's eyes were riveted on the manuscript.

'Where did you get that?' he demanded.

Brent shrugged her shoulders. 'I had been trying to get in touch with Jerry,' she said. 'We had a date last night which he broke. When I 'phoned him here this morning after you left my place, I found he still wasn't home. I decided to come here and wait for him.' She smiled disarmingly. 'I wanted to give him a chance to present his excuses.

'When I got here, I found the door ajar. That's not too unusual. Although I keep telling him that he should be more careful, Jerry's the type that likes to leave everything unlocked. Well, I walked in and made myself at home. I took care of a few things, and then I sat down to read and wait for him, I was reaching for a book when I found this' – she tapped the manuscript with a finger – 'lying on the couch. I started to read it. I had just read the last page of it when you rang the bell.'

She paused and looked at Philip. Her eyes were kind, but inquiring. Philip thought about the contents of the 'Confession'. A deep flush burned its way up his throat to his face.

'I found it very interesting, Philip – extremely interesting.' She hesitated, looked down at the manuscript. 'I don't know quite what to make of it, Philip.'

He tried to speak and could not. He felt completely helpless, as if her words robbed him of everything but his consciousness and this they intensified, focused, so that all of him – his present, past and future – was concentrated in this moment that had stopped, stood still and confronted him.

'Philip, do you really believe all this happened? Is this your version of last night – and the night before?'

'No,' he said, 'that was the way it was to happen. The "Confession" said it would happen that way. But, luckily, it didn't.'

'I don't understand.'

Philip wet his lips. He was breathing more easily now, and his heart had stopped hammering erratically. 'That manuscript,' he began, 'the one you're holding in your lap, came in two parts. I found the first part on my desk Tuesday morning when I came to work. I read it, pondered over it and forgot about it. I thought perhaps that someone was playing a poor joke on me. But when I got home, it began to come true!

'I didn't know that you and Jeremy were coming to dinner at our house that night – I had not met you yet, of course, and I did not know your name. But as soon as I got home Dorothy told me that you were coming, just as the manuscript predicted. And, throughout dinner and afterwards, other little things happened just as they had in the prophecy!

'Some of the events predicted did not occur. But those that did occur were often uncanny. The conversation even turned to Henry Miller, for example. And I did make love to you – although I tried very hard not to!'

'Auto-suggestion,' said Brent, blushing.

'You mean I wrote it myself?' Philip asked. 'I had thought of that. And a psychiatrist I talked to about it said the same thing. But I can't bring myself to accept it.'

'You said the "Confession" was in two parts. What happened the next day?' asked Brent.

'I was coming to that,' said Philip. 'After I left you

that first night, I went down to the office. I intended to sit and wait for whoever was writing the manuscript, if anyone was. I wanted to catch him – or her – red-handed. But when I reached the office, something happened. The next thing I remember it was morning and my secretary was shaking me. I had fallen asleep apparently. My typewriter was open on my desk again, and there was another section of the "Confession" lying beside it. You know what it predicted. You read it.'

Brent nodded her head. Her expression was intense and troubled. Philip looked at her, realizing again how desirable she was to him. 'I tried my best that day – yesterday – to avoid doing what the manuscript predicted. I had lunch with an old friend of mine, a psychiatrist. I went to a movie, usually the safest of activities. I spent the evening drinking. And you know what happened.'

'What did you do this morning after you left me?'

'I went to the office again. This time there was only a blank piece of paper on my desk. I felt relieved . . .'

Brent's hand flew to her mouth. 'A blank piece of paper!' she sighed.

'Why, yes.'

'Oh. Oh, I suppose it's silly of me, but – '

'But what?'

'If this "Confession" were your fate . . . if it really were a record of what is about to happen to you . . . A blank piece of paper might signify . . .'

'My death?' Philip concluded drily.

Brent bit her tongue. 'Something like that,' she admitted.

Philip shuddered. This was one possibility he did not want to consider. He tried to be nonchalant. 'That's a little silly, isn't it?'

'I suppose so.' Brent was not convinced.

'Mere superstition.'

Brent nodded her head. Philip laughed. 'Well, if it is that, there's nothing I can do. I have an appointment with death – and I'll have to keep it.'

196

They looked at each other, and their looks said: 'We're sensible people living in an era of scientific knowledge. If we acknowledge fate, we call it environment or conditioning or determinism – or by some other rational tag. What we are thinking now is fatalistic nonsense. It can't be true!'

The telephone jangled.

Brent reached for it, picked it up, listened a moment and then covered the mouthpiece with her hand. 'It's Jeremy,' she told Philip. 'He says Dorothy is with him. Do you want me to tell them you're here?'

Philip considered this. If he could get Brent, Jeremy and Dorothy together in the same place, he felt sure he could talk the whole tangled affair out – and discover who had been writing the 'Confession' and why.

'Ask them both to come here,' he said. 'I want to get to the bottom of this.'

Brent spoke into the receiver again. After listening a little longer, she said. 'All right, I'll be seeing you,' and hung up. She smiled at Philip. 'They're coming,' she said.

'To get on with my story,' said Philip, 'soon after I reached the office this morning, Miss Grey came in to tell me that she was quitting. She said I had been acting "queer" lately. Then she left. I thought she had gotten her pay and gone for good. But she came back. She confessed that she had been paid to put the manuscripts on my desk!' And then Philip told Brent all about the messengers and the hundred dollar bills.

'Did you check with the messenger service?' Brent asked. 'I should think they would be able to tell you who ordered the messenger.'

'I did that. And I found out who ordered the messenger. A fellow by the name of Philip Banter.'

Brent was thunderstruck. She stood up and walked over to where Philip was sitting. 'But, don't you see, this proves that you must have written the "Confession"?'

Philip held up his hand. 'That's not all the story,' he said. 'When I looked into the drawer of my desk for the manuscripts this morning, I found the drawer had been forced and the manuscripts were missing. This theft must have occurred between the time I left the office yesterday morning and my arrival there today – nearly a twenty-four hour period.'

'Can you account for every minute of that period, every one of your movements?'

'Perhaps not all. But I think I can account for most of them. I had lunch from noon until one-thirty with Dr George Matthews. I was in a barber shop until two-thirty. I walked from the barber shop to the theatre district from two-thirty to three. From three until six I was seeing a movie through twice. After I left the theatre, I went directly across the street to a bar where I drank and talked to a soldier until far after midnight. When the bar closed I took a taxi to your building where I passed out in your presence.'

'And, after I got you inside,' Brent reminded him, 'I left you alone for an hour or more while I went to your apartment to get you a change of clothes – remember? When I came back, you were not where I left you – but asleep in my bed *which you must have made.*'

'You mean I could have gone to my office, stolen the manuscript from myself and taken it here to Jeremy's place, and then returned to your apartment while you were uptown? It's possible. But wasn't I out cold?'

'You were when I dragged you into the apartment. But drunks can do amazing things and not remember a bit of it afterwards. And you could have sobered up. I rather think you had lost most of your liquor.'

Philip nodded his head. It was possible. But – 'If I stole the manuscript myself, why did I have to force the lock on the drawer of my desk?'

Brent smiled. 'I've thought of that, too. Don't forget, I had your keys!'

Steven Foster and Dr Matthews had to wait several minutes before they managed to hail a taxi outside the office building. Then, while Matthews filled the inside of the cab with a thick cloud of rank smoke, the driver proceeded to get into one traffic jam after another. When he finally drew up at the address Foster had given him, it turned out to be a commercial building and obviously not the loft where Jeremy lived. Another five minutes were wasted in finding a drugstore, a telephone book and Jeremy Foulkes' correct address. By the time they reached their destination, a good forty-five minutes had elapsed and their cab parked at the kerb behind another car from which Dorothy and Jeremy had just alighted.

Matthews spoke to them and explained that Foster and he had followed Philip after he had broken away from them in Foster's office. He also told Jeremy that Philip suspected him of having written the 'Confession'. Dorothy wanted to know what Matthews was talking about and, to add to the confusion, Foster came up and solemnly warned both Jeremy and Dorothy that 'Philip is a dangerous madman'.

'But he's alone upstairs with Brent!' cried Jeremy. He brushed past Matthews and began to run up the wide steps two and three at a time. Matthews hesitated an instant, and then ran after him. He caught up with him just as he reached the top of the two long flights. 'Don't break in on him like that,' he said. 'Let us all go in together and give him a chance to explain.'

They did not have to open the door themselves. Philip had heard the commotion on the stairs and he opened the door and asked them in. Brent was standing beside him, obviously unharmed, and much of Jeremy's agitation disappeared. But Steven Foster, still panting from the exertion of climbing the stairs, roared at Philip. 'What have you done!'

Philip was calm now. 'Nothing, I assure you,' he replied and, glancing over his father-in-law's shoulder, said to Matthews, 'If you will ask them all to come into the apartment and let me talk to them for a few minutes, I think I can get to the bottom of all this.'

They all came in and seated themselves in corners of the great loft room. Philip talked for a few minutes and told them briefly about the 'Confession' and the events of the past two days. He handed the manuscript around so each could see it for himself, and while they looked at it he told them of Brent's theory. He said that he found that he could accept every part of it as a theory except the basic premise that he had been writing the 'Confession' himself. To accept this was to admit that he was mad. And, although yesterday he had almost convinced himself of his own insanity, by now he had sufficiently recovered from his nightmarish experience to fight the idea. 'For one thing,' he said, and he looked directly at Dr Matthews, 'too many people seem to want me to think that I am insane.'

Dorothy's reaction to what he had to say was to sit quietly, to withdraw, and – as the story Philip told grew more involved and terrible in its implications – to come over to where he was standing and to take his hand. Jeremy was amazed. 'Why, Philip, that's damnable! Who would play such a rotten trick on you!' he cried.

'One of us here,' Philip replied, looking at each person in turn, Brent, Foster, Jeremy, Dorothy, and, walking to the mirror, at himself. 'Brent may be right and I am just bedevilling myself. If that is so' – and his voice grew lower – 'you may have to follow Dr Matthews' wishes and have me placed in a sanatorium, Dorothy.'

His wife gripped his hand tightly. 'I'll never do that, Philip,' she said.

'However,' he continued, loosening her grip on his hand, 'I am not convinced that I am even neurotic, let alone insane. I think each one of you had a motive, as well as an opportunity, to write the "Confession", steal it and all the rest.'

He glanced at Steven Foster first. 'My father-in-law and I work at the same office – or I should say worked, he discharged me yesterday. As you know, he was my employer. I think I can say that he never approved of me as a son-in-law. I also have my doubts as to whether he would approve of any man as a son-in-law. From what I have observed of his reliationship with my wife he has always loved her deeply.' Philip paused and searched Foster's eyes. The old man did not flinch under the inspection. 'You had the opportunity, Steven,' Philip went on, 'and we need not fool ourselves that you wouldn't rather be rid of me. You certainly knew as much about me as anyone. I know that Dorothy has long made a practice of coming and talking to you about her troubles with me. Yes, I think you would even have known whom we were having to dinner and whether I had read Henry Miller. But, I think, if you had chosen to get rid of me, you would have taken a gun and shot me. You would never have considered as subtle a weapon as the "Confession".'

Philip turned away from Steven Foster, and Dorothy squeezed his hand. Matthews noticed this by-play. Several times so far he had wanted to interrupt but had not because he felt that Philip, of all people, deserved a chance to clear up the muddle. He saw now that Philip had turned his attention to Brent. And Jeremy had noticed that she was the next to be suspected.

Jeremy's florid face grew grim. 'Look here, Philip, you're going too far. If you keep this up, *I'll* say you're insane!'

Philip remained cool. 'Is that a threat, Jerry?'

'Take it any way you damn please. All I'm saying is that Brent has no motive – and that you owe her an apology.'

Philip bowed to Brent. 'I have already made my apologies to Miss Holliday. But I must say that she has a motive for this crime –'

'Crime?' cried Jeremy. 'What crime? Since when is writing a manuscript a crime?'

'Writing a manuscript is not a crime. But when you sign another person's name to it and present it to that person in such a way that it seems the handiwork of his own mind – with the intention of frightening him out of his wits – I call that a crime. Certainly, some of the statements made in the "Confession" are slander as well!'

Jeremy sniffed and walked over to Brent. Now they faced each other across the big room – Jeremy and Brent, Philip and Dorothy.

'Brent loves you, Jeremy. You have talked to her about me. She knows what our relationship is like and what it has been in the past. I rather imagine you have expressed many of the resentments you have felt against me to her. She is a sensitive, artistic person. She is equipped to write a long narrative. She might have conceived of this fiction with harmless intent as a means of shaming me into behaving better towards you.

'But, when she met me, she took a dislike to me. She sensed a conflict, not only between you and me, but also between Dorothy and myself, and impulsively decided that I should be taught a lesson. Knowing enough of psychology to employ it to a bad end, but not enough to realize that the end was bad – she might have written the second chapter of the "Confession" to frighten me even more. After all, she might have reasoned, I am committing no crime – you reasoned that way yourself just now, didn't you, Jerry? – doing no serious harm.'

'You said that the person who wrote this strange manuscript had to have the opportunity, too, didn't you?' Dorothy asked. 'When could Brent have stolen it from your desk? And how would she have known the essential facts about you?'

'She could have stolen it last night. She had my keys, and I know from experience that she could have gotten past the night watchman. Jeremy could, inadvertently, have supplied her with all the information she needed. There is surprisingly little background material in the "Confession" and the most startling aspects of it, the predictions, Brent could have forced to happen.'

Jeremy exploded. He rushed at Philip and shook his fist under his nose. 'I did no damn such thing and she did no damn such thing!' he cried. 'The whole idea is preposterous!'

Philip backed away from his old friend's wrath. It was

becoming more and more difficult for him to hold his temper, Matthews saw. But at the same time, by the very fact that Philip was remaining calm in crisis, he was proving his own contention that he was not unbalanced. 'I didn't say that Brent had done it,' he said. 'I brought up the possibilities so that I could consider them all and then eliminate her. I don't think she did it, although I can't be sure. I think her motivation is weak in comparison to other suspects, and I believe her story. Beyond that, outside of myself, she is the one person who has suffered unpleasant experiences because of this.' Philip stepped forward and gazed directly at Brent. 'Did you write the "Confession", Brent?' he asked.

Her answer came loud and clear, and with a smile. 'I did not.'

Philip motioned to Jeremy. 'You're the next suspect, Jerry. And until I talked to Brent, my most likely. Now I'm not so sure. You had motivation. You've hated me ever since I took Dorothy away from you, to put it bluntly. As to opportunity – well, where were you during the last twenty-four hours?'

Jeremy reddened. He started to stammer when he tried to speak. 'H-h-hate's a h-hard word, Ph-Phil. I was j-jealous of you, I admit. B-but I never hated you.'

Philip's voice was low. 'Where were you yesterday afternoon, last night and this morning, Jerry?'

'I won't say.'

Philip realized that Brent was no longer standing beside Jeremy, that she had slipped away and now was standing closer to himself. Jeremy had gotten up from his chair and was walking towards Philip, his jaw tense, his body in a crouch. Philip heard his wife sigh. He glanced at her and saw that she was excited.

'I wouldn't try anything if I were –' Jeremy was on him, his fist crashing into the pit of his stomach – before Philip could finish his sentence or Matthews could spring between them. Philip spun, crouched, weaved, lashed out with a left, blocked a wild right that Jerry threw with all his might. Then, as Jeremy charged past, Philip hit him on the back of his neck with the side of his hand. Jeremy sprawled on the floor.

Dorothy and Matthews rushed over to him. Philip could see that he was breathing hard, but was completely unconscious. Matthews was taking his pulse. 'I'm sorry I had to do that,' Philip said.

Dorothy stood looking down at Jeremy. Then, savagely, she turned and faced Philip. Her hand stroked at her dark hair, clawed at its abundance, came away leaving it in wild disarray. Her eyes glistened, her lips writhed in anger. 'I'd like to do some accusing now, Philip. I'm not afraid to look you in the face and say you're mad. I've lived with you, shared the experience of marriage with you, and I know your twisted ego!

'You're vain, Philip, vain and ageing. You're slipping, Philip. And you know it. You've built your life on the satisfaction of your senses, taken as much as you've wanted and paid as little as you could for it. But now the pace has begun to tell. Oh, I know – I can see it in your eyes. They look tired, you know. You see it, too. I've watched you look in mirrors. You did it only a little while ago. You've no need to worry, Philip, not for another year or so at least. Some of it's still left, darling. You have a bit more to spend!'

She paused and threw back her dark, disordered mane. 'But not with me, Philip. I shall divorce you. Poor Jeremy wouldn't tell you where he was yesterday, but I shall. He was with me, Philip. We spent the night together. We went down to your office, Philip, yesterday after lunch to tell you – but you weren't there. Then we went to Jeremy's place while he packed a bag. He was with me, Philip, all last night. Now do you understand? Isn't it plain why your weak mind has to invent stories to tell itself to hide the unpleasant facts of your decline? Face up to it, Philip. You've suffered a defeat – I'll never come again to your beck and call!'

Brent had withered in a moment. Her hand was to her

mouth again, but her eyes – those eyes that could be so brave – were piteous. Dorothy did not see what her words had done to Brent. She was watching Philip, and she was dismayed by his passivity. He was actually smiling.

'If I wrote the "Confession", Dorothy – and, mind you, I'm not saying I didn't – how did I know that Brent and Jeremy were coming to our house for dinner when you didn't tell me until I reached home that evening?'

Dorothy was confused. 'But didn't I tell you before that?' she asked. She turned to Brent. 'When did you and Jeremy decide to come to dinner?'

Brent thought for a moment. 'You asked us earlier in the week. You gave us several days' notice.'

'Dorothy,' said Philip. 'You never told me until that night. And you said Jeremy had called up and told you that he was bringing someone to dinner – that you didn't know her name.'

'Really, Philip, you can hardly hold me responsible for so small a thing. How can I vouch for what I said about a detail two days ago? What difference can it make?'

Philip spoke quietly, but his words carried weight. 'It means this much, Dorothy, that if you wrote the "Confession" you made one small mistake. You neglected to tell me about Jeremy and Brent before I read the manuscript.

'You could have done the rest with ease. Like anyone else in this room you could have ordered the messenger service to deliver the manuscripts to Miss Grey by simply writing a letter and forging my name. You just admitted that you visited my office yesterday afternoon. You knew Miss Grey, and she would have let you in to my desk. You forced the lock on my drawer and stole the manuscripts. Then you and Jeremy came back here to his apartment. While he packed, you dropped the manuscript on the couch. I think you wanted someone to discover it so you could use it against me. It was written in the first person singular, wasn't it? To the uninformed reader such a "Confession" would look damning. You planned to hold it over me – perhaps, you wanted to try to win me back by such a threat.

'Behind all this was your own inadequacy – mostly imagined – which forces you to blame me for your coldness, your faults as a wife. Whenever I looked at another woman, instead of trying to attract me, you shrank from the conflict and commiserated with yourself. Your self-inflicted martyrdom grew until it became necessary for you to strike out at me – to have an affair with Jeremy – now to divorce me!'

Dorothy stared at him, and then she laughed. 'Can't you see that what you have just said is only your own neurosis turned inside out? The reflected image of your own narcissism which can never admit its own blemishes but must blame them on the mirror – in this case me? Philip, you wrote that "Confession". You must face that fact if you are not to lose everything!'

At this point, Jeremy groaned and sat up. Dorothy did not notice. Dr Matthews and Brent helped him to his feet and into the kitchen where they began to apply cold cloths to his head. Philip walked to the front of the great room and stood looking down out of the deep windows. He noticed that the frames reached to the floor and that there were no sills. It would be easy to open the latch and just step out . . . he put his hand on the latch . . . and then he withdrew it as he became aware that Steven Foster was watching him.

Philip turned around. Dorothy had lighted a cigarette and was watching him, too. Philip felt trapped, hemmed in by animosities. 'I'll admit there's truth in what you say. And I suppose that I'll never know which one of us was right.' He walked to the chair where he had laid his hat and coat, put them on and walked out the door. Then, as they stood looking at the door, he reappeared in it.

'I'll say this much, Dorothy. If I have hurt you, I'm sorry.'

He closed the door behind him. Dorothy stood staring

at it, unable to move, yet feeling cheated. Dr Matthews came into the room.

'Where is Philip?' he asked.

Dorothy stood clenching and unclenching her hands, her mouth working but no words coming out. Her face was blenched and her eyes were stark, whether from grief or frustration Matthews could not tell.

She put her hand up to her face, cried out inarticulately and ran out of the room and down the stairs. 'She's gone after Philip!' Foster shouted. He grabbed his coat and strode across the room to the door. 'And I've got to stop her!' Matthews heard the door slam, and then heard him pounding down the stairs.

Matthews had gone to the telephone and was calling Lieutenant Anderson. This was a matter for the police.

When he had finished his call, he, too, ran out of the house and up the street.

As he went down the steps of the subway station, Philip had the feeling he was being followed. 'You can't begin that again, old man,' he told himself, 'or the first thing you know you'll be hearing things.' But even as he got change and put his nickel in the turnstile, he could feel the hairs on the back of his neck bristle with the knowledge that someone was behind. Someone was coming down the stairs, pushing his way through the turnstile ... after him?

He stepped onto the platform. A local was rounding the slight curve and came roaring into the station. 'People are always behind you in the subway,' he reassured himself. But as the noise increased, became a din, he heard a voice. 'Philip, you're cra-zee!' The voice seemed to sound in his ear – he though he could feel the moist, warm breath against the sensitive membrane. 'Oh, Philip!' the voice said.

Although he knew he should not do it, Philip swerved quickly around – threw up his hands to protect himself – screamed.

But his scream blended in with the roar of the train.

Epilogue

By the time Dr Matthews reached the subway station, a large crowd had gathered about the entrances, the police emergency squad had arrived and two scout cars were parked across the street. Next to the scout cars Matthews recognized the car of his friend, Lieutenant Anderson, and surmised that the Lieutenant, on the way to the address Matthews had given him on the telephone, had stopped to see what was wrong at the subway station.

The policeman guarding the entrance Matthews entered was one of Anderson's men – he recognized Dr Matthews and let him by, touching his fingers to his visored cap as he did. Inside the station a large crowd had gathered on the edge of the platform where members of the disaster squad were working at uncoupling the cars. Matthews had guessed what had happened when he had seen the curious mob in the street, now he was even more sure. But he looked around for Anderson. He found him at the far end of the platform talking to a pale, shaken Steven Foster. Dorothy was seated beside them on a bench, her face in her hands, sobbing hysterically.

Anderson was a middle-aged man with thin grey hair. His manner was dour, his habit of speaking terse. As he saw Matthews approach, he asked, 'Did you know this was going to happen, George?' He had worked with Matthews many times in the past and they knew and respected each other.

'I can tell you better when you tell me what happened,' Matthews answered.

'But didn't you say that I was to come to a particular address to prevent an accident? Before I got there, I saw

this commotion and investigated. From what he says'
– and he jerked his hand at Steven Foster – 'the fellow
under the train is a friend of yours, Philip Banter.'

Matthews swallowed hard. 'He jumped in front of the
train?' he asked.

Anderson shrugged his shoulders. 'That depends upon
which one of the three witnesses is talking to you. Accord-
ing to Foster there, who I understand is Banter's father-in-
law –' He turned to Steven and said, 'Will you please
repeat your account of what happened, Mr Foster?'

Steven Foster nodded his head and passed his handkerchief over his mouth. His cold eyes twitched and his
forehead was beaded with sweat. 'My son-in-law has
been mentally ill for some time. This morning, in my
office, Dr Matthews and I tried to persuade him to enter
a sanatorium. He ran away from us then and we followed
him to Mr Foulkes' apartment which is down the street a
way.

'He ran away from us a second time, after Mr Foulkes,
my daughter and another friend, Brent Holliday, had
taken turns talking to him. This time my daughter followed him, and then I ran out after her. They both had a
good start on me, so I took a taxi I found in front of Mr
Foulkes' apartment and told the driver to catch up with
them. Before he could, they had both entered the subway
station.

'I paid the driver and entered the station myself. Just
as I reached the foot of the stairs, where I could get a clear
view of the platform –' He paused and mopped at his
brow. Matthews saw that his hand was shaking. 'A train
was coming into the station. Philip must have been standing on the very edge of the platform, his back to me. But
as I watched, he turned. Dorothy was standing behind
him. She must have spoken to him. Anyway, he turned
quickly around – lost his balance – fell in front of the train.
He screamed as he fell. I ran forward, but there was
nothing – absolutely nothing – I could do.'

Anderson broke in. 'Thank you, Mr Foster,' he said.

'I won't make you tell about it again for a while. Why don't you sit down beside your daughter?'

'What is Dorothy's version of what happened?' Matthews asked Anderson.

Anderson looked at him, his eyes quizzical. Matthews knew that the Lieutenant was trying to think out a problem. He wondered how much Anderson knew. But all Anderson said was, 'Mrs Banter corroborates her father's story in every detail, except that she says she did not speak to Philip. Is that right, Mrs Banter?'

Dorothy raised her eyes. Her face was puffed and tear-streaked, and her shoulders drooped. 'I had just reached the platform when Philip turned around. I did not have time to speak to him. I don't think he saw me. He just let himself fall backwards . . .' And she began to sob again.

Anderson walked away from both Dorothy and her father. Matthews walked with him. 'There is one other witness,' Anderson said. 'A blind man who must have been standing near Philip. There were other people on the platform at the time, and plenty more who came downstairs before I put men at the entrances to keep them out – but nobody else saw or heard anything. It's just our luck this man is blind!'

He pointed to a slim negro man who stood talking to another policeman. The man was neatly dressed and his hand held the harness of a sleek, well-fed German Shepherd dog. When Anderson asked him to repeat his story, he said, 'I started to listen when I heard Bozo here growl. Bozo never growls unless there's a reason. Bozo is a good friendly dog. But then I heard a scuffling, and someone panting for breath. All the time the train was coming in and making an awful racket. Bozo backed up and I backed up with him – away from the edge of the platform that is. I knew there was danger or Bozo wouldn't have done that. He's used to trains. Then I heard the voice. It was the nastiest voice I ever did hear. It said, "Philip, you're cra-zee!" – and then it said, "Oh, Philip!" The next thing I heard, a man screamed a terrible sound. And I said to myself, somebody's gone and pushed that poor guy under the train.'

Anderson shrugged his shoulders again. 'Could you tell whether this voice you heard was a man's or a woman's?' Matthews asked.

The fellow thought for a moment. 'That I couldn't do,' he said, smiling blankly. 'All I can tell you is that it was the nastiest – the meanest, cruellest – voice I ever did hear. I hated that voice.'

Anderson thanked the man and told him to give his address to the patrolman and he could go. Then he looked at Matthews.

'This is my mistake, Andy,' Matthews said. 'I had a chance to prevent it, and if I had put things together right I would have prevented it, too. But I put things together wrong - and Philip Banter was murdered.'

Anderson pushed his hat back on his head. 'Murdered, you say? How do you know the blind man's right? He is only telling us what he heard, you know - he couldn't see. I admit there are disparities between his story and that of Dorothy and her father. But if the guy was murdered, who murdered him?'

Matthews smiled tightly. 'If you will get these people together in your office this afternoon, I'll name the murderer.' He gave Anderson a slip of paper on which he had written the names of Jeremy, Brent, Dorothy and Miss Grey. 'Miss Grey works at Brown and Foster. If she isn't there the switchboard girl will tell you how to reach her,' Matthews added.

He took Anderson's arm. 'Why don't you let one of your men round up these people? You and I can have lunch together and I'll bring you up to date on what has happened before this.' Matthews was smiling, but he did not feel the happiness he simulated. He knew that if he had acted more quickly, Philip would not have died. Now all he could do was to make certain that his murderer was brought to justice.

Even psychiatrists sometimes make mistakes.

Anderson's office was sparsely furnished. It usually contained a desk, three chairs and a framed map of the five boroughs of New York City; however, for this occasion several extra stiff-backed chairs had been added. When Matthews and Anderson came into the room, the others were already there. Brent and Jeremy sat together, holding hands. Jeremy's neck was bruised from where Philip had struck him and he kept rubbing this sore spot. Miss Grey sat by herself near the door. She carried a large black purse and her fingers played restlessly with its catch – her nose and eyes were red as if she had been crying. Dorothy and Steven sat near Anderson's desk, but not together. Dorothy had changed into black and by some effort of will she had recovered her poise. Her glossy head was carried high and her gloved hands rested calmly in her lap. Steven Foster was the same as he had been when Matthews first met him: he sat rigidly erect on the edge of his chair, his eyes staring forward, his cane upright between his knees.

Anderson seated himself behind his desk, but George Matthews remained standing. He knew that all of them were looking at him, waiting to hear what he would say. Taking advantage of this interest he turned slowly around and regarded each one of them before he spoke.

'Most of you, I believe, know why you are here. Philip Banter died this morning. He was crushed to death beneath the wheels of a subway train at the 50th Street station of the 8th Avenue Independent Subway. All but one of you were present at the scene in Jeremy's apartment a few minutes before Philip's death, and you know that Philip tried at that time to discover who was writing a "Confession" – a series of threatening, prophetic manuscripts – that had been appearing on his desk.

'I thought, and I know that some of you agreed with me, that Philip was writing these manuscripts himself. I knew him to be neurotic, and alcoholic, and from his wife's testimony as well as his own I knew that he had been experiencing certain schizophrenic symptoms.

Schizophrenics often bedevil themselves by writing diaries or journals with one half of their personality which they do not recognize as their own handiwork during saner intervals. And Philip was a recognizable schizoid type. I went so far as to recommend that he commit himself to an asylum – although only as a cure for his alcoholism.'

Matthews paused and looked around the room again. Lieutenant Anderson had lighted his cigar. Brent was watching him intently. 'Philip uncovered proof this morning that he was not writing the "Confession". Miss Grey admitted that she had received payment on two occasions from a messenger for placing the manuscript on his desk. At the same time that she told him this, however, she resigned her job, saying that she could not stand to work for him any longer. And when Philip called the messenger service, he discovered that so far as that company knew he himself had arranged to have the messenger pay Miss Grey to put the manuscript on his desk.

'I say that Miss Grey's admission that she attended to the delivery of the "Confession", was positive proof that Philip was not writing it. I think it was. For if Philip had been writing the "Confession", why would it have been necessary to go through the complicated business of hiring a messenger service to pay Miss Grey? He would have been writing it at the office, and he would have left it on his desk. But, what had been happening was that someone had been preparing the manuscript and having it placed on his desk so that it looked like he had left it there. And it was the mechanism for simulating this – the business of hiring the messenger service in Philip's name to pay Miss Grey one hundred dollars for placing the manuscript on Banter's desk – that Philip discovered.'

'Yet when he told me about it,' Brent interrupted, 'he made it sound like further evidence that he was writing it himself.'

'And so it was to him, although he denied it in part. It was a shock to him to have the messenger service tell him that he had ordered the deliveries – and he never had the time to reason it through. Shortly afterwards Steven Foster summoned him into his office to talk to me and the whole affair worsened.

'Philip was ambivalent about the "Confession". He knew himself well enough to know that he was a rake, an alcoholic. He knew that he was losing his job at Brown and Foster and that his marriage was breaking up. He knew that he had spells during which he heard voices. But he did not think he was sufficiently insane to write a long narrative that predicted his own future actions, and then forget about it.'

Matthews paused and lighted his pipe. This operation took several minutes of tamping and fussing with the shining meerschaum; during this time he studied his audience. Everyone was listening intently. Miss Grey was the most visibly nervous, Brent and Dorothy were equally calm, old Steven Foster showed his usual hostility.

'It never occurred to Philip that the "Confession" might be a prelude to his murder. Nor, do I think, did it occur to the murderer until a few minutes before his crime. No, Philip thought of the "Confession" as a subtle means of frightening him, perhaps, an attempt to drive him out of his mind. First he suspected Jeremy Foulkes of this. You heard what he had to say in Jeremy's apartment. Jeremy's motive, he thought, was jealousy. Philip had married the girl he loved. Jeremy was throwing Brent at Philip to make Dorothy divorce him, and if in the process Philip had a breakdown – well, that would have complicated matters a little, but the end result might have been the same.

'As you know, Philip rejected this theory. He realized that Jeremy loved Brent, that while he was infatuated with Dorothy he would not go to the extreme of writing the "Confession" to win her away from Philip. Besides, in these times among people in this income category, divorces can be arranged easier than that.

'So Philip turned to Dorothy,' and as he said this Dr Matthews regarded her, too. 'Much of what Philip had

214

to say this afternoon was painful for you to hear, Dorothy. But you know that much of it is true. You *might* have written the "Confession" out of your own feelings of inadequacy, as a neurotic device that you hoped one day would drive Philip from you, and the next day you hoped would bring him back to you. Philip believed you were doing it. And, I think, you were a little afraid – like Philip – that you might be doing it, too, and then forgetting about it.

'You need not have feared that. Philip said that the person who was bedevilling him both hated him and wanted him out of the way, and had the continuing opportunity to place all three instalments of the "Confession" on his desk.' Matthews looked around the room. 'Yes,' he said, 'I said *three*. Each of you could have written the first two instalments, each of you could have hired the messenger service to do its tricks – but only one of you could possibly have placed that blank piece of paper on Philip's desk!' Matthews' eyes swept the room.

'Miss Grey,' he barked, and the girl, startled, jumped to her feet. 'Did you clean and tidy Mr Banter's desk last night before you left?'

The girl stammered, 'Y-yes, s-sir.'

'Did you see a blank piece of paper on his desk then?'

'No, sir.'

'Did you clean his desk this morning before he arrived?'

'Y-yes, sir.'

'Was there a blank piece of paper on it then?'

'N-no sir.'

'Did you sit in your office until Mr Banter arrived?'

'Yes, I did. I wanted to see him early. I wanted to tell him I was quitting.'

'Did you see anyone go into his office from the time you cleaned his desk until he arrived?'

'N-no, sir.'

'No one at all?' Matthews raised his voice an octave on that last syllable.

The girl thought for a moment. 'Only Mr Foster,' she

said. 'He had been paying me extra to tell him all the queer things Mr Banter did. He came in and asked me if I had seen Mr Banter this morning. I told him no. He said I must have seen him since he had come in a good five minutes ago. He said he would just look inside and see . . . he was only inside a minute.'

Steven Foster jumped to his feet and threw his cane at Dr Matthews – all in one movement. Before Anderson could stop him, he had reached the door and jerked it open. But a uniformed policeman stood outside. Foster halted abruptly, gazed at the man for an instant and then slowly turned to face Matthews. His face was a study in disdain. 'I did it,' he said deliberately. 'I killed Philip Banter. He was a rotter and a waster and he did not deserve my daughter!' His face had grown taut and ashen, his eyes protruded.

'Philip came very close, didn't he, Steven?' Matthews asked. 'He said you had the opportunity, and he was right. You were the only one who could have written both sections of the "Confession" and placed the blank piece of paper on his desk. He gave your motive when he said that you had never liked the idea of having a son-in-law and that you had always loved your daughter *deeply*. And who but Philip knew that Dorothy talked to you so frequently and freely? You knew that Brent and Jeremy were coming to visit Philip and Dorothy before Philip did. In fact, you took it for granted that Philip knew, and in so doing made one of your few mistakes.'

Steven Foster, although he stood very straight, seemed to be experiencing difficulty in speaking. 'I saw that he did not honour my daughter. I set about to ruin him. I could only attack him through his vanity, his self-love. Dorothy had told me of Jeremy and Brent, of how Jeremy felt towards Philip. I saw in their visit an opportunity to suggest Brent to Philip. I started to write the "Confession" . . .'

'And, after Philip had read the two instalments, you stole the manuscript from his desk and left it in Jeremy's apartment. Since Jeremy habitually left his door unlocked, you had no trouble getting in. You wanted him to read it, to grow jealous of Philip – to take its slander for truth – you wanted Jeremy to kill Philip. You even misdirected our taxi this morning to delay us and give Philip time to reach Jeremy's apartment in the hope that Jeremy would attack him.

'But several things went wrong. You had not thought it possible that Jeremy was still attracted to Dorothy – that Dorothy would go away with him. So Brent read the "Confession", not Jeremy. And without Dorothy to inform you, you did not know whether Philip had conformed to the "Confession's" predictions last night or not. All you dared place on his desk this morning was a blank piece of paper.'

Matthews was silent, looking at the old man who now swayed as he stood before Anderson's desk. 'Your scheme was ingenious. In many ways it corresponds to the witchcraft of primitive man. Did you get the idea out of Seabrook? I saw his book on your shelf. You should not have relied on a secondary source. Yet it almost worked.

'But Philip, though frightened, was not demoralized. He would not agree to enter the asylum – and leave Dorothy to you! – even with my pressure. He ran away to Jeremy's and questioned each of you in turn – if you could have known the conflict in his mind then, you would realize what an heroic act that was. Dorothy saw, and Dorothy respected him for it. When he left the apartment, she went after him . . .'

'They were coming together again,' sighed Steven Foster. 'I had failed and . . . instead of driving them apart . . . I had driven them together. I hailed a taxi and reached the station before Dorothy did – she lied to the Lieutenant to protect me. I went down the stairs just behind Philip. There was no one on the platform except Philip and a blind man.'

Matthews took it up. 'Philip's back was turned to you. You came close to him and said, "Philip, you're cra-zee!

Oh, Philip!" He must have thought he was hearing the voice again. He turned about, saw you –'

'And I pushed him into the path of the train,' said Steven Foster. His face had grown very pale and his nose had begun to bleed. Matthews stared, fascinated, at his face for an instant; then he sprang to help him. He had recognized the signs of cerebral accident.

Old Foster held up his hand and shook his head. His knees sagged – his mouth gasped. Rigid, even in death, he fell forward on his face.

Dr Matthews knelt beside the body and noted the absence of a pulse. Dorothy, behind him, began to weep. But there was nothing he could do about that . . .

FOR THE BEST IN PAPERBACKS, LOOK FOR THE

In every corner of the world, on every subject under the sun, Penguin represents quality and variety – the very best in publishing today.

For complete information about books available from Penguin – including Pelicans, Puffins, Peregrines and Penguin Classics – and how to order them, write to us at the appropriate address below. Please note that for copyright reasons the selection of books varies from country to country.

In the United Kingdom: Please write to *Dept E.P., Penguin Books Ltd, Harmondsworth, Middlesex, UB7 0DA*

In the United States: Please write to *Dept BA, Penguin, 299 Murray Hill Parkway, East Rutherford, New Jersey 07073*

In Canada: Please write to *Penguin Books Canada Ltd, 2801 John Street, Markham, Ontario L3R 1B4*

In Australia: Please write to the *Marketing Department, Penguin Books Australia Ltd, P.O. Box 257, Ringwood, Victoria 3134*

In New Zealand: Please write to the *Marketing Department, Penguin Books (NZ) Ltd, Private Bag, Takapuna, Auckland 9*

In India: Please write to *Penguin Overseas Ltd, 706 Eros Apartments, 56 Nehru Place, New Delhi, 110019*

In Holland: Please write to *Penguin Books Nederland B.V., Postbus 195, NL–1380AD Weesp, Netherlands*

In Germany: Please write to *Penguin Books Ltd, Friedrichstrasse 10–12, D–6000 Frankfurt Main 1, Federal Republic of Germany*

In Spain: Please write to *Longman Penguin España, Calle San Nicolas 15, E–28013 Madrid, Spain*

In France: Please write to *Penguin Books Ltd, 39 Rue de Montmorency, F-75003, Paris, France*

In Japan: Please write to *Longman Penguin Japan Co Ltd, Yamaguchi Building, 2–12–9 Kanda Jimbocho, Chiyoda-Ku, Tokyo 101, Japan*

FOR THE BEST IN PAPERBACKS, LOOK FOR THE 🐧

CRIME AND MYSTERY IN PENGUINS

Deep Water Patricia Highsmith

Her chilling portrait of a psychopath, from the first faint outline to the full horrors of schizophrenia. 'If you read crime stories at all, or perhaps especially if you don't, you should read *Deep Water*' – Julian Symons in the *Sunday Times*

Farewell, My Lovely Raymond Chandler

Moose Malloy was a big man but not more than six feet five inches tall and not wider than a beer truck. He looked about as inconspicuous as a tarantula on a slice of angel food. Marlowe's greatest case. Chandler's greatest book.

God Save the Child Robert B. Parker

When young Kevin Bartlett disappears, everyone assumes he's run away . . . until the comic strip ransom note arrives . . . 'In classic wisecracking and handfighting tradition, Spenser sorts out the case and wins the love of a fine-boned Jewish Lady . . . who even shares his taste for iced red wine' – Francis Goff in the *Sunday Telegraph*

The Daughter of Time Josephine Tey

Josephine Tey again delves into history to reconstruct a crime. This time it is a crime committed in the tumultuous fifteenth century. 'Most people will find *The Daughter of Time* as interesting and enjoyable a book as they will meet in a month of Sundays' – Marghanita Laski in the *Observer*

The Michael Innes Omnibus

Three tensely exhilarating novels. 'A master – he constructs a plot that twists and turns like an electric eel: it gives you shock upon shock and you cannot let go' – *The Times Literary Supplement*

Killer's Choice Ed McBain

Who killed Annie Boone? Employer, lover, ex-husband, girlfriend? This is a tense, terrifying and tautly written novel from the author of *The Mugger*, *The Pusher*, *Lady Killer* and a dozen other first class thrillers.

CRIME AND MYSTERY IN PENGUINS

Call for the Dead   John Le Carré

The classic work of espionage which introduced the world to George Smiley. 'Brilliant . . . highly intelligent, realistic. Constant suspense. Excellent writing' – *Observer*

Swag   Elmore Leonard

From the bestselling author of *Stick* and *La Brava* comes this wallbanger of a book in which 100,000 dollars' worth of nicely spendable swag sets off a slick, fast-moving chain of events. 'Brilliant' – *The New York Times*

Beast in View   Margaret Millar

'On one level, *Beast in View* is a dazzling conjuring trick. On another it offers a glimpse of bright-eyed madness as disquieting as a shriek in the night. In the whole of Crime Fiction's distinguished sisterhood there is no one quite like Margaret Millar' – *Guardian*

The Julian Symons Omnibus

The Man Who Killed Himself, The Man Whose Dreams Came True, The Man Who Lost His Wife: three novels of cynical humour and cliff-hanging suspense from a master of his craft. 'Exciting and compulsively readable' – *Observer*

Love in Amsterdam   Nicolas Freeling

Inspector Van der Valk's first case involves him in an elaborate cat-and-mouse game with a very wily suspect. 'Has the sinister, spellbinding perfection of a cobra uncoiling. It is a masterpiece of the genre' – Stanley Ellis

Maigret's Pipe   Georges Simenon

Eighteen intriguing cases of mystery and murder to which the pipe-smoking Maigret applies his wit and intuition, his genius for detection and a certain *je ne sais quoi* . . .

PENGUIN CLASSIC CRIME

The Big Knockover and Other Stories   Dashiell Hammett

With these sharp, spare, laconic stories, Hammett invented a new folk hero – the private eye. 'Dashiell Hammett gave murder back to the kind of people that commit it for reasons, not just to provide a corpse; and with the means at hand, not with handwrought duelling pistols, curare, and tropical fish' – Raymond Chandler

Death of a Ghost   Margery Allingham

A picture painted by a dead artist leads to murder . . . and Albert Campion has to face his dearest enemy. With the skill we have come to expect from one of the great crime writers of all time, Margery Allingham weaves an enthralling web of murder, intrigue and suspense.

Fen Country   Edmund Crispin

Dandelions and hearing aids, a bloodstained cat, a Leonardo drawing, a corpse with an alibi, a truly poisonous letter . . . these are just some of the unusual clues that Oxford don/detective Gervase Fen is confronted with in this sparkling collection of short mystery stories by one of the great masters of detective fiction. 'The mystery fan's ideal bedside book' – *Kirkus Reviews*

The Wisdom of Father Brown   G. K. Chesterton

Twelve delightful stories featuring the world's most beloved amateur sleuth. Here Father Brown's adventures take him from London to Cornwall, from Italy to France. He becomes involved with bandits, treason, murder, curses, and an American crime-detection machine.

Five Roundabouts to Heaven   John Bingham

At the heart of this novel is a conflict of human relationships ending in death. Centred around crime, the book is remarkable for its humanity, irony and insight into the motives and weaknesses of men and women, as well as for a tensely exciting plot with a surprise ending. One of the characters, considering reasons for killing, wonders whether the steps of his argument are *Five Roundabouts to Heaven*. Or do they lead to Hell? . . .'

FOR THE BEST IN PAPERBACKS, LOOK FOR THE 🐧

PENGUIN CLASSIC CRIME

Ride the Pink Horse   Dorothy B. Hughes

The tense, taut story of fear and revenge south of the border. It's fiesta time in Mexico but Sailor has his mind on other things – like revenge. Among the gaudy crowd, the twanging guitars and the tawdry carnival lights are three desperate men fighting over a dark and bloody secret.

The Narrowing Circle   Julian Symons

The editor's job at Gross Enterprises' new crime magazine is 'in the bag' for Dave Nelson. Or so he thinks, until the surprising appointment of Willie Strayte. When Strayte is found dead Nelson must struggle to prove his innocence and solve the elaborate puzzle. 'One of our most ingenious and stylish home-grown crime novelists' – *Spectator*

Maigret at the Crossroads   Georges Simenon

Someone has shot Goldberg at the Three Widows Crossroads and Maigret is carrying out a thorough investigation, getting to know the lives of the small community at Three Widows. Although he is suspicious of every-one, he has a hunch about the murder – and that means the case is as good as wrapped up.

The Mind Readers   Margery Allingham

When rumours of a mind-reading device first came out of Godley's research station, Albert Campion found it difficult to take them seriously. Especially as the secret seemed to rest exclusively with two small boys, who were irritatingly stubborn about disclosing their sources . . .

The Daughter of Time   Josephine Tey

Josephine Tey's brilliant reconstruction of the life of Richard III, now known to us as a monster and murderer, is one of the most original pieces of historical fiction ever written, casting new light on one of history's most enduring myths.